# THE BREAKUP PLAN

JENNIFER SUCEVIC

The Breakup Plan

Cover Design by Claudia Lymira at Tease Designs

Editing by Evelyn Summers at Pinpoint Editing

Home | Jennifer Sucevic or www.jennifersucevic.com

Subscribe to my newsletter! Jennifer Sucevic Newsletter (subscribepage.com)

# The Girl Next Door

# WHITNEY

Out of nowhere, a brawny arm slides around my shoulders and hauls me close, anchoring me against a muscular body. Without looking, I know exactly who the culprit pinning me in place is. The woodsy scent is a dead giveaway.

The deep voice confirms my sinking suspicions.

Grayson McNichols.

"Miss me, baby?" he growls against my ear as his warm breath sends shivers skittering down my spine.

There's an edge of humor simmering in his voice that thankfully kills the unwanted attraction that has leapt to life at his proximity. No matter how much I fight against it, he affects me like this every time. It's why I've made it my mission in life to steer clear of Mr. Hellcat Hockey himself.

Needing to create distance between us before I get sucked any further into his orbit, I ram my elbow into his ribs. It's not nearly hard enough to do any real damage, or even to separate myself from him so I can make a quick getaway.

Gray sticks to me like glue.

"Sure did. Almost as much as I'd miss a particularly nasty case of herpes." I brace myself before flicking my eyes in his direction. "No matter what I do, you keep making an unsightly appearance at the worst possible time, just like an incurable STI." I bare my teeth so he won't think I'm being flirty.

He smirks.

My acidic comments are like water off a duck's back.

It's annoying.

Just like him.

"So, what you're really trying to say is that I'm persistent," he waggles his dark brows in a comical manner, "and you find that oddly appealing."

*Please...*

*As if...*

Nothing could be further from the truth. Gray McNichols could eat shit and die, as far as I'm concerned.

He flashes me his trademark smile.

Dimples and all.

*Ugh.*

Those dimples are a real killer. If I have one weakness, it's for a guy with Eddie Cibrian dimples. And Gray has them in spades. Now that I think about it, he kind of resembles Eddie Cibrian, circa early 2000's. I try not to let the smile or—God help me—the dimples affect me, but it's no easy feat.

I've spent years trying to steel myself against his magnetism and charm. To this day, I'm just barely able to hold on to my composure. Most of my behavior is sheer bravado. If he ever pushed me hard enough, the straw house I've built around myself for protection would collapse.

Not only is Gray ridiculously handsome, but he's captain of the Hillsdale Hellcat hockey team, which only ups his hotness factor around campus. My guess is that he's slept his way through half the female population at Hillsdale. All he has to do is smile and girls drop their panties before falling on their backs and spreading their legs wide.

How do I know this?

Here comes the embarrassing part...

Once upon a time, *I* was one of those girls.

Yup, it's sad but true.

I know exactly what it's like to have all that charismatic attention aimed in my direction. It happened second semester of freshman year. I'd seen Gray around campus and was a smitten kitten. And then, one night at a party, we hooked up.

Needless to say, it was a fuck-and-flee situation—the kind that's chock-full of regret in the morning. I blame alcohol for my poor judgment.

Surprise surprise, I never heard a peep from Gray again.

Was I stupid enough to expect more?

Guilty as charged.

He fed me all the lines that are hot guy kryptonite to stupid girls like me, and I fell for it. Hook, line, and sinker.

I know, I know…

*Total.*

*Idiot.*

Trust me, I won't dispute the title. It may have taken a while, but I've come to a place of acceptance. Now, does that mean I'm dumb enough to fall for his easy breezy charm for a second time?

Hell to the no.

Those memories are all it takes to strengthen my resolve.

"What do you want, McNichols?" I hasten my step as we navigate the path that cuts through the heart of campus, but it does no good. I can't separate myself from him. He keeps me trapped at his side.

People wave and shout Gray's name, trying to capture his attention. His celebrity status is irritating. I seem to be one of the few students at Hillsdale who wants no part of him. Like a man who's at ease with his station in life, he acknowledges his clamoring fanbase with a chin lift and a practiced wave of his hand.

What a pompous jerk.

Hillsdale is a Division I hockey school. Every year there are a handful of players drafted to the NHL. There's no question that the muscular defenseman will get snapped up by the pros.

How could he not?

He's the lead scorer three years running.

And yeah, that would be off the ice as well as on it.

Everyone at this school loves him.

Hell, the whole town worships him.

It's nauseating.

He could have accepted a full ride from any top-notch university in the United States—everyone was vying for him—but he chose Hillsdale.

*Lucky us.*

You'd assume with over ten thousand students on campus, the chances of running into him on a nearly daily basis would be astronomically low.

Think again.

I wasn't joking when I likened Gray to an incurable STI. Every time I turn around, there he is, in my face, acting like we're BFF's.

We don't live near each other.

We're not in the same major or in any classes together.

I make it a habit to avoid parties that I suspect he'll be gracing with his esteemed presence. There are a ton of puck bunnies around these parts, but I'm not one of them.

And yet, I can't get away from this guy to save my life.

Thank God this is our senior year. Once we graduate in May, I'll never see Gray again. It's that knowledge that makes it possible for me to get through moments like this.

"Just checking to see if you've changed your mind about us getting together."

I snort at that little bit of ridiculousness. "Umm, I'm sorry. Did Hell happen to freeze over, and I'm the last one to find out?"

He squeezes my shoulder and a jolt of unwanted electricity zips through me. I gnash my teeth against my body's natural response to him.

"You know how much I love it when you play hard to get." He punctuates that sentiment by nipping at my neck.

My heart flutters, and it takes everything I have inside to keep my voice level and not betray the attraction roaring violently through my veins. "I'm not playing hard to get. What I'm playing is *I-don't-want-to-talk-to-you-ever-again*. If you weren't such a meathead, you'd realize the difference and act accordingly." Before he can sweet-talk me into a situation I'll end up regretting, I fire off a pertinent question. "And when was the last time you actually took a girl out on a date?"

I'm not a moron. I know the answer, but I want to hear him say it. It's my ace in the hole, so to speak. Which is a far cry from the ace in the hole *he's* hoping to get.

That won't be happening.

"Never," he admits cheerfully, "but I'd be willing to make an exception for you, Winters."

See what I'm talking about?

Hot guy kryptonite for sure.

But I'm way too smart for him. Plus, I'd like to think that I learn from my mistakes, which is a far cry from some of the other girls around here.

We're about a block away from Thorson Hall, the business building on campus where I'm headed. At this point, I'm practically speed walking. The sooner we get there, the faster I can ditch Gray.

"It's a tempting offer," I lie, "but I'll be taking a hard pass."

His face falls as he presses his hand against his chest.

*And what a magnificent chest it is.*

With gritted teeth, I shove that errant thought away before it can worm its way into my psyche and do permanent damage.

"You wound me, Winters. All I want is one date and you're shooting me down without even considering the offer. Aren't you the least bit curious where I'd take you?"

*Nope.*

*Not even a little.*

"Sure," I snicker. "Let me guess." I tap a finger thoughtfully against my chin. "Would it be a little place called Bonetown? I'm willing to bet it is." I force my voice to fill with boredom. "Been there, done that, have the T-shirt to prove it."

His laugh is rich and low. It strums something deep inside me.

He tugs me closer. "Have I mentioned how much I love your sense of humor?"

"Please," I scoff, uncomfortable with the physical intimacy. My left breast is squashed against his side. The last thing I need is for my nip to pebble and him to feel the physical evidence of my desire. That would only encourage him to pursue me more fervently than he already is.

And that, I couldn't withstand.

I hold my breath, not wanting to inhale anymore of his decadent scent. I need to get away from him before I melt into a puddle. This flirtation is nothing more than a game. It's what Gray is known for.

Why does he insist on messing with me when I've gone out of my way to make my disinterest clear?

Doesn't he realize that there's no shortage of puck bunnies who would be more than happy to shower him with adoration? He could easily score with any number of them. Probably at the same time.

I glance around, noticing quite a number of girls staring in our direction.

It's enough to make me shake my head in disgust.

*Get a grip, ladies! This guy is toxic to the female population!*

"Have you ever considered," he says, breaking into my thoughts, "that what I need is the love of a good woman to change me for the better?"

Laughter wells in my throat before bursting free. "You're so full of shit!"

*The love of a good woman, indeed.*

Ha!

As if...

Gray grins and his dimples pop in tandem. "Maybe."

"Oh, there's no *maybe* about it, McNichols. You're *definitely* full of shit."

I didn't think it was possible for him to tug me closer, but he manages to do it before whispering, "Don't you remember how good it felt when I was buried deep inside you? Come on, Winters. Admit it, you want me."

And there you have it...

The extent of his interest doesn't go any further than him dipping his wick.

I need to get away from Gray before he destroys every shred of my resolve. Deep down, I know he's the worst possible guy for me, but my lady parts are clamoring for his attention.

And that, my friends, would be my cue to leave.

Without warning, I stop and jerk out of his arms. People grumble as they're forced to walk around us.

"Let me make this perfectly clear." I harden my voice, refusing to be taken in by his good looks and easy charm. When it comes down to it, this guy is a predator. If he senses a moment of weakness, he'll take me down before I realize I was being hunted in the first place. And then I'll be lost. "You're the last guy on campus I would sleep with. Your stroke game was mediocre at best, and our encounter was entirely forgettable."

Instead of taking offense, he tilts his head and rubs his chin with his fingers. "Is that so?" He steps closer, his muscular body invading my space yet again, and my body sizzles with the contact. "I find that hard to believe. I've never had any complaints about my," he smirks, "*stroke game.*" His finger finds its way to the curve of my cheek. "But I'd be more than happy to give you an encore performance so you can reevaluate your verdict."

I gulp and step away until his hand falls to his side and I can breathe again.

Oxygen rushes to my deprived brain.

*Seriously?*

How am I supposed to get through to this guy when he refuses to listen to a single word I say?

Unwilling to waste another moment on him, I throw my hands up and stalk toward my one o'clock class.

"So," he shouts at my retreating figure, "you're going to think about it and get back to me, right?"

I flip him the bird and keep walking.

# GRAY

*eak stroke game, my ass.*

If I squint hard enough, I can almost make out the smoke escaping from Whitney's ears. I have a real knack for pissing off that girl. It's not even like I have to try; it just happens naturally.

Does it make me a complete asshole if I were to admit that I enjoy watching her dark eyes flash with anger?

I'm thinking that it probably does.

I'm fairly certain that me poking at Whitney is derailing my efforts to get her back in my bed. Maybe one of these days, I'll resist the temptation I have to torment her and actually make some headway where she's concerned.

Then again, maybe not.

For a moment, I enjoy the view of her storming away. The sway of her ass is one sight I'll never tire of.

"Hey, McNichols. What's going on?"

I snap out of my Whitney Winters-induced fog and glance at my friend and teammate, Collins O'Brien. We share a house off-campus with three other guys from the team. We're notorious for hosting the most outrageous parties at Hillsdale. Although this year, I'm looking to take it down a notch. I've got enough shit going on with graduation and the draft in the spring. This season will be my final one playing hockey for the school. Not only do we need to have a winning record, we need to bring home the Frozen Four Championship.

Goals.

You gotta have them, baby. And I do.

It goes a little something like this: I crush the upcoming season, staying laser focused on hockey. I get snapped up in the first or second round of the draft, play in the pros for a solid decade, nail all the pussy I can, and rake in the money.

Sounds pretty sweet, right?

You bet your ass it does.

Right now, I'm so freaking close to making it happen that I can practically taste it. I've spent the last decade focused on hockey and clawing my way to the NHL. When you have a team of doctors tell you that you'll never achieve your dreams, you find the wherewithal to dig deep and turn said dreams into a reality for the sole purpose of shoving their prognosis down their egotistical throats.

I shake my head, needing to clear away those ugly memories. I don't make a habit of looking backward. Only forward. So, playing at Hillsdale is the sweet buttercream frosting on a triple chocolate cake.

And the NHL will be the fucking cherry on top of it.

A whole goddamn jar of cherries.

"Not much," I respond.

He glances in the direction I'd been staring and smirks. "Looks like you and Monroe have your eye on the same girl."

I straighten to my full height.

*What the hell does that mean?*

My gaze snaps back to Whitney just in time to see her flash a smile at the guy standing next to her near the entrance of Thorson Hall.

*Well, fuck me.*

Looks like Collins is right.

Why haven't I noticed this before?

Evert Monroe is one of my roommates. He's a decent enough guy. Solid hockey player. I've never had any problems with him. That, however, might not be the case moving forward. We'll have to see how this situation shakes out. It's always possible that they're just shooting the shit before class.

Although my instincts tell me otherwise.

Whitney is hot as hell. Long, inky black hair that hits the middle of her back. Dark, chocolatey-colored eyes that dominate her face and are tipped at the corners, giving her an exotic look. She has a slim build that I will fully admit is not my usual type. I like a girl with nice, round titties. Whitney doesn't have much going on in that department, but there's just something about her...

I haven't been able to get her out of my head since we—

Best not to think along those lines. I'll end up getting a chubby, and who needs that? Especially when I'm standing around with another dude.

Collins shifts his weight and grins in her direction. "So, Whitney Winters, huh?"

I scowl and grumble, "Fuck off, O'Brien." I'm embarrassed to be caught ogling a girl. Chicks pant after *me*. Not the other way around.

But Whitney isn't your typical girl. I think she'd be thrilled if I never acknowledged her existence again. Yeah, that's not going to happen. I couldn't stay away from her if I tried.

He chuckles, realizing that he's found a tender spot to poke me in. I don't have too many of those. I usually keep my inner thoughts and feelings tightly under wraps.

With one last look in Whitney's direction, I head off to my next class. Collins falls easily in line with me. "Well, this is an interesting turn of events. Can't say I saw this one coming."

I groan. "You're not going to let this go, are you?"

"Hell, no! I'm just getting started."

# WHITNEY

*D*ad answers my call on the third ring. He's not as readily available as he used to be. I'm not sure what's going on with that. Normally, he picks up on the first ring or texts back within thirty seconds of me messaging.

But the last couple of months?

Not so much.

I chalk it up to him being busy at work.

What else could it be?

"Hey, buttercup!" His voice booms over the line. "How's it going?"

The sound of my childhood nickname sliding off his lips has everything in me settling. Maybe my Spidey senses are off and there's nothing for me to be concerned about.

My gaze is drawn to the apartment door as my roommate, Katelyn, walks in. She smiles, spotting me curled up on the couch. I wave in greeting before pointing to the phone and mouthing the word *Dad* to her before heading to the balcony off our living room for a little privacy. There's just enough space for a small café-style table with two chairs tucked beneath it.

It's early September, and the weather is still seasonal. At eighty degrees, I can close my eyes and almost pretend it's still summer. This is the kind of weather that needs to be savored. Pretty soon autumn will be here, and the leaves will be falling, covering campus like a brightly colored carpet. Instead of shorts and T-shirts, we'll be bundled up in jackets, scarfs, and fuzzy boots. I plunk down on an aluminum chair and kick my feet up on the railing.

"Everything's good." My gaze settles on the setting sun, which is beginning to dip beneath the horizon. The sky looks like it's been painted with red and orange brush strokes. "I tried calling last night, but you didn't pick up."

That comment is greeted with a moment of silence. "Oh, right! I had a meeting that ran late, and then I met up with a few colleagues afterward to discuss an acquisition we're working on in China. There's also a merger..."

My eyes glaze over as he rambles on about whatever the hell he's doing in China. Talking about mergers and acquisitions makes me want to knife myself in the head. I might be a business major, but I'm more interested in personal finance, portfolios, and the stock market.

When I can't take another moment, I cut him off. "Wow, sounds like you've got a lot going on at work." Which is just as I'd suspected.

*See?*

There's absolutely nothing for me to be worried about.

"I was concerned when I couldn't get ahold of you." I'm not going to mention it on the phone, but I'd almost jumped in the car and driven home to check on him. What if he had fallen and couldn't reach his cell phone to call 911?

Who would help him?

For the last nine years, it's been just the two of us. Mom died in a car accident when I was twelve years old. At first, I was scared he would rush out and replace her, but that never happened. Not once has he shown any interest in dating. Maybe it's selfish, but I'm secretly glad. I'm not ready for another woman to step into Mom's shoes.

Obviously, Dad feels the same way.

It's one of the reasons I decided to stay local for college. With Hillsdale being only a thirty-minute drive from home, I'm able to pop home for visits as often as I want. But I'm still far enough away to be on my own.

It's the perfect situation.

"Sorry, Whit," he says quickly, sounding apologetic. "I didn't see your call until it was after midnight, otherwise I would have gotten back to you." Concern fills his voice. "Is everything all right? Did you need something?"

Even though he can't see me, I wave my hand. "No, it's all good. I just wanted to talk." The conversation flows easily between us, but still…something feels off. Although, I'm not able to put my finger on what it is. I'm about to dig a little deeper when he says—

"I'm looking forward to brunch tomorrow."

"Yeah, me too." Dad and I usually meet up for brunch once a month. It's our thing. I always look forward to sitting down and catching up since we don't get to spend much time together. He always reminds me that I can bring Katelyn along, and there are times when I do, but mostly, it's the two of us.

The line goes silent.

Just when I'm about to say his name and make sure we haven't been disconnected, he blurts, "I have some exciting news, but I'm going to wait until tomorrow to spill the beans."

"Dad!" I gripe.

Ugh! I hate when he does this. And he knows it, which is why he chuckles.

My mind immediately cartwheels with possibilities.

What if he's decided to sell the house after all these years?

Or maybe he received a promotion. Didn't he mention about six months ago that there might be an opportunity for him to move to China? I mean, he *has* been doing a lot of work with them lately. He spent two weeks there last summer.

Could that be the big surprise?

Lately, he's been putting in a ton of extra hours. And he's been super distracted. The more I think about it, the more sense it makes.

Ha!

Dad thinks he's so clever, but I figured out the surprise in less than two minutes.

"I think you're going to be excited," he adds, breaking into my thoughts.

I gnaw my bottom lip in contemplation. Him moving isn't necessarily a good thing. Maybe for his career, but not for our relationship. What am I going to do if he leaves for a year or two? I'll be stuck here all by myself. I might be twenty-one years old, but the possibility is a frightening one. Dad is the only family I have.

"How about you just tell me now," I cajole impatiently. "I'm pretty sure I've already figured it out."

"You think so?" His voice turns cagey.

"Yup. So, you might as well spill."

"Nope," he says with humor simmering in his voice. "I'll tell you everything tomorrow over brunch. I want to see the look on your face."

"Dad!" I growl. "Come on!" That's so unfair!

He laughs again, sounding lighter and happier than he has in years.

"Nope." A nervous edge enters his voice. "The cat will be out of the bag soon enough."

*Cat?*

"Don't you mean panda?" I cut in slyly, hoping to knock him off balance.

"Huh?"

"Nothing," I mumble, feeling peeved. "I'm hanging up on you now." I'd much rather he tell me what's going on so we can talk about it instead of making me wait until tomorrow.

Seriously, what's the point of that?

Why is the guy so intent on torturing me? Has he forgotten that I'm his only kid? Who does he think will take care of him in his elderly age?

I should probably remind him of that.

Just as I open my mouth to try to wheedle information out of him one more time, he says, "Whit?"

"Yeah?" I sit up a bit straighter as my breath gets lodged in my throat.

"I love you, buttercup."

My shoulders fall as I slump against the chair. "Right back at you, Dad."

"I'll see you tomorrow morning at ten sharp." Then he adds, "Be there or be square."

Even though he can be corny, it still makes me smile. "I'll be there, and you'll be the one who's square."

He chuckles, and I hit the red end button on the phone before setting it on the glass table.

A few seconds later, the sliding door opens and Katelyn joins me on the patio. She sets a bottle of water in front of me.

"Thanks." I twist off the cap and take a gulp as my roomie slips onto the chair opposite me. She nips her bottom lip between her teeth and eyes me.

*Uh-oh.*

*I know that look.*

"I have a favor to ask," Katelyn says.

Yup…that's *exactly* what that look means.

Do I even want to know what the favor is? After the convo I had with my dad, I'm almost afraid to ask. A hesitant look crosses her face, as if she knows I won't like what she has to say.

"So…" She shifts on the chair and clears her throat. "Any chance you would be up for a party tonight?"

A party?

Everything in me loosens. A night out would definitely take my mind off this whole Dad's-moving-to-China surprise he has planned for tomorrow's brunch.

"Sure," I agree easily. "I'm down for that."

Her eyes widen as she unleashes a grin. "Really?" Thrilled doesn't begin to describe the look on her face. "I thought for sure I'd have to twist your arm."

I wave off her concern. "I had three tests this week. If anyone could use a night out, it's me." Tomorrow, after Dad drops the bomb about taking off to China, my whole world will be rocked. If I'm going to enjoy myself with careless abandon, tonight's the night to do it. I take another sip from my bottle. "Where's the party?"

Here's an even better idea—maybe we can party hop. I'm sure there's more than one happening. Hillsdale is a well-known party school. Not that it slacks where academics are concerned, because it's a rigorous university. At the end of every semester, people drop like flies.

"Oh, didn't I mention it?" She averts her gaze before using her thumbnail to pick at the label of her plastic bottle.

"No, you didn't."

"It's at an off-campus house," she says evasively.

I chuckle. "Where else would it be?" Freshman year, I did hit a few dorm parties. They're the worst. Space is limited, and they never end well. Unless your idea of a good time is spending the evening getting personal with campus police.

Been there, done that.

Not interested in a repeat performance.

We're in the middle of football season and the Hillsdale Hellcats won this afternoon's game, which had the entire campus—not to mention town—going crazy. How much do you want to bet that Katelyn is dragging me to a victory party?

"It's a football party, isn't it? Those guys are a bunch of meatheads." Now, I'm not saying they aren't a bunch of *hot* meatheads, because a number of them are quite swoonworthy. But, for the most part, their idea of fun is chugging beer and smashing aluminum cans against their foreheads. It's amusing to watch for about five minutes, but then I'm bored.

"Nope, it's not a football party." She brightens. "That's good, right?"

"Sure." I shrug as my brows slide together. What other possibilities are there? "Greek?" Hillsdale has a massive Greek system. Fraternity and Sorority Row reads like a bowl of alphabet soup.

"Ummm...no." Katelyn shakes her head. "We're not going Greek tonight."

I straighten on my chair as the edges of my lips tug down. "If it's not the football players or the Greeks, then who—"

That's when it hits me like a ton of bricks.

*Oh, hell no.*

My eyes narrow. "Please tell me that I didn't just agree to a party at the hockey house."

A guilty flush stains her cheeks.

*Son of a monkey!*

"Katelyn!" I snap. "I hate going there!" Honestly, it's not the *there* part that bothers me so much. It's the *who's going to be there* part that drives me over the edge.

"I know, I know," she says hastily, throwing her hands out in a placating manner. "But Evert will be there, and you know I have a serious thing for him."

Ugh!

Even though I make it a rule to steer clear of hockey players, I've always made an exception where Evert is concerned. We met freshman year, and since we're both in the same major, he usually turns up in one of my classes each semester. I've offered to introduce them a ton of times, but Katelyn always ends up chickening out.

She's such a baby!

Those two would be a match made in heaven. If I could get them talking, they'd realize how much they have in common. And if it were at any other house, I'd be on board with the plan. No questions asked.

But...

"Spending the evening with Gray McNichols is definitely not on my to-do list," I grumble.

Her face falls. "Awww, come on, Whit," she whines. "He's not *that* bad."

*Ha!*

"Actually, he's much worse," I accuse.

Katelyn steeples her hands in front of her and begs, "*Pleeeeeeease.* I'll do anything—whatever you want—if you agree to come with me!" Her tongue darts out to moisten her lips. "I'll clean the bathroom for two weeks."

17

It's a tempting offer. Although, as much as I hate scrubbing toilets and showers, it's not enough of an incentive when it comes to that hockey-playing manwhore. I shake my head. "Sorry, no."

A prick of remorse stabs at me when her face crumbles.

"You know how much he bugs me," I say in self-defense. The guy is a total nuisance. It wouldn't be so bad if we could just ignore each other, but he refuses to play along. No matter where we are or what we're doing, he takes a ridiculous amount of pleasure in tap dancing on my very last nerve. It's aggravating as hell. "Tell you what, *I'll* clean the toilets for two weeks if you *don't* make me go to this party."

That's how much I don't want to see Gray.

"*Whitnnnnney,*" Katelyn wails. "If there were anyone else I could drag with me, I would. But Allie went home for the weekend and Tasha has a mandatory sorority thing she can't get out of." She gives me her most pathetic, blinky-eyed look.

God, I hate it when she makes that face. I have a hard time saying no to that expression and she damn well knows it. When I can't stand another moment of her puppy-dog eyes, I fold like a cheap house of cards.

"Fine, I'll go."

"Yay!" She jumps up from her chair and rushes around the table before throwing her arms around my body as if attempting to squeeze the life out of me. "You're the best!" she squeals. "And don't let anyone tell you any different!"

"I have one condition," I wheeze.

Katelyn stops mid-bounce. "What? I'll do anything. Just name it!"

My lips lift, knowing that she won't like my caveat. But that's too bad, because I'm not going to like having to endure Gray's obnoxious presence for the evening.

"If you insist on forcing me to attend this party, then I'm introducing you to Evert." I pause as her breath catches. "And there's no chickening out this time." I give her a steely-edged look. "Got it?"

"You want me to talk to him?" Uncertainty flashes in her eyes as her lips twist into a grimace. "What if I can't do it?" she whispers, sounding as if she's the one now being choked.

"Listen, this little stalker crush you have on him has gone on long enough. If you're dragging me to his house, then you're going to make it worth my while."

"Do I have to?"

"Yup. Otherwise, there's no way I'm stepping foot anywhere near that house." I wave a hand in the air. "The choice is yours."

My lips tilt at the corners with every grumble and groan that escapes from her. One of Katelyn's biggest hurdles in life is her shyness. I don't expect her to get over it in one night, but she's liked Evert for a long time.

Tonight, whether Katelyn likes it or not, I'm going to help her break out of her shell.

When she fails to respond, I ask, "Well? What's it going to be? Because we can always hit a different party."

"No, I'll do it," she mutters before stabbing a finger in my direction. "I don't want to, but I will."

"Are you sure?" I raise a brow, aware of how difficult this step is for her to take. "You don't have to."

Katelyn presses her lips together until they turn bloodless. She looks like she's attempting to gather every bit of courage she possesses to dive headfirst off a skyscraper. "I'm sure." She straightens her shoulders and adds, "God help me, I'm going to talk to Evert."

"Excellent."

If I can get these two together, then something good will have come out of the situation.

I stand up and drag her inside. "Come on, let's find an amazing outfit for you to wear." I'm thinking low-cut and cleavage bearing. Katelyn has big boobs. She usually wears loose-fitting tops that conceal her shape.

Tonight, the girls are coming out to play.

Come hell or high water, Evert's going to take notice.

# GRAY

*I* lift the bottle of beer to my lips and take a swig while scouting the vicinity. It's Saturday night and I've got my arm wrapped around a pretty girl who's more than willing to spend a little quality naked time with yours truly. I glance down at the strawberry blonde-haired girl who's busy pawing at me like a kitten. When our gazes collide, she flutters her lashes and makes a mewling noise.

Savannah is one of my go-to girls.

We have a strict no-strings attached policy.

I'm thinking about taking her up to my room when I catch a flash of dark hair from the corner of my eye. My head snaps in that direction, and I'm surprised I don't come away with whiplash.

My brows shoot up.

*Well, I'll be damned.*

I never thought I'd live to see the day that Whitney Winters willingly graced one of our parties. I'm tempted to check and see if pigs are flying out of someone's ass, because that's the only reasonable explanation I can come up with.

I narrow my eyes, watching her while she's unaware of my scrutiny. I've never been able to figure out what it is about Whitney that I find so damn attractive. Trust me, I've tried. More times than I care to admit. It's aggravating as hell to be into a girl who wants absolutely nothing to do with you. It's like having an itch I can never quite scratch. No matter how many chicks I fuck, I can't evict this particular one from my brain.

"Gray?" Savannah purrs, trying to reclaim my interest. "Do you want to get out of here?" She walks her fingers up my chest.

"Huh?" I hate to say it, but I almost forgot she was there. That's what Whitney does to me. I watch the slim brunette maneuver through the crowd. She's yet to spot me. And when she does, it's highly doubtful she'll be jumping for joy.

More like the opposite.

Everything around me falls away as I watch her with undisguised interest.

"I asked if you wanted to get out of here," Savannah murmurs again, her voice laced with impatience. She's a girl who commands attention and isn't used to being ignored.

When I don't immediately respond, the fingers trailing over my chest settle under my chin before manually turning my face until I have no other choice but to meet her gaze.

*Seriously?*

My forehead furrows.

What I'm not into is bossy chicks.

"Why don't we take this little party upstairs for a while?" The sly look in her eyes hints at all the dirty tricks she's got planned for me. I've been with Savannah enough times to know that she'll make good on those silent promises.

The girl is an absolute beast in bed.

As piqued as my interest had been a few moments ago, I'm going to take a hard pass on what she's offering. She thrusts out her lower lip in a sexy pout when I pry her hand away from my face.

My gaze darts to Whitney as she stops and takes in the chaos unfolding around her. People are drinking and dancing throughout the first floor of the house. The bar is well stocked, and shots are being passed around. There's a group in the corner playing beer pong, and, if the skunky scent permeating the air is any indication, there's more than just alcohol being served this fine evening. Clothing has yet to be shed, but it's only a matter of time before that happens.

Whitney's gaze slides around the room until it collides with mine. That one look sends a bolt of electricity shooting through my body, which is fucking ridiculous, but still...

That's exactly what happens.

Every damn time.

Until I can figure out what it is about her that intrigues me, there's no way I can move on. Been there, done that. Nothing works. Besides, quitting isn't in my nature, and I love a good challenge. And Whitney is nothing if not a challenge. I wouldn't be where I am today if I was willing to throw in the towel every time shit got tough. That thought is enough to have my lips bowing up at the corners.

Making a calculated move that's sure to piss her off, I hold up my beer and tip it in her direction. The girl doesn't disappoint. Her lips flatten as her glare morphs into a scowl. Instead of turning away, she glowers in my direction.

It's like we're engaged in a silent game of chicken from across the room. The longer she holds my gaze, refusing to back down, the more my cock stirs with interest.

Or challenge.

Take your pick.

My attraction for her is seriously perverse.

"Gray," Savannah whines. "I'm bored. Let's get out of here."

There's no way in hell that's happening.

I lift the beer to my lips, draining it before shaking the empty bottle. "Hey, would you mind getting me another one of these?"

"Sure." She nips the bottle from my fingers and disappears through the packed living room. Now that she's gone, I consider my game plan. Before I can take off in Whitney's direction, Collins sidles up to me with a couple of guys from the team.

"Hey," he says.

"What's up?" I ask without taking my gaze away from the dark-haired girl. It would be just my luck to lose her in this jam-packed crowd. I'll be damned if I allow that to happen.

When he elbows me in the side, my gaze shoots to him. Once my attention has been locked in, he grins and waggles his brows like the asshole he is.

Obviously, the object of my interest has not gone unnoticed.

*Great.*

The last thing I need is a captive audience waiting with bated breath for me to crash and burn. Especially with this girl. She's liable to wipe the floor with my ass before handing it back to me. Then I'd never hear the end of it from these jokers.

"Damn, but that girl is *hot* with a capital H," Mike, a sophomore defensive player, says before lifting the beer to his lips and draining half of it. The way he looks her up and down sets me on edge.

And it shouldn't.

I've never cared enough about a chick to feel jealousy where one was concerned. Hell, I've boned a good number of the same girls as my teammates, which is exactly why my number one rule is to wrap it up tight. God only knows what's getting passed around at any given time.

"Yeah, that's definitely one ass I'd like to tap." Justin Tinley gyrates his hips like he's in seventh grade and has no idea what the hell he's doing. "All night long."

My jaw locks as I glare. "Shut the fuck up, Tinley."

Justin glances at me in surprise before jerking his shoulders. "What?" he says, too clueless to understand why I'm jumping down his throat. "I'm just saying I would do her."

Collins smirks. He gets it. "That doesn't mean much, Tinley," Collins laughs. "Show me a girl you *wouldn't* do."

His words break the thick tension that has been gathering in the air like storm clouds, and I roll my shoulders before making a concerted effort to loosen them. I've never had a girl jack me up like this before. Whitney is an anomaly. Most of the time, chicks are interchangeable. One pussy is as good as the next.

"Can't." Justin glances around the crowded first floor of our house. "I'd do all of them."

"Yeah, but the real question is how many of them would *do* you?" Collins shoots back.

Justin gives him a one-fingered salute before muttering, "I'm getting another beer." With that, he stumbles off toward the kitchen.

On his way, he makes the mistake of grabbing a girl's ass. Before he can move on, the chick whirls around and slaps him squarely across the face. Tinley's mouth falls open as Collins and I collapse in laughter.

*Fucking Tinley...*

It wouldn't surprise me in the least to discover that he's a virgin. In fact, I'd be shocked to learn he actually gets some.

As if reading my thoughts, Collins shakes his head. "That guy is never going to get laid."

"I don't see it happening anytime soon," I agree. Which is funny as hell, because most of the guys on the hockey team are drowning in pussy. Girls throw themselves at us. And yet...Justin Tinley can't get laid to save his life.

There's definitely no clitty pity for that guy.

Now that the crowd has dispersed, my gaze darts to Whitney. My brows snap together.

What the fuck?

*Evert Monroe.*

Goddamn that guy.

Already he's homed in on Whitney. I think Collins is right about Evert being interested in her. Normally, that's not something that would bother me. There's nothing I love more than a little competition. Especially when it involves a female.

Bring it on.

But Whitney is different.

I've screwed the pooch, where she's concerned.

Whitney has been on my radar from the moment I stepped foot on campus. She's not one to hang out at the hockey games or parties where we congregate. And she hasn't slept her way through the Hellcat team roster like some of the puck bunnies around here.

If I'd been thinking with the right head when we hooked up, I would have steered clear and found a different chick to blow my wad on. But that's not what happened. A shit ton of shots later, hooking up had seemed like the best damn idea I'd ever had. I wanted to get Whitney out of my system, and screwing her had seemed like the easiest solution.

Unfortunately, that plan backfired spectacularly.

After experiencing the best orgasm of my life, I didn't know what to do. There was no way I was ready to jump into a relationship. And Whitney had monogamy written all over her. Instead of talking to her about it, I pussied out and avoided her like a little bitch.

Sure, I can admit it now. Young, dumb, and full of cum. That'd been me.

So, do I necessarily blame her for hating me?

Nope. Not at all.

I totally get it.

It's just that most girls would have softened their stance over the years. I would have been able to wear them down with my charm. But not Whitney.

If she would give me half a chance, she'd see that I wasn't the same guy I was freshman year. I've grown and matured.

Sort of.

Do I still love to dip my wick?

Guilty.

I won't even try to deny it. But nailing a different woman every weekend gets old. I never thought I'd hear myself say that, but it's true. And the one girl I'm interested in getting to know on a more personal level wants absolutely nothing to do with me.

That, ladies and gentlemen, is what one would call irony.

Sure, I can appreciate it.

Even if it does suck balls.

# WHITNEY

*W*ith Katelyn hot on my heels, I shove my way through the packed party. Unsurprisingly, the place smells like a brewery. Everyone has at least one red Solo cup in their hand. Some have two, which seems like overkill in my opinion. Apparently, the beer gods have smiled down upon this party and blessed it with an abundance of alcohol. There's an ocean of glassy-eyed stares.

As if to punctuate that thought, a guy staggers over and leers. "Hey, baby," he slurs incoherently.

*Sheesh...the things I do for friendship.*

If I could spin around on my heel and walk out of here, I would do it in a heartbeat. The debauchery is even worse than I imagined.

"Not interested," I growl, pushing past him and moving further into the living room.

As much as I want Evert and Katelyn to get together, I'm already regretting this decision. The hockey house is the last place I thought I'd being spending my Saturday night. The only thing I can say is that I've secured an agreement from my bestie to converse with Evert. So, if that means I have to put on my game face and deal with Gray, then so be it.

Hey, who knows?

Maybe I'll get lucky, and our paths won't cross.

Looking for Evert, I scan the crowd until my gaze collides with bright blue eyes. It might be dark in here, but his ocean-colored depths still pop. A little sizzle of awareness skitters across my spine before I lock it down tight. The last thing I need is for this attraction to settle in my core. That's exactly what landed me in this mess with Gray in the first place.

He raises his bottle in my direction, and I scowl in return. The corners of his lips quirk and I grit my teeth in silent aggravation.

Why does he take so much pleasure in messing with me?

What the hell is wrong with the guy?

He could have any girl he wanted. Even now, Savannah Mitchell is clinging to him like a baby rhesus monkey. By the looks of it, baby monkey doesn't appreciate his attention diverted elsewhere.

*Whatever.*

It's not like I care.

As far as I'm concerned, the girl with the overinflated boobs can have him. I have zero interest in tangling with Gray for a second time.

The moment Savannah forces his attention back to her, the unwanted energy humming through my body dissipates. In all the years I've been at Hillsdale, no other guy has ever made me feel this way.

It's disconcerting.

It just goes to show that you can't help who you're attracted to. Apparently, my type is dark-haired, blue-eyed players with muscles galore. I wonder if there's a twelve-step program for that. Lord knows I need it. The attraction I feel for a guy I'm barely able to tolerate is all kinds of wrong.

Ignoring Gray, I rip my gaze from him and continue searching the throng of people partying their asses off until I lock eyes on my target.

*Bingo!*

The sooner I get this over with, the quicker I'll be able to get out of here. With a smile on my face, I turn to Katelyn. "I hope you're ready for this."

"Huh?" Her brows draw together. "What are you talking about?"

I'm sure she was hoping to down a drink or two before we made contact, but the opportunity has presented itself and there's no time like the present. Not bothering to explain, I wave my hand and shout Evert's name to snag his attention.

Katelyn screeches in mortification as she yanks on my arm. "What are you doing?"

"Making good on our agreement," I shout over the music. "You promised to talk with Evert, and I'm about to make that happen." I glance over my shoulder and give her a quick once-over. "Tits out, girl. Lover boy is on his way."

Her eyes go a little wild as she glances around for an exit strategy. "I really hate you right now," she hisses.

I shrug and keep moving through the drunken crowd. "Hey, you're the one who begged me to come along."

"That's a decision I now regret," she grumbles.

My shoulders shake with silent laughter as Evert makes his way to us. His gaze flits from me to Katelyn before settling on me again. My friend tries her best to scooch behind me, but I step out of the way and loop my arm through hers, so she can't escape.

"Hey," Evert says with a smile directed at me. "I didn't expect to see you here tonight."

He slides his fingers through his long, blond hair and pushes a chunk out of his eyes. Katelyn sighs and I press my lips together in an effort not to laugh. But it's difficult. She is so in lust with this guy.

Trying to play it cool, I say, "You're always inviting me to your parties, so Katelyn and I thought we'd come and check it out."

"I'm glad you did." His smile broadens and his bottle green eyes twinkle.

It's not difficult to see why Katelyn is crushing hard on this guy. He's a real cutie.

Step one of this plan was to snag Evert's attention. With that accomplished, we can move on to the second step, which is to get him to take notice of her.

Even though this is going well, Katelyn is slowly trying to inch away from me. I tighten my grip so she can't skedaddle away.

*Not gonna happen, girl. Don't even try it.*

"Evert, have you met my friend, Katelyn?"

His gaze slides to my roommate. He tilts his head, and his hair shifts over his eyes again. "I don't think so." He gives a slight chin lift in greeting. "Nice to meet you."

Katelyn freezes, looking like a deer trapped in the bright headlights of an oncoming vehicle. When she says nothing in response, I squeeze her hand and she startles to attention. "You, too!"

Silence descends, and I clear my throat to keep the conversational ball rolling. "Katelyn is a huge hockey fan." I glance at her expectantly, hoping she'll loosen up and jump in. This interaction is nosediving fast. Maybe I should have plied her with liquor beforehand. "She attended all of the home games last season."

"Oh, yeah?" His brows rise with mild interest.

I wait a beat. When Katelyn remains unresponsive, I dig my nails into her hand. Her breath catches as she bobs her head.

*Sheesh.*

Getting these two together is going to be more challenging than I originally suspected. Maybe I'm the one who should have downed a drink or two. But still, I'm going to give this introduction everything I've got. "In fact, not only does Katelyn enjoy watching hockey, but she actually played in high school." I nudge her shoulder with my own. "She was really good."

My roommate's cheeks flood with color.

Evert perks up at the comment and smiles. "Really? My sister played hockey, too."

Dare I say there's more than just mild curiosity shining in his eyes?

I think we might have actually sparked some genuine interest.

Katelyn draws in a shaky breath and says in a rush, "We're a hockey family. I grew up at the rink."

He nods as if he knows exactly what she means before taking a drink from his bottle of beer. "What position did you play?"

"Right wing." The nervousness threading its way through her voice begins to ebb as she warms to the subject. "I played travel until high school."

My gaze bounces between them as a cautious smile spreads across my face.

"Huh." His eyes ignite with more interest. "Wow. You must have been pretty good. How come you didn't continue playing in college? There are so many scholarship opportunities for women's hockey."

Success!

*Houston, we have liftoff.*

*I repeat—we have liftoff!*

I'm tempted to pump my fist in the air but refrain as Evert asks questions about hockey and Katelyn answers them easily, even managing to throw out a few of her own for him to field.

*Awww, look at that. My baby is finally taking a few wobbly steps on her own.*

Pride fills my chest.

Not wanting to disturb them, I point to the kitchen. "I'm going to hit the bar and grab a drink. I'll be right back."

Not waiting for a reply, I extract myself from the conversation.

A drink is the last thing on my mind, but I'd needed an excuse to make myself scarce. At least for a few minutes. Then I'll pop back over and make sure everything is going smoothly between them.

My goal is for Evert to secure Katelyn's number by the end of the night. Anything more than that is gravy, as far as I'm concerned.

With a smile, I fight my way through the throng of people to the kitchen. Halfway there, I decide to make a pitstop at the bathroom. That should give Katelyn and Evert more than enough time alone. I don't want to toss her to the wolves just yet.

Decision made, I swing around and slam into a hard body. The contact makes me stumble back a step. Before I can crash into those unlucky enough to be in my general vicinity, strong hands shoot out and grab hold of me.

I'm about to apologize and thank the guy who has saved me from making an ass out of myself when my gaze slams into bright blue eyes that are brimming with undisguised humor.

The apology dies a quick death on my lips as I frown.

Of all the people at this party I could have run into, it had to be him.

# GRAY

*H*er scowl has my lips lifting at the corners. I can't help it. It's a natural reaction where Whitney is concerned. My hands are still wrapped around her arms, holding her securely in place. Letting her go is the last thing on my mind. Hell, I'd like nothing more than to pull her closer. But that's not going to happen unless I'm looking for a swift kick in the nuts.

"Hey, if it isn't my favorite girl!" I flash her a disarming smile. "I was hoping you'd make a cameo appearance tonight. And look, here you are." I cock my head and tap my chin thoughtfully. "Coincidence? I think not."

"Hey!" she greets with an equal amount of cheerfulness. Although I'd lay odds that it's forced. "I was really hoping *not* to see you." The smile falls abruptly from her face. "No such luck."

"Come on now," I say playfully, reeling her to me. "We both know that you couldn't stay away if you tried." All I want to do is tug her closer and bury my nose in her hair. Instead of giving in to the impulse, I force down the need.

A garbled sound rushes up from her throat as she attempts to shove me away. "Ugh! Get off me, you big oaf!"

Yeah, that's not going to happen.

Not when I've got Whitney *exactly* where I want her. Instead of relinquishing my hold, I wrap my arms around her slim body and drag her to me before whispering against her ear, "How about we find a nice quiet place upstairs?"

Spine straightening, she rears back. "I'd sooner shoot myself," she mutters between gritted teeth as her palms flatten against my chest.

"Now that's just hurtful."

"You're impossible," she grunts, still trying her to push me away. But like I said, I'm not going anywhere.

And neither is she.

"Yup," I agree easily. "You're better off just giving in to the inevitable."

Whitney glances around my shoulder. "Hey, I just spotted a couple of girls who actually look like they'd be receptive to your manhandling. Maybe you should try your luck with them." Her gaze darts to mine as her lips twist with disdain. "I'm sure you could have all three if you wanted."

I glance in their direction. Just as Whitney claimed, there's a trio of girls watching us with avid expressions. They flash overly toothy smiles and wave ecstatically. Sure, they're pretty enough.

But still…

My eyes slide to hers. "Nah, not my type."

"Please." Whitney snorts with disbelief. "Breathing with a penchant for spreading their legs wide is *exactly* your type."

I take a moment to look her up and down. Her face heats at my slow perusal. "Want to know what my type is?" Releasing her arm, I pick up a lock of her hair and rub the silky strands between my fingers. "Long, dark hair."

With a frown, Whitney slaps my hand away.

"And a killer glare." I grin as her scowl intensifies. "Yup, just like that." I give her a wink. "See how perfect we are for each other?"

The blush staining her cheeks deepens. She gulps and opens her mouth to blast me with what will no doubt be a scathing retort. I'm fully prepared. Hell, bring it on. I'd be lying through my teeth if I didn't admit that my dick is stiffening with anticipation. The more we verbally spar, the more turned-on I get.

For obvious reasons, now isn't the time to dwell on how messed up that is.

The only thing I care about—

"Hey, Gray."

Whitney snaps her mouth shut as we turn at the untimely interruption.

"Hey, Savannah," I greet with forced casualness. When I sent her off to grab another beer, I'd been hoping her interest would get snagged by another guy. It's not like I'm the only hockey player she likes to lavish attention on.

Ignoring Whitney, Savannah flips her long mane of strawberry-blond hair over her shoulder and flashes a sultry smile in my direction before jiggling the cup of beer in her hand. "You ready to head upstairs?"

*Aw, hell.*

I wince as Whitney tenses. Whatever progress I'd painstakingly made with this girl has just been blown to smithereens. Savannah's a cool chick and we've enjoyed each other's company on numerous occasions, but I don't have any real interest in her. "Maybe another time."

Caught off guard by my dismissal, her gaze flicks in Whitney's direction. "But I thought we were going to," she licks her glossy lips suggestively, "*you know.*"

I clear my throat, hoping she'll get the hint and take off. "That sounds fun, but not tonight."

Her brows snap together. "Are you sure?"

"Um, yeah." How much clearer do I have to be?

I'm not interested.

"Actually," Whitney cuts in as she fights her way out of my embrace, "that sounds like a great idea. I was just about to leave." Her gaze slides between the two of us. "Don't let me stand in the way of previous plans."

I have no other choice but to release her. All the warmth she created in my arms disappears. As she takes a few steps away, my hand snakes out to lock around her wrist. If I let her go, she'll disappear into the crowd and I'll never see her again, or she'll leave the party altogether. And then my chance to make headway with her will be gone.

I almost snort.

Whitney has the thickest candy-coating shell I've ever come across. Is there a soft nougat filling buried deep inside?

That's the million-dollar question. One I'm determined to figure out.

The dark-haired girl tugs her arm, trying to break my hold. Her gaze darts to mine before glancing at Savannah.

"Whitney and I have unfinished business to take care of." My attention is solely focused on the brunette. "Don't we, sweetheart?"

Stupid question.

I know better than to ask. Especially with an endearment tacked on. All I'm doing is poking an already irate bear.

Her eyes flash as she frowns. "No—"

"Sure, we do," I cut in.

Savannah's face falls as her gaze narrows on Whitney. She gives her a quick once-over before immediately dismissing her as no competition. "Gray, you can't be serious." A malicious smile curves her lips as she snorts. "She doesn't even have boobs."

*Oh, boy.*

Whitney straightens as if someone has just rammed a two-by-four up her ass. "Excuse me? What did you just say?"

Wanting to diffuse this powder keg of a situation before it explodes in my face, I try to soothe her. "I don't think she meant it like—"

"Yes, I did." Savannah's glittering gaze is fixed on Whitney. "What are you going to do about it?" She folds her arms under her ample breasts, which only makes them appear fuller. Cleavage spills out the front of her low-cut shirt.

Not that I'm looking.

Because I am most definitely *not* looking.

Exactly how stupid do you think I am?

Don't answer that.

I'm staring anywhere *but* at Savannah's tits, which is no easy feat. They're huge. I've spent many an hour playing with them.

Right...moving along.

Instead of backing down from the attack, Whitney takes a step forward. My grip tightens around her wrist as I attempt to hold her back. I don't want her getting within striking distance of Savannah. Not that I think Whitney will do serious damage, but the last thing we need is a catfight breaking out. It would only give Whitney more ammunition to hate me with.

Whitney smirks. "I don't know. Maybe find a pin and pop your inflatables? You might not realize this, but there are people who actually think it's more important to have brains than floatation devices."

Savannah's eyes narrow at the insult. "Are you saying I'm not smart?"

"Maybe the fact that you have to ask the question is answer enough."

All hell is breaking loose in slow motion, and there's not a damn thing I can do about it.

Savannah is just about to open her mouth when she's jostled from behind. Her hand goes flying and the cup of beer she had retrieved ends up splashed across the front of Whitney's shirt.

The dark-haired girl gasps, her back rounding as she stares down with wide eyes.

Savannah nips her lower lip between sharp, white teeth. "Whoops." Laughter simmers in her voice. "Sorry. That was an accident."

Well, shit.

How the hell did we go from bad to worse in two seconds flat?

# WHITNEY

*I* gasp as cold beer douses the front of my shirt and drips down my body before puddling at my feet. People nearby turn and gawk. Laughter fills my ears as others point in my direction.

Oh my God. I want to sink through the floorboards and disappear. My white top is plastered against my chest. I look like I've just entered a wet T-shirt contest.

Whose brilliant idea was it to wear white?

Oh, right. *Mine.*

I glance at Savannah with narrowed eyes. Part of me doubts this was entirely an accident. It was timed perfectly. Plus, there's a smug expression on her face.

What a crazy-ass bitch.

Who does something like that?

With a smirk twisting her lips, Savannah's gaze drops to my chest where it lingers. "I wouldn't worry about it. It's not like you actually have tits."

*Oh no she didn't!*

I tighten my hands and advance on her. I'm not a girl prone to violence, but I'd be willing to make an exception in this instance.

Gray's grip intensifies on my arm. "Take it easy, tiger. It's just beer.

No big deal." He glares in Savannah's direction. "I'm sure it was an accident, right?"

Savannah's tongue darts out to smudge her lips with moisture before she gives Gray a wounded look. "Of course it was!" She waves her hand behind her. "Someone pushed me."

I snort.

*Likely story.*

With a sweet smile on her lips, Savannah says, "Maybe you should run along and change. You're beginning to reek." She gives me a little finger wave. "Tootles!"

Ignoring Savannah, Gray turns to me. "I have a solution."

The last thing I want to do is admit defeat, but Savannah's right. I need to go home and get out of these wet clothes. Not only do I smell gross, but I feel nasty as well. "I'm leaving."

"Nope, that's not necessary." Without further explanation, Gray whips his T-shirt over his head, revealing a ripped chest.

Distracted from my own predicament, my gaze licks over his sculpted pecs and perfectly cut abs. His jeans sit low on his hips, showing off a chiseled V. There's not an ounce of fat on the guy.

The noise of the party fades as I have my own private moment with his body. It's seriously amazing. And yes, it's a painful admittance.

"See something you like?" Humor simmers in his deep voice.

The question has me blinking out of my Gray-induced trance and I wince at being caught staring so blatantly. Even though the damage has been done, I drag my gaze from the sexy ridges of his form to meet his eyes.

Of course, he's grinning from ear to ear.

I fight the heat rising in my cheeks. "Nope, not at all." I'm lying through my teeth, and, by the smirk on his face, he's aware of it. I don't know what's worse—being caught ogling Gray McNichols or standing at this party with a wet shirt plastered against my breasts. I'm tempted to bury my face in my hands, but I need to brazen out this situation or I'll never live it down.

Gray will make certain of it.

"Take it all off, McNichols!" a girl hollers. A mixture of whistles and catcalls fill the air.

"Yeah, don't leave us hanging. We want to see more skin!" another female yells over the thumping beat of the music.

More lewd suggestions follow, but Gray doesn't seem bothered by the comments. Instead, his attention stays pinned to mine. It's like we're the only two people in the room. An unwanted flutter fills my belly as I gulp down my rising panic.

Everyone is staring at us.

Actually, they're ogling Gray.

Maybe I should thank him for that. He's taken the spotlight off me. Was that his intention all along?

I jerk my thumb over my shoulder. "I'm just going to—"

Before I can finish the sentence, he grabs the hem of my shirt and drags it up my body.

For one stunned moment, I allow him to do it until my reflexes kick in. Then I struggle against his movements. "What the hell are you—"

The rest of the words get cut off as the sopping wet shirt is wrestled over my head. I bat at Gray's hands, but it doesn't do any good. He rips the shirt from my body, leaving me exposed.

My mouth falls open and I screech in outrage. As soon as my arms spring up to cover my chest, he whips his dry shirt over my head and yanks it down my torso so that I'm covered. I slip my arms through the holes and stare at him in shock.

"Problem solved. No more wet T-shirt contest." He gives me a sly wink. "Although, I'm not going to lie, I like the wet T-shirt look on you."

*What the hell just happened?*

I shake my head, unsure how to respond. "I don't..."

His grin widens and his dimples pop. "A simple thank you will suffice."

"Thanks," I mumble, shifting my weight.

His smile morphs into a knowing smirk. There's a twinkle in his eyes. "Was that really so difficult?"

39

"Ummm, kind of."

"Yeah," he agrees with a chuckle, "I bet it was."

"Gray," Savannah whines, clearly trying to win back his attention.

"I'm going to take Whitney to the kitchen for a drink. I'd say she's owed one after what happened."

"You are?" I ask.

Nope, that's not a good idea. I need to find Katelyn and get out of here before anything else happens and I'm not able to show my face around campus. This evening has only just begun, and I've already reached my limit.

"Yup, I am." Gray doesn't give me time to argue. Instead, he grabs my hand and tows me to the back of the house. The crowd parts like the Red Sea for him. The power this guy wields is almost impressive. "Tell you what, Winters. You've had a rough night, so I'm going to buy you that drink."

"Isn't the beer free?"

"Maybe." He throws a glance over his shoulder and the muscles of my belly clench. "But that sounded way more chivalrous, didn't it?"

"Sure," I snort. Chivalrous isn't exactly a descriptor I'd use for Gray.

More like cocky.

Or egotistical.

How about aggravating?

We could always go with womanizing.

And those are just a few off the top of my head.

But chivalrous?

Not so much.

As he leads me to the kitchen, I can't help but think that this situation has disaster written all over it.

*The two of us having a drink together?*

*Getting chummy?*

Warning bells go off in my head. I try tugging at my fingers, but it's impossible to break free. Gray stops and swings around to face me. His blue gaze pierces mine.

"I appreciate what you did back there, but I'm going to head out."

40

His hand tightens around mine as he cocks his head. "Come on, Winters. You've got time for one drink. Chill out and have a little fun for once."

I frown at the implication. "I do have fun." Lots of it. Ask anyone and they'll tell you I'm a load of laughs.

"Great. Then we can have a little fun together." He pulls me closer. "Doesn't that sound like a good idea?"

No. What it sounds like is impending doom.

Unsure what to do, I gnaw my lower lip.

One drink...then I can find Katelyn and leave. Hopefully, she and Evert are still hitting it off. If that's the case, then my run-in with Gray and Savannah will have been worth it.

This is me taking one for the team. I hope Katelyn appreciates it.

"Okay," I relent. "One drink and then I'm out of here."

His lips lift into a smile and a flare of attraction leaps to life in my core. No matter how much I try to douse it, it's impossible to stomp out completely.

It's just one drink.

What's the worst that can happen?

# GRAY

*I* crack open an eye and stretch lazily. As I do, I realize there's a warm body snuggled up against my side. One long leg has been thrown over mine.

*Well, hello there morning wood. Nice of you to make an appearance.*

It's certainly not unheard of for me to wake up with a random chick in my bed. Although it doesn't happen nearly as often as it used to. I wrack my brain, trying to recall who the lucky lady is.

It goes without saying that I most likely rocked her world.

Unfortunately, everything from last night is a little murky. I rewind the evening to the beginning. The first thing I remember is Savannah running her hands over my chest. Nothing out of the ordinary there. Then Whitney made an unexpected appearance. I wince, thinking about Savannah dumping her beer down the front of Whitney's shirt. Those pert little nips had stiffened right up, making my mouth water.

And I sure as hell wasn't going to let anyone else ogle her. So, I'd whipped off my shirt, then hers, before sliding mine over her delectable body. She'd tried escaping at that point, but I'd talked her into staying for one drink.

Which turned into two.

Then three.

Christ...didn't we down a couple of tequila shots?

And I seem to recall us playing a game of cups.

The last person I remember being with is—drumroll please —Whitney.

All the fuzziness clouding my brain vanishes and I'm suddenly wide awake.

*There is no way in hell that—*

I turn my head and inhale a sharp breath as I come face-to-face with the girl I've spent three years thinking about.

*Fuck.*

*How the hell did we end up in bed together?*

*Did we...*

I scrub a hand down my face as my mind races, needing to piece together the rest of the evening. I've been trying to talk Whitney back into my bed for a while now, but there's no way I'd knock boots with a girl who's too inebriated to know what she's doing. And Whitney had been feeling no pain by three o'clock in the morning.

Carefully, so as not to wake her, I grab the edge of the blanket and peek beneath it. A pair of sunny-side-up titties greets me. Damn, but they're perky as hell. I'm tempted to reach out and stroke her pretty little nipples, but I resist the temptation.

If Whitney wakes up and finds me groping her, she's liable to go all Loraina Bobbitt on me and cut off my junk. Hell, if I hadn't stepped in last night with Savannah, I think Whitney would have slugged her. That girl can give as good as she gets.

You have to admire her spirit.

Lord knows that I do.

Amongst other attributes. Like those gorgeous titties hiding under the comforter.

I'm certainly not in any rush to finish my perusal. How else am I going to crack this case? My gaze flicks down her lithe body, touching on all that naked skin. The semi I've been rocking becomes full-fledged as they land on an itty-bitty, teeny-weeny polka dot pair of panties.

I collapse against the mattress with relief.

The case has now been closed. I'm fairly confident that if we'd had sex last night, she'd be buck-ass naked. This situation isn't nearly as bad as I first suspected.

That being said, Whitney is going to flip her lid when she wakes up and realizes that she's practically naked in my bed. This is the last place she'd want to find herself. A smile spreads across my face as an idea takes shape. Unable to resist toying with her, I lean over until my lips can brush across hers.

Once.

Twice.

Three times.

I groan, wishing I could do this all day long.

After a moment, she stirs, making a sexy little noise and stretching her body. Her nipples pebble as one breast brushes against my ribs. Unable to suppress my response, a growl rumbles up from my chest. Her dark lashes flutter as she focuses on my grinning face.

She stills as her eyes widen to the point of nearly popping out of her head. I see the exact moment that it dawns on her where she is.

I want to chuckle at the horror-filled expression that morphs across her face. Instead I say, "Morning, sunshine. Sleep well?" I wink, acting like this situation is an everyday occurrence. "I sure did."

Whitney shakes her head as if to clear it. Or, more than likely, to erase the image of me hovering over her.

*Sorry sweetheart, that ain't going to happen.*

"What the hell?" she mumbles, glancing around wildly as she rubs her eyes.

As difficult as it is to keep a straight face, I don't allow the smile to break free. Although, I'm dying inside. "I hope that expression doesn't mean you're already regretting what happened last night."

She squeezes her eyes tightly shut as if trying to block out the implication of those words. "Please," she groans, "tell me we didn't sleep together."

"Oh, you bet your sweet ass we did." I chuckle and smack a kiss against her lips. "For the record, you were a real wildcat in the sack. *So* much better than I remember."

Her eyes fly open, and her mouth forms the perfect O. "*No.*"

I nod and unleash a wicked grin. "Oh yeah, baby. Trust me when I say it was a pleasant surprise to find that you're into anal." I waggle my brows and leer. "*Me likey.*"

The color filling her cheeks drains away as Whitney stares in shock. "You're lying," she whispers.

My guess is that she damn well hopes I am.

"How's that backdoor feeling? I made sure to lube us both up *real* good." I press my pointer finger and thumb together and make an okay sign with my right hand. Then I click my tongue and give her a lewd wink.

Whitney shakes her head furiously back and forth. Her mouth opens and closes like a dying fish gasping for its last breath. Her espresso-colored eyes go a little wild. Any moment, she's going to have a total freak out.

Normally, I wouldn't find that gaping expression attractive on a girl, but this is Whitney Winters we're talking about. Nearly everything she does turns me on. I'm probably enjoying this a little more than I should. There aren't many times I've been able to get something over on her.

Before I can continue with the lie, she throws off the covers and rolls to the side of the bed, hitting the carpeted floor with a loud thump. Laughter bubbles up inside me. I won't be able to hold it back much longer. I peek over the edge of the mattress to see her scrambling backwards as if she's trying to put as much distance between us as she can.

Desperation fills her eyes. "*No, no, no!* This can't be happening," she mumbles more to herself than me. "There's no way I slept with you. I wouldn't do that. *Not again.*"

As tempted as I am to keep running with this, I decide to pull the plug and put Whitney out of her misery before she loses it. "Chill out," I chuckle. "I'm just pulling your leg. We didn't do anything last night."

I point to her pink panties. "You're still wearing underwear. And trust me, if we'd fucked, you'd be waking up naked in my bed."

A loud gasp falls from her lips as she jumps to her feet. She's practically shaking with outrage. The killer glare I've grown to love over the years is now aimed in my direction. I don't think any girl has ever looked at me with so much hostility.

It's kind of hot.

All right, there's no two ways about it. It's sexy as hell.

*"What!"* she screeches at a decibel that could shatter glass. *"You're such an asshole!"* Instead of being relieved that nothing happened, she glances wildly around the room. The moment her gaze lands on the thick tomb of a textbook, she lunges for the nightstand and heaves it in my direction with all her might.

*Incoming!*

Thank God I've got cat-like reflexes. I wouldn't survive very long on the ice if I didn't. I quickly roll to the side as it hits the pillow with a thud.

I blink.

Shit…that could have caused permanent damage.

"I seriously hate you right now!" she growls as her hands tighten.

I toss the covers back and climb out of bed on the other side. A little separation seems like a damn fine idea right about now. It doesn't occur to me that I'm not wearing a stitch of clothing until her gaze drops to my groin and her brows skyrocket across her forehead.

"You're naked," she accuses, pointing a finger at my junk.

That's not usually the response I get. Most girls are more than happy to stare in awe or run their hands over me with giddiness.

But not this one.

I flex my biceps. "You're looking at two hundred and twenty pounds of pure steel and sex appeal." My lips bow suggestively at the corners. "You didn't seem to mind too much last night. In fact, when I woke up, you were cuddled against me, grabbing my—"

"Please," she hisses as color once again blooms in her cheeks.

For a chick so offended by my nudity, she certainly hasn't ripped her attention away from my lengthening erection. I'm so freaking hard right now that I could punch holes through the wall. Especially with the way she's eating me up with her eyes.

Closing the distance between us is a terrible idea.

But that doesn't stop me from stalking around the bed. Sensing my intent, her eyes widen as she scrambles backward until her calves hit the mattress and she collapses on it. I bend forward until I can hover over her nearly naked body.

Heat emanates off her in thick waves. The urge to press myself against her pounds through me. That I don't give in to my body's natural instinct is a testament to the willpower I have. All I want to do is run my hands over her and feel her melt under my touch.

With our gazes locked, I place a hand on either side of her head so that she's caged in and can't escape. Not that she's trying. She remains completely still. All I have to do is close the inch of space between us and I'd feel her slender curves pressed against my hard lines. The breath catches at the back of her throat as my lips ghost over her parted ones. Unable to resist, I stroke my dick against her panty-clad pussy.

*Fuuuuck...that feels amazing.*

A little slice of heaven here on earth.

My jaw locks as I grit my teeth, holding myself in check so I don't take this too far. God, but I want to bury my cock in her softness.

I groan as she tilts her pelvis toward me.

A whimper slides from her lips. "Gray..."

My control snaps as I continue to rub myself against her. The movement is long and languid. I could do this all day. Except...if I don't rein this in, I'm liable to come like a horny teenager.

How embarrassing would that be?

"Yeah, baby?" I growl.

"We can't do this."

I nip her lower lip with my teeth before gently sucking the fullness into my mouth. Her body stills as energy crackles and snaps between us. I give her flesh one last tug and reluctantly release it.

"Then maybe you should stop staring at my cock, because all you're doing is giving me ideas." Backing away is the last thing on my mind, but I don't have any other choice. I've pushed far enough.

For now.

But I'm not finished with her by a long shot.

As soon as I step away, Whitney draws in a deep breath and rolls off the side of the bed. Her feet hit the floor as her gaze flies around the room. Once she spies her clothing crumpled in the corner where it had been shed in the wee hours of the morning, she stumbles toward it.

With shaking fingers, Whitney throws on the shirt I gave her at the party before hauling her crumpled jeans over her thighs and buttoning them. Her long hair slides forward in a silky curtain, shielding her face from view. My fingers itch to tangle in the silky length.

Now that she's dressed, the ever-present invisible shield meant to keep me at a distance has been fully reactivated. With rigidly held shoulders, Whitney wheels back around to face me as she rakes a hand through her hair. Her gaze drops to my still-erect cock before she quickly averts it.

"Could you please cover that thing up?" A scowl twists her lips as she waves her hand in my direction. "I think it's staring at me."

I smirk and stretch my arms overhead, reaching for the ceiling. My muscles ripple and lengthen. Her jaw is locked so tight that it's in imminent danger of shattering, but she doesn't glance away.

Good. I want her to get an eyeful before I cover up.

*Take a long look at what you're missing, sweetheart.*

With unhurried movements, I retrieve a pair of boxer briefs from the dresser and pull them over my junk. Then I throw my arms wide. "Is that better? I certainly wouldn't want to offend your virgin sensibilities."

With a snort, Whitney rolls her eyes. She turns away and searches the room before grumbling, "Have you seen my purse?"

I spy the red leather rectangle lying on the desk. If I point it out, she'll grab it and go. That purse is all that's keeping her from flying out the door. Just as I scoop up the bag, her phone blares from inside and Coldplay's Viva La Vida fills the room.

My brow rises. "Really?"

"It's Coldplay." She folds her arms defensively across her chest and glares. "They're, like, a super band. Everyone knows that."

"Are you crazy? They're nowhere near super band status, but it's cute that you think so."

Her eyes widen as her face goes slack. "Please tell me that you're not being serious right now."

"I'm as serious as a heart attack, sweetheart. Coldplay is mediocre at best. Now, U2? *That's* a super band. Their music spans decades." I shake my head. "Chris Martin will never touch Bono."

She gasps and stabs a finger in my direction. "You take that back right now!"

"Sorry, can't." I shrug. "It's the truth. You're fooling yourself if you think otherwise. I'm sure in about five years, they'll be playing the county fair circuit." Do I really think that? No. But it's fun as hell to wind her up.

With a growl of frustration, she steps forward, swiping at her purse. Again, thanks to my quick reflexes, I jerk it away at the last second and grin.

Her body vibrates with anger as she narrows her eyes and plants her hands on her hips. "Can I *please* have my purse so I can get the hell out of here?"

A smile simmers around the corners of my lips as I deliberately hold it out for her. "See? All you had to do was ask nicely."

Whitney bares her teeth as she reaches out and cautiously nips the small bag from my fingers. Once it's in hand, she huffs out an exasperated breath.

"Thanks," she mutters, shifting her weight and breaking eye contact.

Reluctant to see her go, I ask, "Do you need a ride?"

"From a guy who talks smack about Coldplay?" She shakes her

head. "I don't think so." Whitney rummages around in her purse until she pulls out her cell and glances at the screen. "Shit." She winces and massages her temple with her free hand. "How is it already after nine?"

"That's what happens when you don't go to bed until three in the morning." I arch a brow as an emotion that resembles jealousy ignites in my belly. "Why? You late for a hot date?"

"Yeah," she mumbles before stuffing the phone back inside the bag. "Something like that."

I'm tempted to ask with whom, but I bite back the question at the last moment, knowing damn well that she won't give me any more information. I've irritated the hell out of her this morning.

And yet, I can't bring myself to regret it.

She takes a step toward the door before coming to a halt. "I need my shoes." Her gaze darts around the room. "Then I can leave and forget this ever happened."

There's a shit load of relief flooding through her voice.

Instead of playing any more games, I point them out. Whitney falls on them before sliding her feet into the worn pink Converse sneakers. Once she has them on, she glances at me as if unsure what to say.

I haven't bothered throwing on any clothes. Even though I'm still in my form-fitting boxer briefs, her gaze doesn't deviate from mine. I plow a hand roughly through my hair and flash her a grin. "So, is this the start of a beautiful relationship?"

Whatever tension had been gathering in her body dissipates. Her eyes harden and her upper lip curls. "Over my dead body."

"Your loss." I shrug. "Maybe you should take some time to think it over."

Her gaze drops momentarily to the erection tenting my boxers, and heat slams into her pale cheeks. "That's not necessary," she mutters before stalking to the door.

Just as she steps over the threshold, I call out, "I'll see you around, Winters."

She stops, spine stiffening, but doesn't turn to meet my gaze. Instead, she hastens her step and disappears down the second floor hallway. I hear her footfalls on the staircase before the front door opens and closes with a thud.

A smile of satisfaction springs to my lips.

It might not be much, but I'd say that progress was made in the right direction.

Maybe.

# WHITNEY

*Oh my God!*
Did that seriously happen?
Did I *really* wake up in Gray McNichols' bed?

I groan, because there's no denying the facts. As if that wasn't bad enough, a tiny scrap of material is all that kept me from being naked. I've never been so relieved to be wearing underwear in my life. Gray, on the other hand, hadn't been wearing a stitch. I gulp as that thought worms its way into my brain.

He'd been gloriously naked.

No matter how I feel about the guy, I can't deny that he's a spectacular male specimen. All those thickly corded muscles that look like they've been chiseled from marble... My mouth turns cottony just conjuring up an image of his perfectly sculpted chest, drool-worthy pectorals, and the ridges of his six-pack abs.

Not to mention lower.

*Much lower.*

No. Don't think about his—

*Arghhh!*

*I said don't think about it!*

Gray McNichols is a mistake I narrowly avoided making for a second time. I should be thanking my lucky stars that I managed to escape his evil clutches unscathed.

Instead…

I shake my head to clear it of those unruly thoughts. This is exactly why I'm so adamant about keeping my distance from him. The man is completely dangerous. My brain clicks off whenever he's near, and I start thinking with my lady parts.

While I'm a little sketchy on the details regarding how far Gray and I went last night, I'm one hundred percent positive that we didn't have sex. And I certainly didn't engage in *anal*. My cheeks heat even thinking about it.

*As if…*

For the umpteenth time this morning, an image of his thick cock pops into my head. Yeah…there's not enough lube in the world to make that happen.

It's a ten-minute jog from Gray's house to my apartment building. Thank God I had the good sense to wear sneakers and not a cute pair of heels. By the time I reach the front door of the lobby, my gut is roiling with nausea, and I'm completely out of breath.

Word of advice—jogging after a night of drinking is not a good idea.

I'm going to chalk up this experience as penance for last evening's stupidity and hope it never happens again.

Lesson learned the hard way.

I'm still huffing and puffing as I ride the elevator up to the third floor. I pull out my phone and check the time. A groan escapes. In less than thirty minutes, I'm supposed to meet Dad for brunch. Since I'm alone in the elevator, I lift my arm and do a little sniff test.

It's just as I suspected. There's no way I can leave the apartment without showering. The scent of stale beer wafts off me in suffocating waves. I almost gag. My belly churns like the sea during a storm. That noxious scent has the vomit rising dangerously in my throat. Sweat breaks out across my brow and my mouth fills with saliva.

I've barely been awake for thirty minutes and already this day is a disaster.

The doors open, and I rush out of the car. The first thing I need to do is down half a bottle of Pepto Bismol, otherwise there's no way I'll make it through brunch. The thought of eating greasy food nauseates me.

I step into the hallway and nearly slam into the people waiting for the elevator.

"Oh, I'm so..." My voice trails off as I focus on the two girls wearing tight athletic tops and leggings.

Great.

*Savannah.*

Just the person I *don't* want to see.

Coming face-to-face with her rouses my anger from last night. We both know that what she did wasn't an accident. My gaze shoots from Savannah to the freakishly scary clone standing next to her.

Savannah's eyes light up with recognition. Her lips thin as she looks me over. "Well, well, well...look who's doing the walk of shame."

*Really? That's the best she can do?*

I paste a pleasant smile on my face. I've dealt with enough mean girls in high school to be unfazed by this catty behavior. "And good morning to you, too. I'd love to stay and chat, but I'm kind of in a hurry." I flutter my fingers in her direction, putting an end to the conversation.

Her lips twist as she bares her teeth. "Just an FYI, Gray sleeps with everyone." She gives me a mocking smile that drips with faux innocence before flipping her glossy hair over her shoulder. "I wouldn't want you to think that you're anything special." Again, her eyes take a slow tour of my body. "Because you are most definitely *not.*"

I bristle at the insult. I might be sexually attracted to Gray, but so is half the school. I don't need Savannah throwing that in my face. Gray did a good job of showing me how inconsequential I was after we hooked up freshman year. It's not a lesson I'll soon forget.

But still, even though I want her words to roll off my back, her poisonous dart hits home.

"I'll keep that in mind," I reply sweetly. "It's nice that us girls can look out for each other."

Her jaw tightens. "Don't expect him to remember your name Monday morning. He's probably already forgotten it by now." She glances at the pink sports watch adorning her wrist and smirks. "Especially since we were just on our way to see him."

As impossible as it is to keep the smile glued in place, that's exactly what I do. I'll be damned if I let Savannah and her witless clone push my buttons. "Great! Hope you have fun." I give her a wink as I push past them. "I sure did!"

I hate to admit it, but it feels good to watch the triumphant smile fall from Savannah's face.

Bitchy girls are the worst. Savannah should open her eyes and realize that I have zero interest where Gray is concerned. I'm not competition. She's more than welcome to have at him.

I almost snort.

*Can you imagine?*

How stupid would you have to be to fall for a player like him?

I'm not even going to dignify that question with a response.

I unlock the apartment door and beeline toward the bathroom. I catch Katelyn's surprised gaze from where she's hunkered down on the couch as I rush past.

"Hey! Where have you been?" she calls out, following me into the bathroom.

"Don't ask," I mutter, reaching into the shower stall and turning on the taps. Water sputters to life as I swing around to face Katelyn, who now leans against the doorjamb.

"Listen here, little missy. You have no idea how worried I was!" Her voice rises. I'm trying to decide if she's joking. "No call, no text, nothing at all." She throws her hands up before crossing them over her chest and glaring. "I thought you might have been left for dead along the side of the road!"

There's absolutely nothing funny about this situation, but a chuckle still manages to slip free. "You thought I might be dead along the side of the road?" I cock a brow. "Really?"

Her eyes reluctantly light with humor as her lips twitch. "How about drunk and passed out in some random dude's room? Would that description be more accurate?"

It's unfortunately not all that far from the truth, if you swap out the random dude part. Considering who I ended up in bed with, a faceless stranger would have been preferable. "Nailed it," I mumble, avoiding eye contact.

"Uh-oh."

"Uh-oh is right." I stab a finger in her direction. "I'll have you know that this is all your fault!"

Katelyn straightens to her full height as her eyes widen. She jerks a hand to her chest in disbelief. "What? *Me?* How is it my fault that you ended up in some guy's room last night?" Confusion settles over her features as she shakes her head. Thick blond hair tumbles around her shoulders. "I had no idea what happened to you. One minute you're there and the next you're gone!"

Lifting my hands, I massage my temples. "Gray McNichols is what happened."

Her mouth falls open and her brows lift. *"No!"*

It was Katelyn who picked me up after he broke my—

*No.*

Gray most certainly did not break my heart. He injured my pride and made me feel like a fool. Nothing more. I should probably thank him for it. I've certainly been more discerning as to whom I hook up with after that experience.

Unwilling to discuss the subject, I force out a sigh. "I have to get moving. If I don't jump into the shower now, I'll never make it to the restaurant on time to meet my dad."

Ignoring me, she says, "I can't believe you hooked up with Gray."

I spin toward her and bite out, "We most certainly did *not* hook up!"

*But you wanted to...*

Maybe.

Argh!

I huff out an exasperated breath. "Nothing happened with Gray. I ended up crashing in his bed. That's it. I woke up with my clothes on."

If waking up with your clothes on means wearing only panties, then yes, that totally occurred. There's no way I'm going to mention that Gray, on the other hand, had been naked.

"I don't care." Katelyn is practically salivating as she bounces on the balls of her feet and rubs her hands together. "I want all the juicy deets!"

Pressed for time, I strip off my jeans and shirt. As I do, I realize that I'm not wearing my bra. "There aren't any deets," I reiterate. "Nothing happened. *Absolutely nothing!*"

Great. Aside from my pride, there's another casualty.

My favorite bra.

As if realizing that I'm not wearing the same shirt I left the apartment in, Katelyn's brows draw together as she points to the pile of clothing at my feet. "What happen to your shirt?"

My lips thin at the memory. "Savannah Mitchell spilled beer down the front of it."

Her eyes widen, and she shakes her head in wonder. "Wow. I really *did* miss everything last night."

"I wish I'd missed it as well," I grumble.

Just as I'm about to shimmy out of my panties and hop in the shower, I straighten and remember our sole purpose for visiting the hockey house last night. "What happened with Evert?"

Katelyn blushes and bites her lower lip.

"You dirty girl!" Excitement dances in my eyes. Yes! I knew I could get them together. "Did you two hook up last night?"

She quickly shakes her head. "No, of course not!"

That was probably expecting too much. "So, if you didn't get horizontal, what happened?"

"Well...we talked for a long time."

Excellent. That's definitely a start. Can't go wrong with conversation, right?

But...I'm hoping there might have been a little smooching as well. I make a come-on gesture with my hand. "*Annnnnd?*"

"And…he asked for my number," she squeals, bouncing up and down.

It doesn't matter if I'm nearly naked, I join her in a little celebratory dance. "Yay! Way to go, Katelyn!"

A huge grin lights up her face. "I know! I couldn't believe it!"

I give her a quick hug before jumping in the shower. Knowing that Evert and Katelyn got together makes all the BS that happened with Savannah and Gray worth it. As I move under the hot spray, water sluices over my body and a sigh of contentment slips from my lips. For just a moment, I close my eyes and enjoy the warmth.

I shampoo and condition my hair in record time before scrubbing the rest of my body. The scent of sugary vanilla is a vast improvement over the smell of stale yeast. By the time I blow dry my hair and apply a touch of eyeliner and lip gloss, I feel almost human again. I've got about eight minutes to drive to Calliope's for brunch. There's no way I'm going to make it on time. I fire off a text to my dad and let him know that I'm on my way.

With a quick goodbye thrown over my shoulder at Katelyn, who's on the couch staring at her phone, I race out of the apartment and hop into my trusty Honda Civic before speeding to the restaurant. Thankfully, traffic is light. By the time I pull into the parking lot, I'm ten minutes late.

As I jump out of the car and smooth a hand over my skirt, my gaze gets snagged by a guy exiting a black truck a few rows over. Instead of hightailing it into the restaurant, I take a moment to check him out.

He's definitely tall, topping out somewhere around six foot three.

And broad in the shoulders, which I happen to like.

With thick, dark hair.

So far, he's exactly my type.

*Hmmm…*

That combination sounds suspiciously familiar.

My brows knit together as I frown.

As if sensing my silent perusal, the guy in question swings around and meets my stare head-on.

*No.*
*Freaking.*
*Way.*
My hands go to my hips as I scowl in his direction. "What the hell are *you* doing here?"

# WHITNEY

*A* grin springs to Gray's lips. The way his dimples pop sends my belly into free fall. God, I hate the power he has over me. There has to be a way to get rid of it.

Voodoo.

Witchcraft.

An exorcism.

*Something.*

I could deal with feeling this way about anyone but him.

Naturally, he takes his sweet damn time sauntering over to me. The heat of his gaze slides down my body, leaving me feeling as if I've been physically caressed. The urge to fold my arms around my midsection and protect myself pounds through me, but I keep them glued stiffly to my sides.

Gray gives a low whistle of appreciation that makes the nerves prickle along my flesh. "Looking good, Winters." He gives me a wink. "Although I'll be honest, I preferred how you looked roughly an hour ago, naked and in my bed."

I roll my eyes and hope that my cheeks aren't beet red. I'll bet they are, because it feels like they're on fire. "Oh, shut up." I clear my throat and get back to the original question. "What are you doing here?"

He shrugs and glances toward the entrance of the restaurant. "I'm meeting up with someone for brunch." His blue eyes latch on to mine and energy sizzles in the air between us. "The same as you, I suspect."

Unaffected by our run-in, Gray extends his elbow to me. "Shall we?"

*Please...*

It takes everything I have inside not to scoff.

As if he has one gallant bone in his body.

I'm tempted to refuse the offer but don't. I hate the way he makes me go from zero to bitch in ten seconds flat. Swallowing down my aggravation, I plaster a fake smile across my face. I refuse to let him see how much his presence unsettles me. Then I thread my arm through his and ignore the little flip my belly does at his slightest touch.

If he's shocked by my easy acquiescence, he doesn't show it. Once my arm is wrapped around his firm bicep, we walk through the parking lot toward the entrance.

"You look beautiful," he remarks in a low voice.

Bewildered by the compliment, I mumble out my thanks.

"Who's the lucky guy?"

I glance at him. "What makes you think it's a guy?"

His gaze slides over me again, warming my insides. "Am I wrong?"

I tamp down all the rioting emotions he brings to the surface and remind myself that Gray has this effect on lots of girls. It's not just me. He's a natural born flirt.

Unwilling to play games, I tell him the truth. "My dad." After a beat of silence, I clear my throat and force myself to reciprocate the question. "And you?"

*See?*

I can play nice.

Sometimes.

Gray McNichols means nothing to me. He's an acquaintance from school. In all honesty, running into him this morning is probably the best thing that could have happened. Now I won't have to worry

61

about it occurring on campus in front of a crowd of onlookers. I can put the last twelve hours behind me, where they belong.

In the past.

"My mom," he says, cutting into my thoughts.

Well, that's certainly a strange coincidence. But…Calliope's is one of the best restaurants in town. We have brunch here almost every month. Dad and I have tried other places, but we always end up coming back. It's not unusual to run into people I recognize from campus. Both students and professors.

So, maybe running into Gray isn't so odd after all. Just uncomfortable, considering that I woke up in his bed wearing nothing more than panties.

With any luck, he'll be seated on one side of the dining room and I'll be clear across on the other side. We won't be able to see each other, and I can forget he's there. The less I'm around Gray, the better off I am.

Continuing to play the part of a perfect gentleman—which is a real departure from his usual cocky self—Gray holds open the door for me.

"Thanks," I mutter, catching a whiff of his aftershave as I enter the building. It makes my insides tingle with awareness, and I immediately tamp it down.

"Ouch." He winces with exaggeration. "That sounded painful."

"It was," I mutter, not liking his behavior.

With the hostess station in sight, I huff out a relieved breath.

As I step into the entryway, his fingers wrap around my arm and he steers me to the side. His hand burns my bare flesh. I meet his gaze with an impatient expression, wanting to get away from him. Not to mention all of the feelings he dredges up inside me.

"I almost forgot." A smile curves his lips. "I have something that belongs to you."

Well, I can't imagine what he—

My gaze drops to his hand as it disappears inside his pocket before pulling out the pink polka dot bra that I'd been wearing last night. A hiss escapes from my lips as I swipe it from his hooked finger and glance around to see if anyone has noticed. I shove the silky material inside my purse and zip it closed. "Seriously, what's wrong with you!"

"What?" he laughs. "I thought you'd want it back. Was I mistaken?" He waggles his brows. "Because I'd be more than happy to keep it as a souvenir."

"Of course I want it back," I mutter, barely able to keep the exasperation from my voice. "Why did you have it stuffed in your pocket?" I shake my head as my upper lip curls. "You're such a weirdo."

Gray shrugs. "I was going to swing by your place afterward and drop it off."

I lower my brows and glare, but he doesn't seem affected by it in the least. "Luckily you won't have to do that now."

"No worries, Winters. I'll find another reason to drop by unexpectedly."

"I'd prefer for that not to happen." A shiver runs the length of my body. "I think it would be best if we went back to ignoring each other."

"Have I been ignoring you?" He lifts his fingers to his chin before stroking it. "I'll have to make a concerted effort not to do that. I wouldn't want you to think I'm indifferent."

And just like that, my insides begin to clamor. I grit my teeth against the internal onslaught. Needing to put an end to this conversation before it spirals any further out of control, I change the subject. "As usual, running into you has been a blast, but I really have to go."

He flashes a full-wattage smile and my panties flood with unwanted heat. There doesn't seem to be anything I can do to stop my reaction to him.

"Sure, no problem. I suppose we can discuss this after brunch."

*Over my dead body.*

Not bothering to respond, I stalk to the hostess stand. Gray is right behind me. The young woman behind the podium smiles at the pair of us before her gaze settles on Gray with undisguised interest.

Ugh.

This is the effect he has on all womankind, and I'd be smart to remember that. Gray is a shameless flirt. Just as Savannah felt the need to remind me earlier, I'm nothing special to him.

Not that I want to be.

Please, I'm not that much of a glutton for punishment.

"Hi, can I help you?" Just to be sure that she has Gray's full attention, the woman behind the counter stands up straighter and thrusts out her assets.

"Hi." He flashes her a cordial smile. It's nowhere near full wattage. "I'm Gray McNichols, and this is Whitney Winters. We both have reservations to meet our parents."

Her eyes flare with recognition as she gasps. "Gray McNichols!" She bounces with excitement as her words run together. "*OhmyGod, Iabsolutelyloveyou!*" She bites her lower lip as color floods her cheeks. "I mean," she corrects bashfully, "I love watching you play hockey!" Resting her elbows on the stand, she sighs like a lovesick schoolgirl with her first teenage crush. "You're so amazing on the ice." Unable to contain herself, she squeals. "I can't *wait* for the season to start."

I turn my head just enough to watch Gray from the corner of my eye.

What is it about this guy that makes otherwise sane girls lose their heads?

Sure, he's good looking with short black hair and bright blue eyes that pierce my soul every time he turns them on me. And those dimples are lethal. Then there's his body, which is ripped. His muscles are finely honed from weightlifting and skating. And I've seen him from the backside. The guy has buns of steel.

Fine…I get the attraction.

He's smoking hot.

"Thanks," he says. "This will be my last season with the Hellcats, so I'm hoping it'll be one for the record books. The team is excited to get out there and tear up the ice."

My brows draw together. That's not what I'd been expecting him to say.

Where's the shameless bragging about how great he is?

Shouldn't he be giving her a rundown of his stats?

Even though I don't follow hockey, I know what they are. You can't be a living, breathing human being walking around Hillsdale and not know.

By the enamored expression on the hostess' face, she's already impressed. She takes this opportunity to straighten before leaning forward and treating Gray to an unobstructed view of her cleavage.

Since I have zero desire in staring at this girl's boobs, I peek at Gray. Again, he takes me by surprise. I would have expected him to be enjoying the free show. Instead, his gaze is focused on her face, and his lips are lifted in a polite smile.

It's clear that this woman is dying for him to take her number. She looks like a carbon copy of all the other females who follow him around campus. Big boobs, bright toothy smile, tiny nipped-in waist, and a pretty face.

Why isn't he flirting with her?

Isn't that his usual modus operandi?

It's obvious that he wouldn't have to work very hard to lure this one into bed.

I'm not sure what to make of this behavior.

Although, it's doubtful that it means anything. He'll probably circle back later to get her number.

Gray is exactly the guy I think he is.

Didn't he prove that freshman year?

My spine straightens at the thought.

"So, about that reservation…" Gray's voice trails off as he hikes up a brow.

When it becomes apparent that he isn't going to flirt, the hostess clears her throat and pries her gaze from him to scan the iPad she's using to check us in. "Of course." She grabs two menus and steps around the podium. "If you'll both follow me, I'll show you to your table."

*I'm sorry…come again?*

Surely, she meant to say *tables*. Right?

As in, separate tables.

Across the restaurant from each other.

A confused expression flashes across my face as I glance at Gray. He shrugs, looking equally perplexed. Maybe she plans to show one of us to our table, then she'll seat the other?

I mean, that makes sense.

Except…as we walk through the main dining room, I catch sight of my dad. He's seated at a square table with four place settings. What's weird is that he isn't alone.

A dark-haired woman with a sleek, shoulder-length bob is parked next to him. Their heads are bent together, and a smile curves his lips. A pit the size of Rhode Island settles at the bottom of my belly as I catch a few wisps of her throaty laughter.

Gray's long-legged stride slows, and his expression darkens before he glances at me. "I take it that's your father?"

*Uh-oh.*

My shoulders stiffen. It feels like someone has wrapped their fingers around my throat and is slowly squeezing the life out of me. "Yeah," I rasp. "And that would be your mother?"

*Say no.*

*Say no.*

*Say no.*

Even though I silently chant the refrain in my head, I realize the chances of that happening are slim to none.

He gives me a sharp nod. "You got it."

As if the scene in front of us wasn't disturbing enough, I watch in shock as Dad closes the distance between them and plants a kiss on her lips.

*My eyes! My eyes! Someone make it stop!*

"Tell me that didn't just happen," he grumbles, sounding as traumatized as I feel.

"I wish I could." Frowning, I press my fingers to my lips to keep everything inside. "Ugh…I just threw up in my mouth."

And it's not from overindulging last night, either.

Every time I think this day can't get any worse, I manage to jackhammer to an all-new low.

How is it possible that my father is playing kissy face with Gray McNichols' mother?

Unaware that my world has just imploded, the hostess arrives at the table with a smile. She waits a beat, but Dad doesn't stop locking lips with the woman seated next to him. To make matters worse, I can't stop staring. It's like a horrific car accident I can't rip my eyes away from.

Someone needs to make this stop.

Thankfully, Gray takes matters into his own hands by clearing his throat.

Loudly.

Our parents jump apart like a pair of guilty teenagers. Both of their gazes shoot to us in surprise, like they weren't expecting company. Dad chuckles as his cheeks flood with ruddy color. Instead of apologizing, he squeezes her hand before rising to his feet. A goofy smile lights up his face, making him look years younger.

"Whit!" he crows enthusiastically.

"Hi, Dad," I mutter, unsure how to act. My joints feel rusty, and my movements are awkward. I plaster a smile across my face and hope it doesn't look as forced as it feels. My gaze darts to the woman seated so close to him that they might as well be sharing a chair. "Um, hello." I give a slight wave of my hand. "I'm Whitney."

If there's proper protocol that should be followed when being introduced to the woman your dad was just sucking face with in public, I have no idea what it is. It's a small consolation when Dad snaps out of his befuddled daze. I'm having a difficult time reconciling the guy in front of me with the man I've known all my life. This is not normal David Winters behavior. The Dad I know is shy and reserved. And he certainly doesn't engage in PDA.

*Who the hell is this man?*

Has Dad been invaded by body snatchers?

That's the only logical explanation.

Gray's mother rises to her feet and shimmies around the table toward me. A second wave of shock washes over me.

*Ummm, what's she doing?*

67

*Why is she headed my way?*

*Please tell me she's not going in for a hug.*

I stiffen as she wraps her arms around me.

"It's so good to finally meet you! Your father talks about you all the time, Whitney. I already feel like I know you." She pulls away and air rushes back into my lungs as her friendly gaze locks on mine. Then she laughs and shakes her head. "I should probably introduce myself first. I'm Veronica, a friend of your dad's." She points to Gray, who stands next to me with his hands shoved in the pockets of his khakis. "I'm also Gray's mother."

My mouth opens and closes as I grapple for words.

*She's heard so much about me?*

*She already feels like she knows me?*

Up until two minutes ago, I had no idea this woman even existed. My head swims.

As soon as Veronica releases her hold, she greets her son with a warm embrace. Gray's arms wrap around her as he holds her close. He bends his head, and his lips move against her ear. When she pulls back to nod, there's a strained expression marring her face.

By Gray's reaction, I imagine he's just as blindsided by their relationship as I am.

My father sweeps his hand anxiously toward the table. "Let's sit down." Belatedly he smiles at Gray, reaching out to shake his hand. "I'm David, by the way. Whitney's father."

The two men shake, and Gray's lips stay pressed in a thin line.

I don't claim to know him well, but he looks on the verge of losing his shit. I certainly can't blame him for being upset. I feel the same way.

Before I can lay a hand on his arm to get his attention, he snaps, "What the hell is going on?"

# GRAY

*W*hitney winces as the words explode from my mouth. Barely do I notice that her fingers are wrapped tightly around my forearm. Which is ironic. Any other time, I'd give her a smile in hopes of charming this girl into forgiving me for acting like a major douchebag freshman year. It's not often that she lays her hands on me of her own volition. Actually, she never touches me. That alone should tell you how pissed off I am.

Bewildered by the outburst, Mom stiffens as her eyes flare. All of the nervous energy she'd been exuding vanishes. "Grayson Aloysius McNichols, watch your language!"

I'm embarrassed to admit that Whitney isn't the only one who flinches. Mom's razor-sharp tone coupled with the fact that she's trotting out the middle name are enough to remind me that she's not a woman who puts up with nonsense.

"Sorry," I mumble like a chastised ten-year-old. It only adds insult to injury that Whitney and her dad are here to witness it.

David clears his throat and glances around the table. Silence ensues as we all shift on our respective chairs, unsure where to go from here.

"Perhaps," he mutters, "it would have been better if Ronnie and I had spoken to each of you in private."

*Ronnie?*

My gaze swings to Mom, who's back to wearing a besotted expression on her face. I've never heard anyone call her that. Not even my father. Speaking of which...I thought those two were trying to get back together? Isn't that what he told me this summer?

I grind my back teeth, feeling my temper spike again.

David's gaze darts between his daughter and me before he shakes his head. "Oh, Whit, I almost forgot." He raises a hand in my direction. "This is Grayson! You're both seniors at Hillsdale." A hopeful note threads its way through his voice. It's as if he's grasping at straws, trying to right this listing ship.

But that's not going to happen.

I almost feel bad for him.

*Almost.*

"Isn't that a coincidence?" he goes on to say as Whitney and I glance at each other.

"Yeah, Dad," she says drily. "I know who Grayson is."

Caught off guard by the admission, he asks, "Wait a minute, you two are friends?"

"Yup," I cut in swiftly before she can beat me to the punch. "We sure are."

I'm tempted to tell David just how well acquainted I am with his daughter. If for no other reason than to see the look on his face.

But I don't. No matter how much of a dick I've been in the past, I won't hurt Whitney in order to lash out at our parents. It's obvious that she's just as much a victim in this farce as I am.

Although...that doesn't mean I can't have a little fun at her expense.

"Huh," David says. "Isn't that a coincidence?"

"It certainly is." I settle against my chair. "Whitney's a *huge* hockey fan. She attended every home game last season." A smirk twists my lips. "In fact, I seem to recall her having a bit of a crush on me in freshman year." I tilt my head and flick my gaze in her direction. "Isn't that right, *Whit?*"

Instead of answering, she gnashes her teeth together and glares.

"Really?" David chuckles and shakes his head. "That's so cute. My little girl with a crush."

Whitney's face goes up in flames as she rams the toe of her shoe into my shin under the table.

Twice.

Damn, that hurts.

I swivel my legs away before she can inflict further damage. Pain radiates throughout my shin, but the glowering look on her face is well worth the price of admission.

"I did *not* have a crush on him," she snaps.

"Ohhhh, I'm pretty sure you did," I interject in an obnoxious sing-song voice. "Don't you remember that party—"

"Fine!" she barks, cutting me off. "I liked you for all of a week. Then I came to my senses."

"If I'd known you liked hockey so much, we could have attended a few games together," David says, interrupting our back-and-forth before it can escalate. "I guess that's something we'll be able to do this season." David glances at me before his gaze settles on Mom and another dopey smile overtakes his face. "How much fun will that be?"

Whitney gives me a well-honed death stare. "Tons."

"Well, I'm glad that you two are already friends," he says, sounding more relaxed. "That certainly makes circumstances easier."

I almost laugh out loud at her father's description of our relationship. If he only knew! The last thing I'm interested in being is Whitney's friend. All I want—

*Wait a minute.*

Why the hell does it matter if Whitney and I are friends?

I don't like the direction this conversation has swerved in. What I should probably do is sit back and assess the situation. But with each second that slowly ticks by, my agitation continues to grow until I blurt, "What does us being friends make easier?"

An awkward silence descends.

When neither of them utters a peep, my narrowed gaze swings from David, who has gone radio silent, to my mother, who sits with her hands folded primly in her lap.

"Oh, um, well—" she begins before being interrupted by our waitress, who takes our drink and food orders. I rattle off something but have no idea what. Brunch is the last thing on my mind.

Once she disappears, I stare at Mom and wait. I have a feeling that I know what's coming down the pike, but I want to hear her say it.

Actually, I hope to God I'm wrong.

The table—hell, the entire restaurant—fades to the background as Mom moistens her lips.

"David and I wanted to share with both of you that we've been seeing each other for a few months—"

"A few *months?*" Whitney gasps, echoing my sentiments perfectly.

*What.*

*The.*

*Actual.*

*Fuck?*

Mom bites her lower lip and nods. "We've been dating for three wonderful months—"

David leans toward her and murmurs, "They have been wonderful, haven't they, Ronnie?"

"Yes, they've been amazing." Her eyes go soft as she becomes trapped in his gaze. It's almost more than I can stomach. Thankfully, she shakes herself out of the trance and continues. "And it's become quite serious." She pauses, her gaze meeting mine and then Whitney's. "Serious enough that we thought you two should meet one another." Mom hoists a nervous smile as she exclaims, "But here you are, already friends."

When we both remain silent, she rushes on. "I know this might seem out of the blue, but it's really not."

"I've actually known Ronnie since high school," David pipes up, "and she's just as beautiful now as she was then."

Mom blushes at the compliment, and it takes everything I have inside not to roll my eyes. The guy certainly likes to lay it on thick.

I glance at Whitney, only to find her confused gaze already pinned to mine. With wide eyes, she shakes her head as if to say *what the hell is going on here?* I raise my brows and shrug. I haven't the slightest clue.

David wraps his fingers around Mom's hand and squeezes. I'm tempted to wipe the dopey smile off his face. With my fist.

"Ronnie and I are planning a trip to the Virgin Islands." He glances at Whitney and then me. "Isn't that exciting?"

No, it's totally messed up. How is Mom supposed to get back together with Dad if she's dating this joker?

I slump on my seat as they chatter excitedly about their upcoming vacay. From the corner of my eye, I catch our waitress and raise my hand to flag her down. Clearly, I'm going to need a stiff drink to get through the rest of this meal.

Actually, make it a double.

# WHITNEY

"Can you believe that?" I spear a piece of fruit with my fork and pop it into my mouth. Katelyn and I are grabbing lunch at the student union on campus.

She shakes her head and takes a massive bite of her burger. Once she's swallowed the masticated meat, she says, "Nope." Another bite disappears in her mouth as she chews it thoughtfully. "If anything, you have to give David props for putting himself out there after all this time."

Has she heard one word that I've said?

This isn't a good thing.

My brows lower. "No, actually I don't. It's not like I want him to be alone for the rest of his life, but—"

"You just don't want another woman taking your mom's place," Katelyn finishes for me.

"I don't know." My shoulders droop as she cuts right to the heart of matters. "Maybe."

We eat in silence as her comment circles around my head.

A few minutes later, she picks up a fry and points it at me. "I don't think anyone will ever take the place of your mom, Whit. But she's been gone for a while, and I'm sure he's lonely. Your dad probably wants someone to spend time with. Can you blame him?"

"I guess not," I say glumly.

I mean, he *did* seem pretty happy at brunch. I wrack my brain, trying to remember the last time I saw him smile so much. Even though my appetite has pulled a disappearing act, I stab a piece of cantaloupe with my fork. Instead of taking a bite, I push it around the bowl. It's not like I don't see the logic in what she's saying.

"It's seriously crazy that David is seeing Gray McNichol's mom." She waggles her brows and grins. "If you play your cards right, the two of you could end up being stepsiblings." More laughter bubbles up from her throat. "How hilarious would that be?"

She's kidding, right?

My expression contorts with horror. I don't know why, but I hadn't even considered the possibility of that happening. Maybe because I'm still trying to wrap my head around the fact that my dad has been dating someone on the sly for three months and I knew nothing about it. Even though I try tamping it down, hurt flares to life inside me. I thought we were close and shared everything. Okay, maybe not *everything*. There are some things you just can't share with your dad. But still...secretly dating someone for three months is huge. This relationship would be a lot easier to accept if I'd known about it from the beginning and been able to watch it grow instead of finding out about it when they've already planned a romantic getaway. I feel like I've been dropped into an episode of *The Twilight Zone.*

"Bite your tongue!" I grab a fry from her plate and pelt it in her direction. How dare she say something like that to me? I'd rather slit my own throat than allow that to happen.

My plans after graduation involve never seeing Gray McNichols again. And that can't happen if our parents are dating, or—God forbid —in a serious relationship.

She shrugs. "I'm just saying that it would be funny."

I narrow my gaze. "You can be a real jerk sometimes."

"True statement," she agrees.

"No," I correct. "*All the time.*" Okay, I'm being a bit harsh. Katelyn is a good friend and I'm lucky to have her.

"Do you have any idea," she says, interrupting my thoughts, "just how many girls on this campus would yank out their hair extensions to have Gray as a stepbrother?"

I roll my eyes and pop the speared chunk of cantaloupe into my mouth. "Well, they can have him. I'm not interested."

Katelyn tilts her head as she considers me silently from across the table. I don't like the searching look now aimed in my direction. The last thing I need is for her to dig deeper and discover that I really do have—

"Hmm." Another pause. "Are you sure there isn't a tiny flame flickering deep inside for the guy?"

I give her my best *are you crazy* look and shake my head emphatically. "Nope. Can't stand him."

"Okay. If you say so." She shrugs but doesn't necessarily look convinced. "Honestly, I don't think you have anything to worry about." She picks up her diet cola and takes a sip. "What are the chances of this relationship turning into something that lasts?"

*Exactly!*

I latch on to the comment like it's a lifeline.

"Give it a couple of months," she continues. "I bet they'll break up and move on." Her face grows serious. "Although, you're going to have to accept that the horse is out of the barn and there ain't no putting him back inside."

Ugh. She's right. Maybe it was foolish to expect Dad to never date again. To live a celibate—

*Woah.*

I slam on the mental brakes before that thought can go any further. Traveling down that road will only lead to years of therapy. And that, I don't need. As far as I'm concerned, Dad doesn't have a sex life.

"His relationship with Gray's mom will probably fizzle out in a couple of months," Katelyn continues. "But I doubt he'll stop dating. So, you better prepare yourself for the fact that he'll be bringing other women around."

"Yeah, I know. But I'd rather he get serious with just about anyone else."

"Don't worry about it." She waves a hand. "At this point, they're still in the honeymoon phase of their relationship. Once shit gets real, she'll be running for the hills. You just need to sit back and wait for it to happen. Your dad has been single and living on his own for a while. I'm sure he has a ton of bad habits that would drive any sane woman crazy."

Katelyn's probably right about that.

What am I freaking out about?

The pit that has been sitting at the bottom of my gut since Sunday morning finally dissipates.

For the first time in days, I can breathe again. And it feels *so* good. "I take back everything I just said about you not being a good friend."

"Thanks. I knew you'd come around eventually." Katelyn grins and takes another gigantic bite of her burger.

How she manages to fit so much in her mouth is almost impressive. I shake my head and scrunch my nose in disgust. I'm just about to make a pithy comment about the amount of meat in her mouth (wink-wink) when her gaze gets snagged by something over my shoulder.

Her eyes bulge as she squeaks around her mouthful of burger. But it's so garbled, I can't make out what she's saying. Katelyn excitedly draws in a sharp breath, which sends the burger shooting down the wrong tube. Eyes widening, she immediately coughs and thumps her chest.

"Oh my God, are you okay?" Panic fills me as she continues pounding on her chest. "Do you need the Heimlich?" I shoot out of my seat. "Nod your head if that's a yes." I lace my hands together and crack my knuckles. "I'll do my best not to break any ribs."

With her eyes watering, Katelyn shakes her head and points frantically over my shoulder again.

"What is it, Lassie?" I tilt my head, trying to figure out what has her so worked up. "Has Timmy fallen down the well again?"

She gives me a sour look and swallows the chunk stuck in her throat before collapsing against the bench. Huffing out a breath, she grabs her drink and sucks down half of it. "Oh my God, that's so much better." She pokers up and accuses me as if I'm to blame for her biting off more than she could chew. "I almost died!"

I splay my hands wide. "And I offered to help."

"You said you might crack ribs."

"Umm, it's called a heroic measure for a reason." I grab my bottle of water and tip it to my lips before asking, "So, what's got you all worked up?"

A dreamy look settles over her face. "Evert."

"Oh?" I hike a brow with interest. Katelyn has been obsessed with her phone ever since the party Saturday night, but he has yet to text or call. I'm not sure if he's playing it cool or if he's just not interested. "Go over and talk to him," I encourage.

Instead of taking my advice, dismay washes over her features and she shakes her head, signaling that my idea is a no-go.

"Come on, Kate," I cajole. "Go say hi. It doesn't have to be a big deal. Just pretend to bump into him. It's easy."

Her shoulders hunch as she frantically shakes her head.

"You are such a baby," I grumble, making an executive decision that she won't be pleased about. I swivel on my seat and catch sight of Evert, who is busy talking with a few friends outside the cafeteria.

"Evert!" I bellow at the top of my lungs.

"*Ohmygod! What are you doing, Whit!*" Katelyn hisses as Evert turns in our direction. He spots us, and she gasps. "Oh no! He's headed this way! I'm going to die!" She rips her gaze from Evert to glare at me. "But first, I'm going to kill you."

Unconcerned with the threat, I wave off her comments. "Please, you'll thank me for this later." I grin and glance at Evert, who's making his way toward us. Katelyn needs to chill out and roll with this. "Take a deep breath and remember to smile," I advise. "Everything will be fine."

She doesn't have time to blast me with a reply before Evert arrives on the scene and slides into the booth next to me. His hip bumps against mine and I scoot over to make room for him.

I was kind of hoping he would sit next to Katelyn, but I suppose this works. Now they can make eye contact while chatting.

"Hey, Whitney." He smiles at me before glancing at my roommate. "It's Katelyn, right?"

Color blooms in my roommate's cheeks as she lights up like a Christmas tree.

I raise my brows and smile, hoping that's all the encouragement she needs to loosen up.

But no...she remains mute. Which is exactly why I kick her in the shin under the table.

"Ouch." She jerks up in her seat. "I mean, yes, that's right." Then she takes my advice and beams in his direction.

I have to hand it to myself. Sure, Evert has only just sat down, but this is going amazingly—

I squint at Katelyn.

What the hell is that?

Is it—

*Oh.*

*Sweet.*

*Baby.*

*Jesus.*

There's a piece of lettuce wedged in her teeth. At least it's not her front teeth, but still...this is bad.

Is it possible that Evert won't notice?

What am I saying?

Of course he will.

It's massive.

And bright green.

It's all but waving and screaming, *Hey! Look at me!*

I want to smack my head against the table for allowing this to happen. Katelyn has threatened to kill me in the past, but I suspect she might make good on it when she finds out about this.

"Did you guys have fun at the party the other night?" Evert's gaze bounces between the pair of us.

I wish he'd just stare in Katelyn's direction, so I could pantomime to her that there's food stuck in her teeth. But then again, I don't want him to look at Katelyn with lettuce stuck in her teeth!

This has turned out to be a disaster.

"Yeah," I say, "we had a great time."

"It was so much fun," my roommate enthuses. For the first time in her life, she has a perma-grin plastered across her face. It's not helping the situation. Now that I know the lettuce is there, I can't stop staring.

I clear my throat loudly and Katelyn's gaze swings toward me. I widen my eyes and smile, all the while rubbing my finger against my teeth.

Her gaze turns questioning before it slides back to Evert as he asks us another question. But I can't focus on what he's saying, because I'm too busy coming up with an alternate plan. Whatever he says makes Katelyn laugh, and I wince as the salad stuck in her pearly whites winks at me.

Enough is enough. I can't let this situation continue. We don't have any other choice but to abort the mission.

"What are you doing after this?" Katelyn asks. "Do you have class?"

*There is no damn way I can allow her to take off with him.*

Just as Evert opens his mouth to answer, I make a production out of picking up my phone and glancing at the screen. "Oh my gosh, Katelyn, we've got to go! We're late!"

"Late?" Her brows slide together as she frowns. "What are we late for? I thought we had thirty minutes until we had to leave."

She should know me well enough by now to realize that I wouldn't drag her away from Evert unless there was a damn good reason. "Um, no," I grit out slowly, widening my eyes, hoping we'll have a moment of telepathic understanding. "We have to go *now*. Right now! We've got that *thing* we were talking about earlier."

"*Thing?*" Her face scrunches in confusion as she shakes her head. "Whitney, what are you talking about?"

*Grrrrr.*

Since telepathy isn't working, I turn to Evert with a cheerful smile. "Well…it was super great running into you, but we've got to go."

"Oh...okay, sure." He moves out of the booth and I hurry after him, popping to my feet.

Katelyn, on the other hand, is lollygagging, wanting to squeeze every last drop out of this interaction. She reluctantly slides out and gathers up her belongings.

I dump our food tray and grab Katelyn's arm, giving Evert one last wave. "Okay, I'll catch you in class."

"For sure," he calls back.

Katelyn gives a wave of her own. I drag her away before she can beam another smile in his direction. As soon as we're a few steps away, she whispers furiously from the side of her mouth, "Are you employing the leave-them-wanting-more tactic? Is that what's going on? Because I thought everything was going really well. I don't understand why you rushed us out of there."

Instead of answering, I push through the ladies' room door and haul Katelyn in front of the mirror. She stares at me like I've lost my ever-loving mind. I brace myself for impact before pointing to the silver glass that stretches across the wall in front of the sinks and give one command. "Smile."

With a furrowed brow, her gaze shifts to the mirror and she bares her teeth.

Her eyes widen as she spots the leaf. She sucks in a sharp breath and screeches at the top of her lungs, *"Oh my God! Please tell me that wasn't there the whole time I was talking to Evert!"*

I bite my lip, not having the heart to confirm her worst fears.

She groans and picks the lettuce from her pearly whites. "Well, that settles it. I'm never talking to him again."

I rub her back with comforting strokes. "I don't think it's that bad."

"Easy for you to say. You didn't have a whole salad wedged in your teeth!"

I wince.

Poor Katelyn...

# GRAY

*I* catch sight of Whitney in the crowd about twenty feet ahead of me as she moves across campus. My gaze drops to the sway of her ass. Before she can get away, I pick up my pace and pull alongside her. She flicks a quick glance in my direction as I fall in step with her.

"Hey," I greet with a smile.

In true Whitney fashion, she grimaces, looking less than thrilled by my presence. And just in case I wasn't clear about her feelings, she grunts, "Ugh. It's you."

I huff out a laugh and shake my head. "There you go again, stroking my ego."

"Please," she scoffs. "Your ego is just fine." She waves her hand toward a few chicks staring in our direction. "There are plenty of girls who would like nothing better than to fawn all over you."

She's right about that. But Whitney is the only one I want attention from. Which is a real kick in the ass.

When I don't immediately launch into my reason for seeking her out, she grows impatient. "Is there something you needed, or can I look forward to you stalking me in plain sight from now on?"

Her sharp tone makes a smile spring to my lips. Is it perverse that I enjoy our verbal sparring?

Probably.

It's like a twisted version of foreplay that gets me hard.

"I'd be more than happy to discuss my stalker tendencies at a later date, but right now we've got more pressing matters to hash out." I give her a bit of side-eye. "You got a few minutes to talk?"

"I suppose."

Her unenthusiastic tone suggests that a preferable pastime would be having her fingernails yanked out one by one.

"I was just about to head home." Her lips pull down at the corners as her eyes fill with suspicion. "What could we possibly have to discuss?"

"Oh, lots of stuff." Unable to help myself, I sling my arm around Whitney's shoulder and haul her close. She stiffens. The scent of her floral perfume makes me want to suck in a big breath of her. Instead, I dig deep and find the willpower to refrain. "Let's go to my place."

Whitney's feet grind to a halt as she turns and glares. "This better not be a ploy to get me into bed again, McNichols."

I swing my hand in a wide arc and snap my fingers. "Awww damn, you caught me." I shake my head and chuckle. "I can't slip anything past you, Winters." I pause for a beat and admit, "As much as I'd love to lure you back into my bed, we've got shit to work out." When she says nothing, I jog her memory with two words. "Our parents."

"So that wasn't a bad dream?"

My lips quirk. "No such luck, sweetheart. Our parents dating each other is disturbingly real."

With my arm still wrapped around Whitney, we walk toward the northern end of campus. The house I rent is conveniently located across the street. Most mornings, if I don't have an early practice, I can roll out of bed and haul ass to class in less than fifteen minutes flat.

I unlock the front door and hold it open for Whitney. Surprise fills her eyes as she silently walks through. You better believe my mama raised me right. Holding open a door for the fairer sex was drilled into my head at a young age.

As we hit the entryway, I notice Evert and Collins kicked back on the couch in the living room playing NHL on the Xbox. Their attention is glued to the large screen TV mounted on the wall as their thumbs flick over the controllers with lightning-quick movements.

"Hey," I call out.

Collins grunts out a barely intelligible greeting, his eyes laser focused on the action. Evert catches sight of the slim brunette at my side and his attention immediately gets snagged. I can't blame him, but that doesn't mean I like it. It only confirms Collins' earlier comments about Evert having a thing for Whitney.

The moment Evert gets distracted, a grin breaks out across Collins' face as his avatar races up the ice and dekes out the goalie. He drops the controller and punches both fists in the air. "Suck it, loser!"

Evert grumbles and tosses the wireless controller onto the couch. "I'm getting a Gatorade."

"Sure, I'll take one, too," Collins smirks. "Thanks for asking."

Instead of bypassing us and heading straight to the kitchen, Evert stops and gives Whitney a chin lift in greeting—which is more than she gets from Collins, who is still on the couch doing some kind of douchey victory dance.

"Hey, nice to see you." Evert's mouth curves as his gaze locks on her. Apparently, the game he was just trounced in is already forgotten.

My eyes narrow at the easy smile that springs to Whitney's lips as she returns the greeting.

Well hell, I don't think Whitney has ever looked at me like that. A kernel of jealousy flares to life in the pit of my gut, which is ridiculous. There's no reason for it. Just like Whitney claimed earlier, I've got more girls than I know what to do with ready to stroke my oversized ego.

Not to mention other oversized parts of me. I shouldn't give a damn if these two want to get flirty with one another. But if the burning in my belly is any indication, I care. More than I'm willing to admit.

Evert shifts his weight and stuffs his hands into the pockets of his jeans. "I didn't know you'd be stopping by."

Whitney flicks a glance my way. Other than a brief look in my direction, that's all the attention I'm given. "Me neither."

It's like I'm a third wheel they wish would get lost. I'm not trying to sound like a conceited asshole, but girls don't ignore me. Let alone forget that I'm standing next to them.

"So, I was wondering—" Evert begins.

*What the hell does this guy think he's doing?*

Oh hell no. I can see what's coming from a mile away, and it's not going to happen on my watch.

The nerve of this guy...trying to highjack the girl I brought over. Have I entered a parallel universe?

Not allowing him to finish, I clap Evert on the back none-to-gently. Honestly, with my luck, Whitney would agree to go out with him right on the spot.

"Well, it was great talking to you, Monroe, but Winters and I have important business to discuss." I give him a sly wink and grab Whitney's hand, dragging her up the staircase. "In private," I add, just in case he doesn't get it.

With that, my cockblock is complete.

Once we reach the second story, Whitney tugs her hand free from mine and I have no other choice but to let go.

"That was rude," she grumbles.

I shrug, not really giving a damn if it was rude or not. Evert Monroe needs to back the fuck off.

"And did you seriously wink at him?" she snaps in outrage before sputtering, "Like we're going up here to do something *other* than talk?"

"Nope." I shake my head and deny exactly what I did. "Don't know what you're talking about."

A growl of annoyance escapes her lips as a barely suppressed smile tugs at the corners of mine. There's a little voice in my head cautioning that if I want to make progress with this girl, I need to stop provoking her at every turn.

But it's so completely satisfying when she glowers at me.

Pulling the key from my pocket, I unlock my bedroom door and hold it open for her. I extend my arm with a flourish and a smirk. "Ladies first."

"Please." She rolls her eyes, unimpressed with my gallantry.

*See?*

This is exactly why chivalry is dead.

No one appreciates it anymore.

Her gaze bounces around the room before she strides to the desk and sets her messenger bag down on the floor. Then she takes a seat on the chair as her attention settles on me expectantly.

With a grin, I drop my backpack next to the bed and fall on it with a bounce. Unable to resist teasing her, I pat the mattress. "Want to come sit over here?"

Her lips flatten as she folds her arms across her chest. "As tempting as the offer is, I'll pass."

I tilt my head. "You sure about that? We could snuggle while talking. Maybe hit two birds with one stone."

Whitney shakes her head, not looking the least bit tempted. "No, thanks."

Clearly, she isn't going to budge on the matter. "Suit yourself."

When I don't immediately launch into my reasons for dragging her here, she clears her throat and impatiently circles her hand in a *let's get this over with* motion. "I have a packed schedule today, McNichols. So, if we could get on with this, that would be awesome."

Shifting my weight, I lean forward and rest my elbows on my thighs. It's been a few days since Whitney and I were ambushed by our parents at Calliope's. During that time, I've come up with a foolproof plan.

Without further ado, I drop the bomb. "We need to break up our parents."

Her eyes widen. "Seriously?"

Apparently, that *wasn't* what she was expecting me to say.

"As a freaking heart attack," I confirm with a nod.

"I..." Whitney shakes her head and frowns. "I don't know." Her lower lip finds its way between her teeth until she's able to worry it.

My cock stirs to life as my focus gets snagged by her mouth.

"Don't you think we should wait this out? Odds are they'll break up on their own."

I lift a brow. "Are you really willing to take that chance?"

Just remembering the sappy looks on their faces and how lovey-dovey they were at the restaurant is enough to induce nausea.

Nope. This romance can't be allowed to flourish. It's way better to break them up now than later down the road when their feelings have become more entrenched. I'm shocked that Whitney isn't jumping on board with the idea.

Obviously, it's time to trot out the big guns.

"Huh. I didn't realize how much you were looking forward to having me as your stepbrother. Think about how much quality time we'll be able to spend with each other when they move in together." I let those words hang in the air before adding with an evil grin. "Holidays, family gatherings, vacations..."

She blanches and shakes her head with vehemence.

"What?" I ask innocently. "That's *not* where you saw this headed?"

"No."

"Their relationship must be pretty damn serious if they decided that we needed to be introduced."

*How is she not seeing this?*

Whitney raises her hand until she can massage her forehead. "I don't know if I want to get involved in any nefarious schemes you've hatched."

I point a finger at her. "For starters, I like your use of nefarious. Good job."

Even though the circumstances are dire, her eyes spark with humor as a small smile trembles around the corners of her lips.

"And second, the plan couldn't be simpler. I'll do all the heavy lifting." I spread my arms wide. "You just have to follow my lead and play along."

She glances at the ceiling as if searching for divine intervention. "And that's exactly when this plan of yours will backfire and turn to shit."

87

I snort. "Please, have a little faith. Nothing will go wrong. I told you, it's simple. We barely have to do anything."

When that's not enough to secure an agreement from her, I decide to attack this from a different angle. In order for my plan to work, I need her cooperation. Otherwise, we're screwed.

And not in a good way.

If I don't want our parents dating because I'm hoping that my mom and dad will finally get their shit together, maybe Whitney feels the same. It's worth a chance, right?

"What's the deal with your mom? Are your parents divorced?"

Emotion darkens her eyes before she quickly glances away. "No," she says softly. Just when I wonder if Whitney will continue, she clears her throat. "My mom died nine years ago. It's been me and my dad ever since."

*Well, shit.*

I scrub a hand over my face, feeling like a complete dickhead. I had no idea that she'd lost her mother. It only drives home the fact that Whitney and I don't know each other.

Not on a personal level. It's disconcerting to realize that I want to delve deeper with this girl.

Shaking the thought away, I mumble, "Sorry. I didn't know."

Her shoulders hunch as if she's trying to steel herself against the pain. A strange protectiveness surges through me. I'm tempted to close the distance between us and wrap my arms around her. Instead, I remain firmly planted on the bed. It's highly doubtful she'd accept any comfort from the likes of me.

"Don't worry about it," she says.

Silence falls over us as a far-off expression settles on Whitney's face. Her gaze stays trained out the window. The urge to make this situation better bubbles up inside me, but I don't know how to do that. The fact that I've dredged up a painful memory from her past kills me.

Not sure what to say, I blurt, "My parents divorced about a year ago. Over the summer, they grabbed dinner a few times, so I thought…" I shrug as my voice trails off. A protective layer that I don't expose to many gets peeled away.

Her gaze finds its way to mine. "You thought they might get back together."

"Yeah." Uncomfortable with the change in topic, I shift my weight and look away. "Maybe." Just because I'm revealing this information of my own free will, doesn't make it easy.

"And that won't happen if my dad and your mom are getting serious with one another," she adds softly.

My hooded gaze flickers to her. "Doesn't seem too likely, now does it?"

She shakes her head as a small puff of air escapes from her lips. "I can see why you wouldn't be thrilled by the situation."

"You can't be either," I shoot back.

"No, I'm not. But I don't see how we can break them up."

The intimacy we've just shared gets forced back into the darkness where it belongs as I lean forward. The vulnerability vanishes from her eyes and it once again feels like we're on even terrain. "Have a little faith, Winters. I already told you; not only is this plan simple, but it's foolproof."

"Then why do I feel so frightened?"

One side of my mouth crooks. "All you have to do is trust me." By the time I'm done describing the plan in detail, she's back to furiously gnawing on her lip.

"I don't know, Gray."

"Or," I say easily, "we can leave it up to fate. I'm sure spending Christmas together as a blended family will be a shitload of fun." I give her a wink to seal the deal. "Right, sis?"

I know I've hit a nerve when she shudders.

"So," I push, "are you in or out?"

Whitney huffs out a restless breath and rises to her feet before grabbing her bag from the floor. "Give me a few days to think it over and I'll get back to you." She hikes the black bag onto her shoulder and strides toward the bedroom door.

Just as she's about to twist the knob with her fingers, I say, "I wouldn't take too much time. Their relationship seems to be in hyperdrive. And Thanksgiving will be here before you know it."

She glances at me with a sober expression and jerks her head in a tight nod. "Okay."

# WHITNEY

*G*ray's words buzz annoyingly around my head for the next couple of days. No matter what I do, I can't stop dwelling on them. The problem is, I want no part of breaking up Dad and Veronica. I'd much rather let their relationship fall naturally by the wayside.

What are the chances of them staying together for the long haul?

Slim to none, is what I'm guessing. So, I'm leaning toward telling Gray to count me out.

But still…

It's probably best to do a little recon on my own before putting the kibosh on his plans, which is exactly why I've decided to head home for an impromptu visit. Disconcerting doesn't begin to describe what it was like to see Dad so besotted at brunch last weekend.

I stop at Oceana, our favorite local Chinese restaurant, on the way home after my last class on Friday. We have yet to discuss the situation since brunch. Dad texted a couple of times during the week wanting to talk, but I told him I was busy.

It's not a total lie.

I'm taking five upper-level business classes this semester, and they're all challenging. But I think we both know that I'm avoiding the topic. So, I've decided to put on my big girl panties and talk to him.

How else am I going to figure out how serious the situation is?

It seems ridiculous that Dad would want to tie himself down to the first woman he's dated since Mom. My parents were married for fifteen years; it has to be at least twenty-five since he's gone out with someone else. Now that he's dipped his toe in the dating pond, isn't he going to want to play the field for a bit before settling down?

A shiver scuttles down my spine. Uncomfortable with the thought, I shove it away before I can inspect it too closely. Parents and sex don't mix.

I'm pretty confident in my assessment that this relationship won't make it past the six-month mark. Gray is jumping the gun and getting bent around the axel over nothing. The guy needs to chill out and relax.

By the time I pull on to our street, I've convinced myself that this relationship with Gray's mom is no big deal. In hindsight, it's ridiculous that I allowed Gray to jack me up. They've been dating for three months. That's only twelve weeks! Give me a break. I've dated several people for that length of time, and we certainly didn't get hitched. Not even close.

This behavior is perfectly normal, single dad stuff. I'm not going to stress about it. Katelyn is probably right. I'll have to get used to the idea of Dad bringing girlfriends around every now and again.

My brows draw together when I see Dad's silver BMW parked in the garage. I thought for sure I'd beat him home from work.

This works out even better. The food is hot. We can sit down and talk over Chinese and then I'll head back to campus. I need to figure out a way to get Katelyn and Evert back on track and put the whole *lettuce stuck in the teeth* episode behind us. With those thoughts circling through my head, I shove the housekey in the front door and let myself in. Silence greets me as I step inside the foyer.

That's odd. I know he's here. His car is parked in the drive. I peek into the living room and then the dining room, only to find both empty.

"Dad?" I call out before waiting for a response. Maybe he's in the basement tinkering around in his workshop. "Are you here?"

As I head down the hallway with the bag of Chinese tucked under one arm, I hear footfalls on the second floor right before they hit the staircase. I set the grocery bag on the granite counter and swing back around to the entryway.

"Whit?" Dad says in surprise. "Is that you?"

"Yeah." I snort and shake my head. "Who else would it be?"

As he reaches the landing, I realize that he's wearing his navy plaid robe. Concern floods through me. I frown and take in his disheveled appearance. His normally combed hair is mussed and sticking up at the back.

"Are you feeling all right?" I'm not going to lie, there are times when I feel bad that Dad lives alone. Last year, when he got a nasty case of the flu, I stayed at the house for the week and traveled back and forth to school so I could take care of him. "Did you stay home from work today?"

"Ummm..." An odd expression flits across his face. It's like he's trying to come up with a response. The floorboards creek from above again and another set of footsteps slowly pads down the staircase. Dad's cheeks flood with color.

My forehead scrunches in surprise. "*Who—*"

Just as the word escapes from my lips, Veronica comes into view. Her movements are cautious as she meets my bewildered gaze. Unlike my father, she's fully dressed. Although her hair looks equally tousled. She's wearing the same embarrassed expression that my father does. With fluttering fingers, she tucks a stray lock of hair behind her ear and smiles brightly.

It's only when I pick my jaw up off the floor that it hits me what these two were up to.

*Oh.*

*My.*

*God.*

*I've just walked in on my dad having sex.*

"I should probably go." She points to the front door, hesitantly inching toward it.

"Ronnie," Dad protests, "you don't have to leave."

Unsure what to do, I shuffle my feet. Could this moment be more awkward?

"Maybe I'm the one who should leave," I mutter, wanting to be anywhere but here. I can't believe that my dad and her were—

A thick tremor slides through my body.

*Stop thinking about it!*

"No, no!" Veronica says, waving me off. "You stay." She pauses next to Dad and gives him a peck on the lips before her voice drops to a husky murmur. "I'll see you tomorrow."

"Okay." The same smitten look from the other day transforms his face as a dopey smile curves his lips. "Drive safe and text me when you get home," he adds as she walks to the front door.

I'm tempted to roll my eyes. Give me a break. The woman has to be in her mid-forties. I think she can find her way home in one piece.

With one last wave, Veronica—or *Ronnie,* as Dad likes to call her— closes the door softly behind her. My dad stares forlornly at it as if expecting her to return for him. After about twenty seconds of silence, I grow impatient and clear my throat. His eyes swivel to me in surprise, like he forgot I was there.

*Un-freaking-believable!*

I've been home for approximately five minutes, and what I've officially ascertained of the situation is that it's worse than I originally assumed.

*Much worse.*

"So, ah, you decided to pop home for a visit?" he says with a small smile.

It couldn't be more obvious that I've ruined his plans for the evening.

I try to wrangle my emotions back under control. If there are any positives to be found in this situation, it's that I now understand what I'm up against. I never thought I'd say this, but Gray was right. We need to put a stop to this relationship before it becomes permanent.

"Yeah," I say with forced cheerfulness, "I brought Chinese. I thought we could have dinner and talk."

He perks up. At least he no longer looks like his favorite dog just ran away, which is a considerable improvement.

Although not much.

"Great." He rubs his belly with exaggeration. "I'm starving."

*Right...*

That only makes me think about how he worked up an appetite in the first place. I wince, not wanting to go there.

We head to the back of the house in silence. The kitchen hasn't been altered since Mom was alive. Instead of finding it drab or outdated, it's comforting. When I close my eyes, I can still see her bustling around the small space, making dinner or helping me with my homework at the table. It never fails to make me feel closer to her.

Except now. After what just happened, Veronica's image is super-imposed over Mom's.

How many times has she been in our house?

Does she keep clothes tucked away in the drawers Mom once used?

The muscles in my belly contract painfully. As hungry as I'd been when I picked up the food, my appetite is now gone.

Dad grabs two plates from the cabinet and silverware from the drawer. I pull out a can of Orange Crush for myself and a lime LaCroix for him from the fridge. We open the containers of rice, sweet and sour chicken, wonton soup, and vegetable egg rolls before sitting down and digging in.

The rich and pungent scent makes me nauseous. Not knowing what else to do, I take a little of everything and push it around my plate. Every time I glance at Dad—who sits across from me in his robe —I'm reminded of how quickly everything has changed. The silence that falls over us is brutal. It's never been like this, and I hate it. I want our relationship to go back to the way it was before Veronica crashed unwantedly into our lives.

When I can't stand another moment, I set my fork down. "I guess we should probably talk about Veronica."

As terrible as it sounds, I really hope he'll chuckle and tell me that they're just having a bit of fun.

His wide gaze flies to mine as his soup-filled spoon pauses mid-air. Carefully, he lowers the utensil to the bowl again. "You're right, we should." The air deflates from his lungs as he drags a hand through his mussed hair. "I'm sorry, Whit. I'm not very good at this."

*You're telling me.*

He shifts on his chair, looking so uncomfortable that I almost feel sorry for him.

"I'm trying to understand what's going on here, Dad. You just introduced me to this woman last weekend and said you've been dating for a couple of months, which made me think this relationship was in the early stages, but that's not the case, is it?"

His gaze flits away from mine before coming back to rest on me again. "I held off on telling you because in the beginning I wasn't sure how serious it would get. And Ronnie has only been divorced for a year." He shrugs. "I wasn't sure if she was ready for another relationship."

"But…she is?"

The corners of his lips lift, and his eyes brighten. "We're both on the same page with moving forward." A wistful expression settles on his face. "It's been a long time since I've felt this way about a woman." His voice lowers as he adds softly, "Not since your mom."

This isn't what I wanted him to say.

"Whitney?" He straightens, his brow crinkling with concern. "Are you okay? I know this is a lot to take in."

"Yeah," I admit weakly as I stare at my plate, "I'm fine." I swallow down the thick lump wedged in the middle of my throat. "I thought you were moving to China for your job," I mumble.

"I'm sure you're glad that didn't turn out to be the case," he says with a chuckle.

Well, that's debatable. At the moment, China seems like the lesser of two evils. Especially since one of those evils involves Gray McNichols.

Dad fiddles with his spoon before admitting, "You'll probably think I'm moving too fast, but I've decided to propose to Ronnie when we're in the Virgin Islands."

*"What! You can't be serious!"*

Startled by my outburst, Dad's eyes widen.

*I need to calm down. Flying off the handle isn't going to solve anything.*

I draw in a deep breath before forcing it out. Then I repeat the process. Several times. But it's not working. I press my fingers to my eyes and shake my head, wishing the situation would disappear.

"Dad," I say carefully, "you just got involved with this woman. You can't possibly propose after dating for a couple of months." I lower my hands and meet his dark eyes. When he remains silent, I sputter, "That's crazy!"

*Oh my God! How doesn't he see that?*

His expression doesn't alter in the slightest. My father has always had a calm demeanor. Most of the time, I can appreciate that. But right now, it's driving me nuts.

"Actually," he says, "I've known Ronnie for most of my life." He picks up my hand and squeezes it. "This might be difficult for you to understand, but this relationship is right. Nothing has felt this good in a long time, and I don't want to lose it." His eyes plead with mine. "I want you to be happy for me, Whit. I think this is going to be a positive change for all of us." He nods as if to punctuate his thoughts. "I really do."

"Okay, I get that you like her and want to spend time together. Does that necessarily mean you have to rush out and get engaged?" I feel like I'm grasping at straws. "Why not take your time and see how it goes?"

A heavy sigh leaves his lips. "Because I'm almost fifty years old, and I've lived the last nine years alone. I almost forgot what it felt like to be part of a couple. To have a woman in my life who cares about me."

Everything in me deflates. Only now do I realize that nothing I say will get him to slow-track this relationship.

"You'll see," he adds. "After a month or so, it'll feel like Ronnie has always been part of our lives."

I bite my lip to keep from arguing. It's obvious that Dad isn't going to see reason any time soon, which means the only option I have left is Gray.

And his hairbrained scheme to break them up.

# GRAY

*I* lift the bottle of beer to my lips and watch the NHL action as it unfolds on the seventy-inch, high-def screen in our living room. Detroit and Chicago are tied in the third period. It's been a tight game. Every time one team scores, the other comes back to even it up.

My money is still riding on Chicago. The Blackhawks have always been my favorite team.

Sharp fingernails graze my bicep and I rip my eyes from the television to find Savannah standing next to the recliner I'm parked in.

"Hey, Gray," she purrs, shifting her weight and leaning over, giving me a glimpse down the front of her shirt. I'm not going to lie, it's a damn fine view. Once Savannah has snared my attention, she smiles. "Good game, huh?"

Sure it is, but I'd be shocked if Savannah knew which teams were duking it out on the ice. She's more interested in hockey players than the sport itself. There are a lot of girls like her on campus. And once I hit the pros, there'll be even more puck bunnies throwing themselves at me. I used to consider the jersey chasers another perk of being a high-profile college athlete.

Play hard on the ice, party even harder off it.

That's always been my motto.

I've plowed my way through more girls than I can remember. First during the two years I spent playing juniors, and then here at Hillsdale. When a gorgeous chick spreads her legs, offering no-strings-attached sex, do you really turn it down?

Hell, no.

I think half these guys play college sports just to get their choice of pussy. But I'm kind of over it. Casual encounters no longer hold the same appeal as they used to. I'm not sure when that changed.

"Yup." Since I'm not too interested in what Savannah is offering up, my gaze meanders to the game. I don't want to miss a moment of the action.

Detroit scoops up the puck and suddenly their left wing is rushing toward Chicago's goal. I sit up and lean forward as his blades dig into the ice. He's a fast motherfucker. If one of Detroit's defensemen doesn't catch him, they'll score.

Shouts erupt all around me. We're a mix of Red Wings and Black-hawks fans, so you have guys cheering for both teams, which always makes for a lot of trash talk. The wing takes a shot, and the goalie drops to his knees, effectively blocking it. I slump against the chair in relief as the game cuts away to a commercial.

"Wow," Savannah coos, still at my side, "that was so exciting!"

I grin as our gazes collide.

That's one of the reasons I love hockey. The action is always fast paced. Constant racing back and forth across the ice. There's never any downtime. I love watching it just as much as I enjoy playing it. I could live at the hockey rink and never grow tired of it. Next year, if all goes according to plan, that's exactly what I'll be doing.

My life revolves around hockey.

There was a time not so long ago when I thought it had been taken away from me and now...

Every day that I'm out on the ice is a fucking gift.

One I'll never take for granted.

Before I realize it, Savannah has settled herself on my lap. My hands go to her hips as she wiggles her ass against my cock. Taking that as an invitation to proceed, her arms snake around my neck and she pulls me closer, thrusting her breasts under my chin.

Subtly is a lost art when it comes to this girl.

I'm about to break it to her that I'm not in the mood when the game resumes and I'm sucked back into the action.

When the doorbell rings, no one budges. Everyone's ass is glued to their spot. You blink, and a goal could be scored. When the bell peels for a second time, someone grumbles and jumps off the couch to answer it.

People come and go from this place at all hours of the day, so I don't give it much thought. We have an open-door policy with our teammates. I may be in a hockey-induced trance, but the moment I hear her voice, it dissolves, and my head whips in that direction.

"Um, hi. Is Gray here?"

"Sure, he's watching the game," Collins says. "Wanna come in?"

As soon as Whitney steps into the entryway, she glances around before her gaze locks on mine. After a beat, she eyes up the girl perched on my lap.

*Well, shit.*

I almost forgot about her. Savannah, unaware of our audience, continues to nibble at my neck. My brows beetle together.

When the hell did that happen?

Whitney's expression hardens as she shoves her hands into the pockets of her hoodie and clears her throat. "Obviously, you're super busy right now, but we need to talk."

My first impulse is to shove Savannah off my lap, but I resist the urge. Instead, my hands tighten around her waist. With my attention focused on Whitney, I whisper in Savannah's ear that I've got business to take care of and we can get back to it afterward.

I have zero intention of doing anything with Savannah. But Whitney doesn't need to know that.

Savannah wriggles her backside against me before shooting a sly look in the other girl's direction. Just as the auburn-haired girl saunters away, I give her ass a little slap. She jumps with a squeal and a high-pitched giggle that hurts my ears.

Whitney rolls her eyes and shakes her head. "You're such an egotistical pig."

Maybe. But I'm more interested to see if she's bothered by another girl sitting on my lap. From all outward appearances, she couldn't give a rip.

Bummer.

Wanting to push her buttons, I tap my thigh as one corner of my mouth hitches. "You looking to fill the spot that was just vacated?"

"Hardly." She makes a point of glancing at her phone and saying in a voice laced with boredom, "Look, I don't have all night. Can we get this over with?"

With a shrug, I rise to my feet. Whitney trails after me as I head into the kitchen. Going to the fridge, I pull out two bottles of water before tossing one to her. She catches it easily in her hands.

As I settle against the counter, I pull off the cap and take a swig. "What's up?"

Because there has to be something. There's no way in hell she would show up on my doorstep without a damn good reason.

I'm interested to discover what it is.

"I stopped home and saw my dad today," she says.

"Oh?"

"He's planning to propose to your mom while they're on vacation."

I blink, hoping that I misheard her. She couldn't have possibly said—

"Propose?" I pause for a confused beat. "As in...*marriage?*"

A ghost of a smile flits around Whitney's lips. "Well, he's not gonna propose that they play a game of canasta."

"Fuck." I plow a hand roughly through my hair.

*Marriage?*

No way that's happening.

"You can say that again." Whitney snorts and sets the bottle of water on the counter. "I'm sure I'll end up regretting this at some point, but your plan? Count me in."

I give her a smug smile. "What happened to not wanting to get involved?"

She jerks her shoulders and lifts her chin. "Obviously, I've changed my mind."

"Not as enamored by having me for a stepbrother as you'd originally suspected, huh?"

"Good Lord, no." She shudders, and I'm not sure if it's for real or show. "So, when are we going to put this into motion?"

My lips twist into a smile. "As soon as possible." Then I add, "Don't worry about a thing. Just leave it all to me."

Whitney shakes her head and groans, "Famous last words."

I snort.

She doesn't know the half of it.

# WHITNEY

$\mathcal{M}$y belly clenches as my phone dings with an incoming text message. I don't have to glance at the screen to know that it's Gray. He's waiting downstairs in his truck. We're going to dinner.

At his mom's house.

I smooth my fingers over the thigh-length skirt and glance nervously in the mirror. Now that it's the moment of truth, I'm not sure if I can go through with it.

But it's too late to back out. Plus…what's the alternative?

Having Gray McNichols for a stepbrother?

Nope. That can't be allowed to happen. With my luck, Dad and Veronica will get married and live happily ever after. And I'll be tied to Gray—a guy I can barely stand—for the rest of my life.

Decision made, I swipe my purse off the dresser and head for the door. Two minutes later, I slide into the passenger side of Gray's truck. The dome light illuminates the cab as his bright blue eyes sweep over the length of me. I try to steel myself against it, but the way his gaze touches upon every part of me feels like an intimate caress.

"You look nice."

The deep timbre of his voice explodes like a firework in the pit of my belly. I shift uncomfortably, not wanting him to see the way he affects me. Best to keep that under wraps.

"Thanks," I mumble, avoiding eye contact at all costs.

I wish I could say that I didn't notice how good he looks, but that would be a lie. He's wearing a blue and white striped button-down paired with khaki pants that stretch across his muscular thighs. There's a chunky silver watch wrapped around his wrist and he smells damn near edible.

I clench my thighs together to stifle the growing ache. Spending an entire evening together is going to suck.

Gray pulls out of the parking lot and into the flow of traffic. Once we're away from campus, he glances in my direction. "You're clear on the plan?"

I take another peek at him and give a curt nod.

Yeah...I'm clear on how this is supposed to go down. I just don't like it. But I've been back and forth a million times. There isn't an alternative.

And Gray's right. It'll be simple. I just need to play along.

It takes about fifteen minutes to reach Veronica's house where the four of us are having dinner together. My nerves continue to leap and dance, making my belly prickle with unease. As we park along the curb in front of a small Cape Cod, I spot Dad's silver BMW parked in the drive. A thick shudder works its way through me as I'm inundated with memories of surprising them last Friday.

At four o'clock in the afternoon.

*Who knocks boots at four in the afternoon?*

*Apparently, these two.*

*Gross.*

I blink back to the present when Gray opens the passenger side door for me.

A smirk lifts the corners of his lips. "Milady."

As ridiculous as it sounds, his cocky grin makes everything in me settle. This situation is easier to deal with when I'm annoyed.

Before I can retaliate with a snappy comment, Gray extends his hand. "Ready to do this?"

Anxiety spirals through me and I draw in a sharp breath, cautiously placing my fingers in his. "As I'll ever be."

His warm hand swallows mine up as we walk to the front door.

"Everything's going to be fine," he says as if sensing my growing unease. "All you have to do is follow my lead."

"If you say so," I mumble, hoping he's right.

Instead of knocking on the beveled glass door, Gray turns the handle and thrusts it open. We step inside and I glance around, taking in the rooms from where I stand in the beautifully decorated foyer. A cozy living room is to the right with a sleek white couch, colorful turquoise pillows, and two matching chairs. A trio of different sized mirrors adorns the far wall. All of the accents are silver, glass, and the same blue-green hue.

The result is sophisticated and classy.

Impressed with her style, I remember Dad mentioning that Veronica is an interior designer. From the little I've seen of her house, she's obviously talented.

"Hello?" Gray calls out. "Mom? We're here." He whispers so that only I can hear, "It's showtime."

Gray gives me a wink as if we're co-conspirators and my belly trembles in response. I push away the unwanted feelings as my father saunters out of the kitchen with a crystal tumbler of amber liquid in his hand.

He looks perfectly at ease in Veronica's house.

I glance at Gray, wondering if he's noticed the same thing. By the tightening of his shadowed jaw and the furrowing of his brow, my guess is that he has. He probably doesn't like seeing my dad in his home any more than I liked seeing Veronica in mine. This might be the first thing we have in common.

With a smile on his face, Dad glances between the two of us before reaching out to shake Gray's hand. "It's nice to see you again."

Gray nods, his lips lifting just enough to appear pleasant. "You, too."

Dad pulls me into his arms and gives me a quick hug. "Hey, Whit. I'm so glad you could make it tonight."

"Yeah," I say with forced enthusiasm. "This should be fun."

*Not.*

Once we pull apart, Dad's gaze bounces from Gray to me before he waggles a finger at us. "Did you two come together?"

"Ummm..." My mind empties and I glance wide-eyed at Gray for assistance. Lying and subterfuge have never been my strong suits. I've been here less than two minutes and already my armpits are damp with perspiration. It's doubtful I'll make it through the evening without falling apart.

"Yup." Gray steps in smoothly, spearing me with a quick glance. "We only live a couple of blocks from each other."

Accepting the explanation at face value, Dad's posture relaxes, and he claps Gray heartily on the shoulder. "That was nice of you to give Whitney a lift over here."

"No problem." Gray's lips bow into an easy smile. He looks like a cat about to pounce on an unsuspecting canary.

I glance around, wishing there was some way to air out my armpits. It feels like a million degrees in here. I'm sweating buckets. Maybe we should call this off and just let the cards fall. Would having Gray as a stepbrother really be so bad?

Probably.

As my dad waves us toward the back of the house, he glances at Gray. "Your mom is in the kitchen making chicken marsala. Dinner should be ready in about fifteen minutes." He beams. "She's a fantastic cook."

Gray's jaw ticks as we trail after my dad. "Yeah, I'm aware of that."

Not taking notice of Gray's curt tone, Dad continues. "I'll have to make more of an effort to hit the gym. I've already packed on a few pounds."

I squeeze Gray's fingers to pull his attention back to me. When his gaze meets mine, I widen my eyes. He jerks his head in a tight nod as if he understands that I'm silently telling him to calm down. Once we're in the kitchen, I greet Veronica and Gray heads to the minifridge tucked in the island. He rattles off ten different drink choices.

I perk up at the last one. "You have Orange Crush?"

"Um, yeah." He gives me a legit *are you crazy* look. "Of course we do. It's my favorite."

My brows beetle together as I reluctantly admit, "Yeah, mine too."

"See how much you guys have in common?" Dad says with obvious delight as his gaze ping-pongs between us. He looks like he's waiting for us to wrap our arms around each other and sing 'Kumbaya.'

*Poor Dad. He's about to get sucker punched and doesn't even realize it.*

Gray pops open both cans of soda before passing one to me. Our gazes lock as we each take a sip. For the next twenty minutes, the three of us stand around the kitchen island while Veronica puts the finishing touches on dinner. By the time we sit down at the beautifully set table in the dining room, my nerves have settled, and I've almost forgotten that Gray and I are in cahoots to break them up.

Veronica flutters around the table, making sure that we have everything we need. Just like the kitchen and living room, her dining room is stunning. It could be photographed for a spread in a glossy decorating magazine. The theme of silver, glass, and turquoise has been carried out in here as well.

The chicken and mushroom dish Veronica prepared is served over a bed of wild rice with steamed asparagus on the side. Normally, I'm not a fan of the green stalks, but these are surprisingly yummy. I suspect it's the hollandaise sauce I've drenched them in.

I sigh in frustration.

*This woman is good.*

I want to find something not to like about her, but I can't. She's perfect. And surprisingly nice.

How she raised such a cocky jerk like Gray I'll never understand.

If Veronica weren't Gray's mom, it's doubtful I'd have as many reservations about them being together. It's not that I'm suddenly on board with another woman taking Mom's place, but there are worse women than Veronica that Dad could have gotten involved with. She's taken the time this evening to get to know me, asking questions about school and what my plans are after college. She seems genuinely interested.

The conversation throughout dinner is light and casual. Everyone is enjoying themselves. Every so often, I glance at Gray from the corner of my eye and wonder if he's changed his mind about going nuclear on their relationship.

Dad breaks into my thoughts when he picks up his glass of wine and raises it in the air for a toast. His eyes are focused on Veronica, as if he can't bear to look away from her for even a moment.

Yeah, it's nauseating, but there's something sweet about it as well.

He clears his throat as a smile curves his lips. "Ronnie, I just want to say that these past couple of months with you have been the best I've experienced in a long time. I can't believe that we—"

Gray shoots to his feet and my eyes widen.

"Whitney and I have an announcement to make," he cuts in abruptly.

*Oh God...we do?*

It takes effort to swallow the chicken marsala that's sitting in my throat like a lump of wet sawdust. My eyes water as I choke it down. I'm deathly afraid of what's going to pop out of Gray's mouth next. Both Dad and Veronica turn to stare at Gray with matching quizzical expressions.

I'm rooted in place as Gray's blue gaze lands on me.

"Whitney and I have been seeing each other."

A deafening silence follows that announcement.

Dad and Veronica share a confused look before he lowers his wine glass to the table. His brows snap together when Gray lays his hand over my clenched one.

"Whitney?" Dad's gaze bounces from our clasped hands to my face. "Is this true?"

My tongue darts out to moisten my lips.

*Ahhhhhh.*

Gray's fingers tighten around mine when I remain silent. Anytime I'm forced to fib, I break out in hives. Gray squeezes my fingers—harder this time—and I wince from the pressure.

"Yes, it's true," I blurt and sneak a peek at Gray. "We're together." Laughter bubbles up from my throat. It comes out sounding high-pitched and nervous. "He's my boyfriend."

Dad shakes his head as a frown settles across his features. If I were trying to erase the love-stricken look from his face, this has done the trick. "I don't understand." He rests his elbows on the table and cocks his head. "When did this happen?"

"Ummm…" I gulp. *Details. Of course, they want details.* Unfortunately, we never discussed those.

"About two months ago," Gray answers smoothly.

I practically collapse against the chair in relief. I'm ready for this inquisition—I mean dinner—to be over with.

"Why didn't you mention this before?" Hurt flashes in Dad's eyes, which only makes me feel worse.

"Um…well…your announcement at brunch kind of threw us for a loop." Gray watches me steadily as I press onward. "We weren't sure what to do and needed time to discuss the situation."

My face feels like it's on fire as my neck begins to itch. I reach up and scratch my collarbone.

Dad's eyes narrow. "Are you breaking out?"

*"What?"* I push out a high-pitched cackle that makes me sound manic. Gray's eyes widen, and I wince in embarrassment. "No, of course not." But that doesn't stop me from scratching my skin frantically before forcing my hands to my lap.

This was a horrible idea.

*Just look at me! I'm a mess. A sweaty, hive-ridden mess!*

This is all Gray's fault.

He's to blame.

"Whitney and I weren't sure if we should continue seeing each other in light of your relationship, but we decided that we just can't be apart. The feelings we have for each other are too strong." The soft expression he aims in my direction is disconcerting. He turns back to our parents. "I'm sure this complicates matters for you guys, but hopefully you can be as happy for us as we are for you."

My eyes widen.

*Oh...he's good.*

I watch as they silently digest this information.

Gray relaxes against his chair as a triumphant smile curves his lips.

"Well, I certainly didn't see this coming," Veronica muses before taking a sip of her wine.

Dad shakes his head, still looking stunned. "Me neither."

For the first time since walking into Veronica's house, I wonder if Gray was right. Throw a monkey wrench into their budding relationship and they'll be broken up in a couple of days.

Problem solved.

But then Veronica smiles. "There's no reason we shouldn't be delighted. I'll admit that it's an unusual situation, but who cares?" She glances at my dad with a gooey expression in her eyes. "We'll work through it."

Dad takes a cue from his new squeeze regarding our relationship and bobs his head in agreement. "You're absolutely right, Ronnie, my love." He picks up her hand and brushes a soft kiss against her knuckles.

As they share an intimate look, I take this opportunity to glance at Gray. He appears none too pleased by this new development and rolls his eyes as I smother a chuckle. If he was hoping to put a damper on their grand love affair, it's turned out to be an epic fail.

Just as Dad leans toward Veronica, Gray clears his throat. "Now that our relationship is out in the open, it shouldn't be a problem if Whitney and I talk about moving in together next semester."

Dad jerks away from Veronica and glares at a now smiling Gray. I bury my face in my hands and pray that the floorboards will open up and swallow me whole.

Gray better enjoy his meal, because I'm going to strangle him when this is over.

# GRAY

$\mathcal{J}$f the death glare aimed in my direction is any indication, Whitney's father isn't thrilled with the idea of me shacking up with his little girl.

Oh, well.

I'd thought for sure that us dating would have been enough to cause a few problems in paradise, but Mom took it in stride, looking genuinely happy for us. And Whitney's father followed suit.

So, what other choice did I have but to up the ante?

"We'll discuss your living situation at a later date," David replies gruffly.

I give him a wide smile and pull Whitney's chair closer before slipping an arm around her shoulders. "Sure, no problem. Why don't you think about it and get back to us?"

David's jaw locks and Mom places her hand over his as if trying to walk him back from the ledge. He looks ready to reach across the table and wring my neck.

Operation *break-up-the-parents* has finally gained some much-needed traction.

The remainder of dinner is stilted and uncomfortable. Mom tries her best to shift the conversation, but we're never able to recover from the bomb I dropped. David sits across from me with a pinched expression on his face. He keeps stealing looks at his daughter. Every time he does, I make sure to touch her or tug her closer.

"So," Mom says brightly, "David and I are looking forward to your first scrimmage next Thursday."

Hockey…right.

"Yeah, me too. We're playing the Ice Hawks. Should be a good game." Considering how important this year is for me, hockey should be the only thing on my brain. Unfortunately, because of this situation, it's not.

Mom turns to Whitney, wanting to pull her into the conversation. "Will you be joining us?"

The question throws her off guard. Her eyes grow wide as her fork pauses mid-air. "At the game?" she squeaks, as if she has no idea why Mom would be asking her that.

I slip my hand under the table and squeeze her thigh. The gesture doesn't go unnoticed and David scowls.

Who knew Whitney was such a terrible liar? She really needs to pull herself together. Every time a question is volleyed in her direction, she panics, looking like a deer caught in headlights. If the situation weren't so dire, I'd be laughing my ass off.

"Yes," I say, widening my eyes and giving her a penetrating stare. "The scrimmage on Thursday. Remember we talked about it? You told me you'd be there to cheer me on."

It takes a moment before she straightens on the chair. "Oh, um, yeah! Of course, the *hockey* game."

I almost shake my head as I turn back to our parents. "Whitney's my number-one fan. Aren't you, sugar-booger?"

She scowls. "You bet I am."

"I still can't believe you like watching hockey." David narrows his eyes. "You never mentioned it. Not once." There's an uncomfortable pause. "Don't you think that's odd?"

Whitney's face reddens, and the splotchiness around her collarbone grows as she gulps. "Oh, well, I—"

"Actually, she's always been a Hellcat fan, but now she's really into it," I cut in, taking pity on her.

Instead of agreeing, Whitney scratches her neck and glances around as if searching for an escape route. A hunted look fills her eyes. Any moment, she's going to crack under the mounting pressure, and I can't allow that to happen. We've made a decent amount of headway tonight. I need to get Whitney out of here before she blows like Mount Vesuvius and ruins everything.

"Well folks, it's getting late." I turn to Whitney. "How about we grab another Orange Crush for the road?"

Whitney wilts in relief like I've just thrown her a lifeline.

"You're leaving already?" Mom frowns. "We haven't eaten dessert yet."

I shrug. "Would you mind boxing it up for us? Whitney and I were planning to hit the library tonight. We both have a ton of homework to plow through."

Mom smiles even though she's disappointed the evening is getting cut short. "Sure. Of course, that's not a problem."

Whitney practically jumps up from the table and stumbles over her feet in her haste to get away. I'm tempted to laugh, but I have a feeling she'd junk punch me if I did.

Within ten minutes, two thick wedges of homemade chocolate cake have been packaged up and we're at the front door, saying our goodbyes.

David pulls Whitney in for a hug and murmurs, "We'll talk soon." Then he gives her a look chock-full of meaning.

Her face falls as she gulps, reluctantly nodding in response.

I kiss Mom on the cheek and tell her that dinner was great before heading outside with Whitney in tow. As soon as the door closes behind us, Whitney huffs out a breath and doubles over as if she's going to be sick.

"All in all, I think that went pretty well," I say cheerfully. "What about you?"

In answer, she straightens and punches me in the arm.

"I'm shocked at you, sugar-booger." I chuckle and rub the spot she just hit. "Haven't you learned that violence is never the answer?"

This time, she wallops me harder. "Stop calling me that!"

"What? You don't like it?" My eyes widen in feigned surprise. "It's my cutesy pet name for you."

She growls as her face grows red.

Changing the subject, I add, "FYI—you have to be one of the worst liars I've ever seen."

"Most people would view that as a positive characteristic." She buries her face in her hands. "That was the most awful dinner of my life." She glares at me through the cracks between her fingers. "No thanks to you!"

I click the locks on the truck and hold open the passenger side door. As soon as she slides inside, I jog around the front and set our desserts in the backseat before starting up the engine and pulling onto the road.

"Why did you tell him we were moving in together?" Before I can answer, she continues. "Oh my God! Did you see the look on his face?" Whitney groans. "Now I'm going to have to sit down and have a conversation with him about this!" She shoots me an accusing look. "Do you have any idea how uncomfortable that's going to be?"

"Sheesh, I never pegged you for a drama queen. Bring it down a notch." I glance at her. "It's not that bad."

"Are you kidding," she shrieks. "It's terrible!"

"What else was I supposed to do? I had to up the stakes." I shrug. "Who knew they'd be cool with us dating?"

"And your answer was to tell them we're moving in together?" Her voice escalates as she throws her arms wide. "That's the best you could come up with?"

I smile smugly. "It certainly did the trick, didn't it?"

By the time I pull into the parking lot of her building, it's obvious that Whitney is about to erupt. Smoke is practically pouring out of her ears. I park the truck and cut the engine before turning to face her. Clearly, I have some placating to do. Although, I'm not sure what she's so bent out of shape about.

Who cares if we told a few small, white lies?

It's not a big deal. She needs to stay focused on the big picture.

"Look, the point of all this was to break up our parents. I'm sorry if I took it too far. But the good news is that I think we made a dent in their relationship."

Her lips flatten. "Yeah, we'll see about that."

"Are you still on board with the plan?"

Breaking eye contact, Whitney glances away and nibbles at her lower lip.

Does she have any idea how sexy I find that?

I'm tempted to lean over and suck the fullness into my mouth. My cock stirs at the idea. "Trust me," I mutter, still focused on her lips, "we both want this."

I have no idea if I'm talking about kissing her or breaking up our parents. It's a toss-up.

A flicker of doubt crosses Whitney's face. "They seem really happy together." There's a pause. "Maybe we should just forget about it."

Oh, hell no.

I shouldn't be surprised that Whitney's getting cold feet. I arch a brow. "Is that really what you want, *sis*?"

She winces. "Fine," she snaps. "I don't want them together."

A slow smile spreads across my face. I had a feeling that would do the trick. "Yeah, I didn't think so."

Whitney falls silent and stares out the windshield. She seems oblivious to my presence, so I'm free to look my fill. It's funny...I'm around chicks who dress as scantily as possible in order to capture my attention and yet this one, who looks like a nun in comparison, is the one I want. The gray and white striped sweater she's wearing isn't overly tight, but it accentuates the soft curves of her breasts. The navy skirt with gold buttons down the front hits about mid-thigh, leaving quite a bit of sun-kissed skin on display.

My mouth salivates and I tighten my hands in an effort not to touch her. With any other girl, this is exactly when I'd be making my big move. But this isn't just any girl. It's Whitney Winters.

As if sensing the direction of my wayward thoughts, Whitney

grows impossibly still before swinging around to stare at me. With narrowed eyes, she jabs a finger in my direction and growls, "I know what you're thinking, McNichols, and you can forget about it!"

A chuckle escapes as I hold my hands up in a gesture of surrender and lie through my teeth. "I have no idea what you're talking about." I tilt my head and squint. "Maybe you're the one who's having inappropriate thoughts about me." I pause for a beat as if considering the merit of my words. "Isn't there a term for that?" I snap my fingers and point at her. "Projection. I think you might be projecting your own desires onto me."

She gasps, and her eyes widen to the point of looking like they might fall right out of her head.

It's kind of hilarious.

Before she can protest, I shrug. "Hey, you're the one bringing it up. The thought never crossed my mind." I shake my head and smirk, unable to resist pushing her buttons. "You're such a naughty girl for trying to take advantage of this situation."

Whitney screeches at the top of her lungs and I burst out laughing.

"You're such an asshole!" she seethes before swiveling around and staring straight out the windshield. A deafening silence follows as she gives me a bit of side-eye. "Jerk."

"Oh, come on, Winters," I chuckle. "You know you love me."

"Nothing could be further from the truth."

"Are you sure about that?" I lower my voice until it's more of a purr.

"I've never been more certain about anything in my life," she responds icily.

"Hmmm, now why does that sound like a challenge?"

Her head whips toward me again. "*What?* No! Of course, it isn't! You're crazy!"

"Nope," I murmur, my gaze falling to her lips as I place my fingers beneath her chin. "It *definitely* sounded like a challenge. And you may not realize this, but I have a hard time resisting one of those."

Whitney draws in a sharp breath and knocks my hand away. A

flash of heat flares to life in her eyes before being snuffed out. "Then I guess it's good that one wasn't issued."

"All right." I shrug, pulling away from her. "If you say so."

Releasing a pent-up breath, she gradually relaxes against the leather seat. "I do."

I pause for a beat. "Since you brought up kissing—"

"Oh my God," she grounds out. "I did *not* bring up kissing!"

"Whatever. It's okay if you want to kiss me." I grin. "Most girls do."

She makes a strangled noise deep in her throat.

"Anyway, it would probably be a good idea if we practice." When that suggestion is met with a deafening silence, I add, "It's like acting. We have to be able to sell it and make it believable."

Whitney's gaze darts around the truck as she shifts on the seat. "Do you really think that's necessary?"

Hell yeah, it's necessary.

In fact, it couldn't be *more* necessary.

"Absolutely." I reach out and stroke a long strand of her hair. It feels like silk against my fingers. "You almost blew it for us tonight. That can't happen again. We told our parents that we've been together for two months. We've got to act like it."

She jerks her shoulders until they're somewhere in the vicinity of her ears. Her fingers tangle in the hem of her sweater, twisting the fabric. "I did not almost blow it," she whispers, but her voice lacks conviction.

I scoff. "You were a nervous wreck." My gaze drops to her collarbone. The blotchy rash that had broken out on her neck is almost gone.

"I don't like lying," she mumbles in self-defense. "Especially to my dad." Her tongue darts out to moisten her lips.

And that, ladies and gentlemen, is all it takes to snap my tightly-leashed control. I reach out and pull Whitney into my arms. I fully expect her to flatten her palms against my chest and shove me away, but she doesn't.

"I've wanted to kiss you since you first slid into my truck tonight," I murmur right before my lips crash onto hers. I don't want to scare

118

her away, but I can't help myself. I want to lay my hands all over this girl and claim her for my own.

But I can't do that just yet. I need to proceed with caution, or she'll be out of the truck so fast my head will spin. It requires a herculean effort on my part to soften the pressure of my mouth. She moans, becoming more pliant in my arms.

Now that I know she isn't going to push me away, I allow the kiss to unfold at a more leisurely pace. There's a teasing quality to the way my tongue dances with hers. When she makes soft, little mewling noises that are sexy as hell, I want to pump my fist in the air.

After a few minutes, I change the angle of my head and lick at her lips. My hand squeezes her hip, gripping it possessively. She whimpers as my tongue invades her mouth, plundering the sweetness. My fingers inch their way up to her waist, sliding around the band of her skirt to the taut flesh beneath.

I stroke along her bare belly before gliding toward her ribcage. Then further upward until I find the lacy cups that are molded against her breasts. A thick shiver slides through her as I trail my fingers teasingly over the edge of the material. When she arches, trying to get closer, I slip my fingers inside the cup and squeeze the warm weight of her breast.

The idea of taking this further is so damn tempting. All I want is to bury myself balls-deep in her tight pussy and fuck her right out of my system once and for all. I have the feeling that if I played with her body long enough, she'd let me. Instead of doing that, I pull back and ease my hand out of her bra before flattening my palm against her lower abdomen.

When I meet Whitney's gaze, there's a dazed expression on her face.

I lick my lips, still able to taste her sweetness. The urge to dive back in is strong. It pounds through me like that of a steady drumbeat. "I'd say that was definitely believable."

The sound of my voice breaks the spell that had fallen over her.

"Oh!" She shakes her head as her fingers scrabble for the door handle. "I, um, should go."

There's just enough light flooding inside the cab of the truck from the posts in the parking lot to see the hot rush of color that fills her cheeks.

"Yeah," I agree reluctantly, "you probably should."

Just as Whitney pops open the door, I reach around to give her the dessert Mom packed for us. "Wait, take this with you."

"No, that's all right." She sucks in a gulp of air, looking like she wants to flee the situation. "You can have it."

I shake my head. "Stop arguing and just take it."

"Are you sure?" She nibbles at her lower lip, which is swollen from my kisses as she considers my offer.

I fucking love the muddled look on her face. It's such a difference from the usual iciness she shoots in my direction.

And I'm the one who put it there.

*Me.*

That thought makes my dick strain against my khakis.

"Mom makes a wicked good chocolate cake. You'll enjoy it."

A reluctant smile curves her lips as she takes the bag from me. "Thanks."

"No problem."

She steps out of the truck and onto the pavement with her purse and dessert in hand. Just as she's about to slam the door, I call her name. "Whitney?"

Her gaze darts to mine. "Yeah?"

I give her a wink, unable to resist one last parting shot. "Don't worry about convincing them, you totally sold it."

The confused look evaporates as she narrows her eyes and slams the door in my face. I chuckle and watch as she hustles to the apartment building without another look in my direction. Once she's safely inside, I take off.

This evening went better than expected.

On both fronts.

# WHITNEY

"*D*id I show you this one already?" Veronica scrolls through the photos on her phone as we sit in the stands at the arena. It's about ten minutes until the puck drops and the Hellcats are on the ice finishing warmups. Even though I'm trying to focus on the pictures, my attention continues to get snagged by Gray as he circles their half of the ice.

No matter how much I keep reprimanding myself, I can't help it.

Why am I so preoccupied with him?

I almost wince. Stupid question. I know *exactly* why. It's that damn kiss we shared. It's been days and I still can't stop thinking about it. I clear my throat as well as those thoughts from my mind. Just like he said, it was nothing more than practice.

"No, I don't think so." I force myself to focus on the picture of Veronica and my dad at an apple orchard. They're both grinning as Gray's mother holds the phone for a selfie.

"Here we are, picking apples at Miller's Orchard last weekend." She glances at my dad with a look of adoration.

Katelyn, who I talked into joining us, crowds me from the other side to get a better look at the photo. "Seems like fun, Mrs. McNichols."

121

Gray's mother flashes a smile in Katelyn's direction and nods her head. "It was great, and we couldn't have asked for better weather. We'll have to do it again next year." She glances at my dad. "Right, David?"

"Absolutely," he agrees, face lighting up. "We can make it a tradition." His eyes drift to mine. "Maybe next fall, you can join us."

Unease pricks at my conscience. If Gray has his way, that won't be happening. When I don't respond, Katelyn elbows me in the side and I straighten. "Sure. That sounds great."

Dad doesn't seem to notice that anything is amiss. He's in his own little world, distracted by the woman next to him.

"Ronnie baked two pies from the apples we picked." He pats his belly. "I've already eaten my way through one of them. Tomorrow I'm starting on the other."

Veronica laughs as she leans into my father and scolds, "It's not a challenge, David! You have to pace yourself."

He gives her a sly look and whispers loud enough for me to overhear, "You know I have a hard time resisting your pie."

*Nooooooooo!*

*Please tell me he did not just say that!*

Horror fills my face as I glance at Katelyn. Even though she wears a matching expression, her shoulders shake with mirth. Sure, if it wasn't my parent, I'd be laughing my ass off as well.

But it *is* my parent. And I can never unhear those words again.

Veronica bats playfully at his chest and tells him to hush.

Then she straightens, turning back to me with a blush staining her cheeks. "We're either giving the other pie to you and Gray or your father will take it to work. If we leave it at home, he'll end up eating it all himself."

Unhappy with the idea, Dad frowns and grumbles, "*What!* You made those for me."

"Too much of a good thing can be bad for you," she reminds pertly.

I swear to God, if they make any more innuendos regarding their sex life, I'm out of here. I'm still trying to get over the last comment.

"Goodness, I almost forgot this picture was on my phone," Veronica murmurs, more to herself than to me.

Snapping back to the conversation, I glance at her cell, expecting another cutesy pic of her and Dad. Instead, I find an image of a sullen teenager with dark, messy hair sitting in a hospital bed. My brows slam together as I do a double take.

*No...it can't be.*

I blink, but the image stays the same. "Is that Gray?"

All of the lighthearted happiness filling Veronica's blue eyes as she chatted about the apple orchard disappears. Left in its place is a somber expression. "Yes," she says quietly, "it is."

With my eyes glued to the screen, I wait for her to fill in the details. When she remains silent, lost in thought, I find myself asking, "What happened?"

"Gray hasn't told you?"

Surprise flickers across her face as I shake my head. Only then do I remember that we're supposed to be a couple.

Veronica's brow furrows as she stares silently at the photo. The noise of the arena fades as I wait for an explanation.

By the time she clears her throat, I'm sitting on the edge of my seat. "When Gray was thirteen, we took a skiing trip to Colorado over spring break." Her lips lift at the corners as she gets lost in the memory. "Gray loved to ski and was a natural at it. The way he'd fly down the slopes," she muses, shaking her head. "Skiing and hockey were his passion. His father and I had just bought him a new pair of skis for his birthday, and he was so excited to try them out. Gray was skiing down a double black diamond when another skier lost control and collided with him." Her tone sharpens. "That man had no business being on such an advanced trail. He came out of it without any serious injuries, but Grayson wasn't so lucky. He broke his leg in two places and fractured his pelvis." Moisture gathers in her eyes. "It's by the grace of God that the damage wasn't more severe."

My heart thumps painfully as the photograph of Gray in the hospital bed swims in front of my eyes. "That's horrible," I whisper. "I had no idea."

"His recovery was a difficult time for all of us. Gray had always been such an active kid. Constantly on the go, playing sports, or hanging out with his friends. They would skate, ski, and snowboard. For months, he couldn't do anything but lay in bed and recover. He was miserable." Her lips twist, and again, I have the feeling that she's getting sucked into the memories. But then she blinks back to the present and the look disappears. "The doctors told him that it would take months of physical therapy for him to walk again but, with the injuries he sustained, playing hockey would be out of the question."

My eyes lift, immediately fastening on Gray as he circles the ice. His stick rests against his broad shoulders as he stretches, twisting his torso from side to side. Just as he comes around the bend, his gaze collides with mine. A jolt of electricity zips through my body, making the nerve endings beneath my skin come alive.

"That's difficult to believe," I murmur.

This time when she smiles, it's full of pride. "I know. He worked so hard to prove them wrong. It consumed him. Months and months spent in physical therapy. It took more than a year before Gray was ready to get back on the ice. Of course, his doctors cautioned against it, but Gray refused to listen. His dream was to play in the NHL, and he wasn't going to let anyone tell him that he couldn't make it a reality."

My gaze seeks out Gray as he glides across the ice. Every movement is smooth and fluid. If his mom hadn't told me about the accident, I would have never believed it.

The Gray I know is so cocky and full of himself. I wouldn't have suspected that he'd struggled with anything in his young life and yet, he's already overcome a massive obstacle. He refused to accept the fate he'd been dealt. The accident, a fractured pelvis and broken leg...I can't imagine how much grit and determination it must have taken to get where he is today. As much as I don't want to find any admirable qualities in Gray, how can I not?

Is it possible that he's not as one-dimensional as I'd always assumed?

Trust me, it's a bitter pill to swallow.

"You know," Veronica says in a hushed tone, interrupting the thoughts that whirl through my head, "I was surprised when Gray told us you two were dating."

My brows rise, and I shift on my seat, uncomfortable with the lie. "Oh?"

"He's never brought home a girl for me to meet." Her smile morphs into a grin as she shrugs. "Gray's always been so focused on hockey, there's never been time for anything else." Her hand finds mine before giving it a gentle squeeze. "I'm glad he's finally realized that there's more to life than hockey." She pauses. "There's love."

Oh God…why did she have to say that?

Gray and I aren't in love. We don't even like each other. This is all a cooked-up charade to break them up.

*Ughhhhhhh.*

It's on the tip of my tongue to blurt out the truth, but I bite it back when the referee drops the puck and the game gets underway. Our attention is pulled to the ice, and our previous conversation is pushed to the backburner.

Katelyn leans toward me and whispers, "You're in deep shit, girl."

I groan because she's right.

I'm practically drowning in it.

125

# GRAY

$\mathcal{W}$e might have pulled off a win against the Ice Hawks, but Coach still chewed our asses out. As much as I hate to admit it, the guy is right. There's no way that game should have been as close as it was.

Some of the blame for that falls squarely on my shoulders. Having Whitney in the stands was distracting as hell. Throughout the game, I kept stealing glances at her to see if she was watching the action.

Fine. I wanted to know if she was watching *me*. I shake my head and slam my locker door shut.

For years, Whitney has been simmering in the back of my brain. Up until now, I've been able to go about my business and focus on what's important—hockey. But that's no longer the case. Now she's front and center and all I can think about. For the first time since I came up with this whole fake-dating scheme, I'm having second thoughts. All of this forced proximity is messing with my mojo. And that's the last thing I need. I've got way too much riding on this season to fuck it up now.

"Hey, are we still on for Dive Town?" Collins asks, pulling up alongside me.

"You bet your ass we are," I grunt with more force than necessary. A drink is exactly what I need.

Maybe a chick. And not the one I've been fake dating, either. Whitney is the only girl I've met who's capable of messing with my mind. It would be so much easier if I could simply screw her and move on.

But that's not the case.

So, yeah…meeting up with the team at Dive Town, a local bar near campus which lives up to its name, is *exactly* what we're gonna do.

More importantly, it's tradition.

If we win a game, we go to Dive Town to gloat. If we lose a game, we skate suicides and then head to Dive Town to piss and moan about it. And I'm not one to break tradition. Especially after a win.

Even if it was by the skin of our teeth.

"Excellent. I'm in the mood for a little pussy," he says conversationally as we push through the locker room door and into the brightly lit hallway.

I roll my eyes and snort as my muscles loosen. "When the hell aren't you in the mood for pussy?"

A thoughtful expression crosses his face, and he flashes a grin. "Never."

We turn the corner and I skid to a halt as soon as my gaze falls on Whitney. She looks fucking amazing in a soft blue sweater and skinny jeans. All it takes is one glance and I'm salivating like one of Pavlov's dogs.

I drag a hand through my hair.

She's standing with my mom, her dad, and friend, Katelyn. I wasn't expecting them to wait around. I thought they'd be long gone by now. Especially since I've noticed that Whitney has been avoiding me after the kiss we shared in my truck.

The urge to wrap my hands around her and drag her close before locking lips with her pounds through my blood. All thoughts of hooking up with other girls to forget about this one is tossed by the wayside.

Whitney is the only girl I want. And I'm just fooling myself by thinking otherwise.

"Can I just say," Collins remarks, breaking into my thoughts, "that your mom is seriously hot?"

*What the fuck?*

I scowl and shake my head, hoping to hell that I didn't hear him correctly.

I rip my gaze from Whitney to glare at Collins before slapping him upside the head. He grunts as my hand makes contact. "Jesus H. Christ!" I grumble. "No, you can't say that!"

"All right." With a frown, he rubs the side of his head. "Noted."

For good measure, I add, "You ever mention my mom again, and you'll be slurping your food through a straw for the foreseeable future. Got it?"

"Yeah...got it," he mumbles, changing the subject. "Hey, isn't Monroe talking to your girl again?"

My gaze shoots back to Whitney. And wouldn't you know it, Evert is parked beside her, yapping her damn ear off.

With narrowed eyes, I stalk toward the group. It only takes a few moments for me to pull up alongside Whitney, slide my arm around her, and tug her close, away from Evert.

"Hey, Monroe." I give him a chin lift in greeting and lay claim to what's mine. "Thanks for keeping my girl company." I'm tempted to add *now beat it* but resist the urge. It doesn't escape me that this is the first time I've ever felt territorial. Usually, girls are a dime a dozen and easily interchangeable.

But I don't feel that way about Whitney.

I frown, unsure what to make of the strange emotions brewing inside me.

Evert shifts his weight as his gaze flicks between us. *"Your girl?"* he repeats, sounding surprised.

The group goes silent. All conversations cease to flow as people turn in our direction.

"Yup." I pull Whitney closer until she's practically wedged against my side and hold my breath, hoping like hell she doesn't decide to balk at the forced proximity. Muscles that I hadn't realized were tense loosen when she doesn't shove me away. "That's right. We've decided to go public with this relationship." I give Whitney a bit of side-eye, wondering exactly how far I can push this. "Right, babe?"

The silence that follows is a real killer. Even though I'm freshly showered, sweat breaks out across my forehead.

After what feels like an eternity, Whitney slips her arm around my waist. "Yup. It's finally out in the open."

I wince, keeping the smile plastered across my face as she slips her hand beneath my shirt and grabs a chunk of skin between her fingers, giving it a pinch.

*Fuck me, that hurts!*

"Congratulations," Evert mumbles, looking less than thrilled.

"When you find the right one," I add loudly so everyone can hear, "you need to lock that shit down."

David glares as a muffled growl vibrates from Whitney's throat and she redoubles her efforts to damage my flesh. I have the sneaking suspicion that my waist will be covered in bruises come the morning.

"Great," Collins says enthusiastically. "You can come to Dive Town with us."

"Oh…" Whitney glances at me and shakes her head. "I don't think that's—"

"Of course she's coming. You wouldn't want to miss celebrating a win with us, would you, honey-bunny?"

Whitney clenches her teeth and glares.

"Well, I guess we should head home, Ronnie, and leave all this cele-brating to the kids," David says, eyeing his daughter with a frown.

Mom nods her head. There's a delighted smile simmering around the edges of her lips.

"Sure you don't want a ride home, Whit?" her dad asks. I get the feeling David is trying to save his daughter from my evil clutches.

Whitney opens her mouth to respond, but I cut her off. "Nah, she's good, David. I'll make sure she gets home at a reasonable hour."

He straightens to his full height, which is still a few inches shorter than me. "Please see that she does," he says in a clipped tone.

"Dad," Whitney mutters in embarrassment, "I'm twenty-one years old. I can take care of myself."

"You'll always be my little girl, buttercup," he grumbles.

Clearly, Operation Break-up-the-Parents is alive and well. I grin and give her a little squeeze. "Don't you worry, I'll take real good care of her."

Whitney pinches me again and I wince.

Damn, but that girl has wicked fingernails. I think she might have drawn blood.

David and my mom take off and the rest of the group disperses with plans to meet up at Dive Town.

"Katelyn," Whitney whispers, catching her friend's gaze and nodding in Evert's direction as he walks toward the glass doors that lead to the parking lot.

Katelyn glances at Evert and shakes her head. Whitney widens her eyes and points.

*Ahhhhhh. I see what's going on here. This is a situation I'm more than happy to assist with.*

"Hey, Evert," I yell.

Two sets of wide-eyed gazes swing toward me. Katelyn's mouth falls open in horror as my teammate turns our way.

"Would you mind giving Katelyn a lift to the bar?" I flash him a grin. "Whitney and I need a little alone time, if you catch my drift."

He glares at me before shifting his gaze to Katelyn and shrugging. "No problem."

Her face lights up. "Are you sure you don't mind?"

This time his lips curve into more of a genuine smile. "Not at all." He hitches his head toward the parking lot. "Come on."

She grins at Whitney before jogging over to where Evert waits.

"I'll see you in a couple minutes," Whitney calls after her.

"Your little chickadee will be just fine, *Mom*," I snort. "You don't have to worry."

As soon as Evert and Katelyn push through the glass doors,

Whitney smacks me in the chest. Her brows lower as she growls, "You can be such an ass."

"Don't worry," I assure her, "you'll get used to it." Slinging my arm around her shoulders again, I pull her toward the arena doors that lead into the chilly night air.

"I really hope that won't be necessary," she grumbles.

# WHITNEY

*D*ive Town is a well-known Hillsdale hockey hangout, so it's stuffed full of fans by the time we arrive. Two long tables in the back have been shoved together and saved for the team. The music is always loud, beer and shots are cheap, and on Monday nights, there's karaoke.

I glance at Gray as we walk through the door, still unable to believe that I'm here with him. How did I get tangled up in this situation? It doesn't make any sense. I've spent years avoiding Grayson McNichols. Now, I can't seem to get away from the guy.

People scurry out of Gray's way as we maneuver through the packed bar. I can't blame them. Even if he weren't captain of the Hellcats, he's still a force to be reckoned with.

One brawny arm is wrapped around my shoulder, anchoring me against him. There's no way for me to escape. Hands reach out for a fist bump or to slap him on the back in congratulations as we move through the crowd. Fandemonium ensues as people tell Gray what a great game he had. Heads swivel in our direction. It's an odd sensation to have so many sets of eyes watching every move you make when you're not used to the attention. I've done my best to fly under the radar for the past three years. With Gray stuck to my side like a barnacle, I'm anything but inconspicuous.

Needing distance, I slip from beneath his arm. When he glances at me, I point to the restroom across the bar. "I'll be right back."

He jerks his head toward the far end of the room. "We'll be over there." He winks. "Don't be long. Otherwise, I'll be forced to track you down."

Hmmm. That sounded suspiciously like a threat.

"I'll do my best."

As soon as I'm a few steps away from Gray, I draw a breath of fresh air —all right, more like stale beer and sweat—into my lungs before exhaling.

I hate myself for noticing how good Gray smells. It's something woodsy and masculine that's uniquely his. And right now, it's playing havoc with my libido. Every time I'm around the guy, my panties dampen, and I'm tempted to rub against him like a cat in heat. How am I going to get through the next couple of hours in his company?

Inhaling his delicious scent? Reliving what it felt like when his lips were roving over mine? His hand palming my breasts?

I shake my head to clear it. Best case scenario, I feign a headache in about thirty minutes and Uber it to the safety of my apartment.

Yes. That's exactly what I'm going to do.

Decision made, I head to the bathroom and take care of business, giving myself a silent pep talk. By the time I return, all of my emotions have been locked down tight and I feel more in control. Nothing is going to happen between us. I'm more than capable of keeping Gray at a distance. One drink and I'm out of here.

I push my way through the throng of people, searching for the dark-haired, blue-eyed devil. The back of the bar is crowded with hockey players. And we can't forget about the puck bunnies that turn out in droves to party with the team.

It only takes a moment to find him. My feet grind to a halt when I spot Savannah snuggled up on Gray's lap.

*Grrrr.*

*That girl...*

Every time I see her, she's hanging all over him. Naturally, he's lapping up her adoration like the attention-seeking whore that he is. Those two are perfect for each other, which begs the question...

*What am I doing here?*

Maybe I should take this opportunity to skedaddle before Gray realizes I've disappeared. *If* he notices. For just a minute, I consider skipping out on this victory party.

But...if I do that, then I can't turn the tables on him for a change. And I don't want to deny myself the pleasure of seeing the look on his face when I send his little puck bunny packing. With a determined stride, I proceed toward the couple until I reach the chair Gray is lounging on.

This is payback for all the times he's embarrassed me. Except neither one of them is paying attention and my arrival goes unnoticed.

I clear my throat.

But that doesn't do it either.

So, I clear it more loudly, and that does the trick. Their gazes turn my way. Savannah looks mildly surprised to find me there, while Gray's expression becomes hooded. I have no idea what he's thinking.

I jerk my thumb toward Gray as I stare at Savannah. "Did lover boy happen to mention that he's been officially taken off the market?"

Her brows slam together as she frowns. "What are you talking about?"

I unleash a sweet smile. "Grayson McNichols will no longer be hooking up with the likes of you. That's what I'm talking about."

She flinches as her disbelieving gaze swings to Gray. "Is that true? Do you have a girlfriend?"

With his gaze locked on mine, he doesn't bother to spare Savannah one glance. "Yup, Winters and I are now an item."

"But-but," the other girl sputters. "You told me that you weren't interested in being exclusive!"

He shrugs. "Guess I changed my mind."

When she doesn't immediately vacate his lap, Gray says, "You should probably move it along." He tips his dark head toward me.

"Winters has quite the jealous streak. I've seen her lose her shit, it's not pretty."

I arch a brow when Savannah gives me a death glare.

"Fine." Without another word, she flounces away, pushing through the crowd until she disappears from sight. I have little doubt that she'll find another hockey player to hook up with for the evening.

Now that it's just the two of us, I'm not quite sure what to do. I didn't think beyond what would happen after confronting him and Savannah. As I take a step backward in retreat, Gray's hand snakes out and wraps around my wrist. He tugs me forward and I lose my balance before tumbling onto his lap with a loud *oomph*. My arms slide around his neck in order to steady myself as his hands lock on my waist to hold me in place.

With our faces scant inches apart, his gaze sears into mine, holding me captive. We might be in the middle of a jam-packed bar, but everything around us fades, making our closeness feel much too intimate.

"I'll have you know," he says, voice dropping, "that Savannah likes to help me celebrate after a win." He allows that comment to sink in. "Guess that's up to you now."

My mind tumbles back to the way his lips felt coasting over mine the other night.

I hate to admit this, but Gray is an amazing kisser.

Actually, he's phenomenal at everything. I might have only knocked boots with him once, but it was more than enough to singe every moment of the encounter into my brain. And contrary to what I told him, he certainly doesn't have a weak stroke game.

I blink, and his face looms closer. My breath catches as his mouth ghosts over mine.

Once.

Twice.

Three times.

A whimper escapes from me. I ache to feel the pressure of his lips against mine, but they never quite touch. It would be so easy to close the distance that separates us. If I lean just a bit to the—

*What the hell am I doing?*

Snapping out of my Gray-induced haze, I flatten my palms against his chest and blurt, "Your mom showed me a picture of you in the hospital."

I think we're both shocked by the comment.

His eyes turn distant as he leans against the chair, creating space between us. "She told you about that, huh?"

I nod. Even though disappointment surges through me, I know that putting the kibosh on what was about to transpire was the right thing to do. Gray and I shouldn't be kissing. We shouldn't be doing *anything* together.

"Yeah." I nod. "She was surprised that you hadn't shared the details yourself, considering that we're now a couple."

Gray studies me for a long moment before glancing away. My body wilts in relief as soon as his eyes release mine. No one has ever stirred me up inside like this. I don't know what to make of it. More importantly, I don't know how to make it go away.

The attraction buzzing wildly through my system is a major problem. One that needs to be nipped in the bud so that it doesn't blaze out of control.

Just as I begin to relax, his gaze returns, impaling mine. "What did she tell you?"

The seductiveness that had been threading its way through his deep voice earlier is long gone. In its place is an unfathomable distance. One that I'm strangely tempted to breach.

Which doesn't make sense.

Distance is exactly what I need between us.

Maybe bringing up his injury wasn't such a great idea. But it's much too late to backtrack.

I shrug and downplay the situation, hoping we can gloss over the details and move on to a lighter subject. "Just that you had a skiing accident when you were younger and broke your leg and pelvis." The photo of the teenager he used to be materializes in my brain. It's still difficult to believe that he was involved in such a serious accident. I watched him skate during the game and couldn't detect the slightest hitch in his step. My voice lowers as if we're sharing secrets. "The doctors said that you would never play hockey again."

"Two of them told me that I would never walk without a limp," he adds, voice turning bitter.

It's an odd emotion on him. Grayson McNichols has a happy-go-lucky persona that he portrays to the outside world. It's strange to scratch the surface and realize there's more to him than that.

"But you proved them wrong." As much as I don't want to be impressed by what he's been through and overcome, I am.

He jerks his shoulders as if that minor miracle is nothing more than a pesky detail. "What other choice did I have?" His gaze travels around the dark bar as if he's deliberately avoiding eye contact.

"A lot of people in your situation would have given up."

It's impossible to imagine Gray as a young teenager lying helpless and broken in a hospital bed, told by the adults in charge of his care that he would never be able to play the sport he loved. He's just too cocky, talented, and driven to ever let something—or someone—stand in his way.

"That was never an option."

It sucks to admit that his determination is ridiculously sexy.

Without considering the ramifications, one hand slides along his jawline until I'm able to cup the side of his face in my palm. "What you've overcome is amazing."

His shuttered gaze meets mine before dipping to my lips. My hand continues to cradle his strong jaw. The heat of his skin burns the tips of my fingers. I should pull away. It feels like everything in my body is about to burst into flame, and I don't think I'm ready for that. When his mouth slowly descends, I blink, snapping out of my haze before jumping off Gray's lap. On wobbly legs, I stumble back a step. My hand flies out to grab his chair and steady myself.

Desperate to get away, I point to the bar. "I'll get us drinks." My voice comes out sounding high-pitched and panicky.

Gray arches a brow. "I'm sure the waitress will be by to take our order."

I shake my head and gulp.

*Nope, I can't wait that long.*

I have to get out of here or I'll self-combust. "It's not a big deal." Already headed toward the bar, I toss the words over my shoulder. "I'll be back."

Only then am I able to draw in a full breath of air.

# GRAY

$\mathcal{I}$ plow a hand through my hair and watch Whitney push her way through the crowd. It's like she can't get away from me fast enough.

Just as I'm about to go after her, a pouty voice says, "Gray? Can we talk?"

I force my attention away from Whitney, only to find Savannah staring down at me. Her lower lip is tucked between her teeth. I groan inwardly, knowing that she wants to discuss my newly minted boyfriend status. I'm not an idiot. I know she was hoping that if I ever decided to get serious, it would be with her.

"Ahhhh…" Unfortunately, my brain chooses that moment to malfunction and I'm unable to come up with an excuse as to why now isn't the right time.

"Good."

Before I realize what's happening, she's already settled on my lap. With her arms twined around my neck, she stares deeply into my eyes.

"I don't understand, Gray." Her fingers slide into my hair. "How are you with that girl?" Her face scrunches as she shakes her head. "She's not even your type."

"Oh?" I arch a brow. "And what's my type?"

Her look turns coy as she watches me from beneath the fringe of her lashes. A smug smile curves her lips. "Me, of course. I'm *exactly* your type."

I wish I could tell her that she's wrong, but I can't. In the past, chicks like Savannah were precisely what I went for. Long thick hair (check), pretty face (check), big boobs (check), nice round ass (check), and the ability to keep our relationship status casual (the most important criteria of all).

Savannah checked all those boxes with flying colors.

My gaze slides to Whitney, who stands at the long stretch of bar with her back to me. The length of her dark hair hangs like a shiny curtain down her back. Even though my hands are wrapped around a girl, she's not the one I want.

My fingers ache to tangle in Whitney's silky strands. Her body is slim. She doesn't have much going on upstairs. And her ass might be kind of flat, but it's still fucking hot. I like the way she fills out her jeans.

It's no secret that I want to lay my hands all over her.

Whitney is the opposite of every girl I've found myself attracted to, and yet she's the one I haven't been able to stop thinking about since we hooked up freshman year. Riddle me that, because I can't make heads or tails of it. I just know that it's the truth and I'm tired of fighting it.

Which brings me to the chick on my lap. The last thing I want to do is be an asshole. I like amicable partings. That being said, she needs to understand that what we had is over. Whether Savannah wants to admit it or not, we were never serious. Promises were never made.

"I guess my tastes have changed," I say lightly, hoping she'll drop the subject.

Instead of taking the hint, she rakes her fingernails against the back of my skull and attempts to pull me closer. "But that doesn't make any sense."

I shrug, already tiring of this conversation. "It is what it is, Savannah."

"Are you sure there's nothing I can do to change your mind?" She bats her mascara-laden lashes at me. "I can be very persuasive when I want."

You're damn right she can be. Many a times I've been on the receiving end of her particular brand of persuasion. It's nothing short of impressive. She can suck the chrome off the bumper of a car like nobody's business.

It's like winning the fucking lottery.

But still...I'm not interested.

My gaze flickers to Whitney just in time to see her smile at Evert, who has sidled up beside her.

*Seriously?*

My teammate and I have never had any beefs, or we wouldn't be sharing a house, but I'll tell you what...that guy is going to get it. I don't know how much clearer I need to make it that Whitney is no longer a free agent. The dude needs to move on.

*Where the hell is Katelyn when you need her?*

I shoot out of the chair and rise to my feet. Savannah gasps as she tumbles off my lap. My hands go to her upper arms to steady her.

"Sorry," I mumble. All of my attention is focused on Whitney. And Evert, who just tucked an errant lock of hair behind her ear.

*Son of a—*

That's it. Someone's getting the piss beat out of them tonight. And that someone is gonna be Evert. When his fingers are broken, we'll see how easy it is for him to lay hands on my girl.

Whether Whitney realizes it or not, that's exactly what she is.

*My girl.*

Maybe she always has been.

I have no idea.

Ever since the accident, I've avoided any kind of serious emotional entanglements. I was too focused on proving those asshole doctors wrong and turning my dreams into a reality. For the first time in my life, I feel like something is missing.

By the time I reach Whitney and Evert at the bar, I'm coming in hot. As soon as I'm in striking distance, I slide my arm around Whitney and haul her close, glaring at Evert the entire time.

"Missed you, babe," I say tightly. "Thought you were bringing drinks back to the table?"

Whitney stares at me owlishly as if uncertain what to say. "I, um, was—"

Not interested in an explanation, I tilt her chin and press my lips against hers. When she gasps in surprise, my tongue slips inside the warm recesses of her mouth. Her palms flatten against my chest as she struggles to break free. I shift my body and continue caressing her. That's all it takes to have her melting against me. Instead of trying to push me away, her fingers curl into my shirt as she tugs me closer.

Now that she's no longer fighting me, I slow things down, taking my time, showing her the side benefits to us being involved. When she moans, I pull away, knowing that I've proven my point. It takes all of my self-control not to grin at the dazed expression on her face. I'm also pleasantly surprised to notice that Evert fucking Monroe has made himself scarce.

This is turning out to be a banner night for me. I scored two goals during the game. And I'm about to score one off the ice.

"You ready to take off?" I growl.

All I can think about is getting Whitney alone and putting my hands on her.

She nods, looking like she doesn't know what the hell just happened.

"Good. Let's get out of here." With that, I grab her hand and tow her out the backdoor of the bar.

And there you have it, folks. A hat trick scored by yours truly.

# WHITNEY

For the second time in as many minutes, my fingers feather across my lips.

*Did that just happen?*

This relationship was supposed to be strictly pretend. Instead... everyone on campus now thinks we're a couple. I'm not sure how this happened. One day I'm hating on the guy, and the next we're fake-dating and he's announcing—to my father, no less—that we're shopping around for an apartment. This whole situation feels like a runaway train barreling down the tracks, and I'm not sure if there's any way to stop it.

*Do I even want to?*

I quickly shove that thought away before I can inspect it too closely and glance at Gray from the corner of my eye as he drives us back to my apartment. A heavy silence has fallen over us. It's thick with tension. You can practically see the sparks flying between us. My fingers twist nervously in my lap as I shift on the leather seat. I wrack my brain for something that will defuse the intensity swirling through the air, but it remains frustratingly blank.

Actually, that's not entirely true.

My mind continues to circle back to the kiss at the bar. But I sure as hell can't bring that up. The best thing we can do at this point is put an end to this whole fake-dating scenario.

I blink back to the present as Gray pulls his pickup truck into the parking lot of my building. He finds an empty space and slides into it before turning off the engine. Then he angles his body toward mine.

The urge to flee the vehicle jolts through me, but I hold my ground. We need to talk, and there's no better time than the present. But that doesn't stop the nerves from skittering along my skin. He must have the same idea because we both end up speaking at the same time.

"We should end this," I blurt.

"We should have sex," he says.

We stare at each other silently as I scrunch my face.

*Huh?*

Air gets clogged in my throat. "I'm sorry, what did you say?"

His lips lift into a sexy smile. "I think we should sleep together," he repeats idly. Except there's nothing lazy about the way his eyes are eating me up.

*Have sex?*

*With him?*

*Again?*

*No way.*

"You can't be serious," I squeak.

Gray's gaze drops to my lips and attraction awakens before fluttering to life in the pit of my belly. "Actually, I couldn't be more serious." He tilts his head and studies me carefully. "Are you going to deny the chemistry between us?" He pauses for a beat. "Or that you want me?"

I gulp, wishing I could do exactly that.

Unsure how to proceed, a high-pitched laugh falls from my lips as I try to brazen out this awkward conversation. "Fine, I'll admit it...I want you." I shrug with a forced casualness that I don't feel. "So what? That doesn't necessarily mean we should sleep together."

My admittance has the heat in his eyes leaping to life. He moves closer, one hand lifting to stroke the curve of my cheek. "Sure it does.

How much simpler could it be? You want me, and I *definitely* want you." His voice drops, becoming low and husky. "I've wanted you since freshman year. One time wasn't nearly enough."

When he presses closer, I place a palm against his chest to ward him off. His proximity clouds my judgment. It would be all too easy to give in to Gray. But sleeping with a guy like him isn't smart, and I've been burned before.

With my hormones clamoring, I pretend not to give a damn. "All you want is a warm body in your bed. You don't necessarily care that it's me." It may hurt to admit the sentiment out loud, but it's the truth. And I can't allow myself to forget it.

Not even for a minute.

"That's not true." He pulls back. The heat clears from his eyes as a new kind of intensity takes hold. He almost looks...*offended*. "Is that seriously what you think?"

*One hundred percent!*

I laugh, but the sound comes out thick and raspy. "It's what I know. You're a player." I shrug. "You can't help yourself. You'll sleep with anyone."

He grows uncharacteristically silent. "Okay," he admits softly. "You're right. Maybe in the past that's exactly what I've done."

"What do you consider the past?" I arch a brow, feeling like my feet have finally found steady ground again. All of the attraction humming dangerously through my system dissipates. "Twenty-four hours ago?"

One side of his mouth reluctantly quirks.

Why does he have to be so damn adorable?

As much as I try to fight it, another arrow of lust explodes in my belly. Fine. It explodes much lower.

"Touché." He pauses. "Have you ever considered that I'm capable of change?"

*"Change!"* I hoot with a grin. "You have to be joking."

"Actually," he mutters, "I'm not."

"Of course you haven't changed! Every time I run into you, Savannah Mitchell is hanging all over you."

He shrugs and flattens a hand to his chest. "Is it my fault that chicks find me so irresistible?"

"Please." I roll my eyes. "Feed those lines to a girl stupid enough to believe them." Which would sadly be most of the female population on this campus. "I'm not as gullible as I was freshman year."

The smile simmering around the edges of his lips falls away as his voice turns serious. "You were never stupid, Whitney."

The air in the truck shifts.

It was a tactical error on my part to bring up our past. It took me a long time to get over Gray. I refuse to backpedal at this point. "Yes," I admit coldly. "I was. Sleeping with you was a mistake." I give him a pointed look. "One I won't be repeating."

His voice lowers. "I never meant to hurt you."

I force my gaze from his, not wanting Gray to chisel away at the wall I've built around myself where he's concerned. "You didn't," I lie.

"Good," he says softly, his hand rising until his thumb can trace over my lower lip. "Because that's the last thing I'd ever want to do."

I brush off his apology, not wanting to read too much into it. "It doesn't matter anymore. I've moved on."

"Have you?"

"Absolutely." Even as I force the response from my lips, I realize it's yet another lie I've been telling myself. Although, Gray doesn't need to know that.

"Okay." His voice takes on a silky quality. One that sends warning bells peeling throughout my head. "Then it shouldn't matter if we make out, right? Because you're totally over it."

"Wait...what?"

Gray's hand slides from the side of my face to the back of my neck before pulling me closer. Just like earlier this evening, his mouth slants over mine. When his tongue licks at the seam of my lips, I groan and open for him. He slips easily inside my mouth, wreaking havoc on my senses.

Then I'm lost to the feel of him as he drags me under.

*Damn Grayson McNichols and his addictive kisses!*

Will I ever learn my lesson where he's concerned?

# GRAY

*R*emember that kissing game kids used to play at parties in middle school?

I think it was called seven minutes in heaven.

Yeah…that's exactly what the thirty minutes spent fooling around in my truck with Whitney feel like.

Absolute fucking heaven.

When I can't take another moment, I send her packing before my control snaps and I lose it. As soon as the sexy haze clears from her face, she bolts from the truck and races for the apartment building like the hounds of hell are nipping at her heels.

Once she disappears inside, I sit for another ten minutes, willing the monster erection in my pants to deflate. I consider going after her but, in the end, where would that get me?

Sure…inside that sweet pussy of hers, but that's not all I'm looking for.

Not anymore.

If I want to make headway with Whitney, then I'm going to have to pump the brakes and not go for instant gratification. It's a totally foreign concept.

And the blue balls I'm currently sporting?

Never experienced that, either.

As I pull up in front of my house, the entire first floor is lit up. It appears the party has moved from Dive Town to our place. For once in my life, I'm not in the mood to drink and carouse. I'd hoped to come back to a little peace and quiet, maybe hit the sack early.

Guess that's not going to happen.

We might have won the game tonight, but we still have practice at the butt crack of dawn tomorrow morning. And I know Coach is going to skate the hell out of us for not playing better. Apparently, none of these jackasses care about that.

As I walk through the front door, the music is turned up and a few of my teammates are getting busy on the couch. A naked titty catches my attention. Yup, we've reached the clothing optional portion of the evening. A couple years ago, that would have been me making out in front of everyone.

Who the hell am I kidding?

That was me last year.

But now...

I don't know. Maybe I want more than just a quick fuck. I shake my head and beeline for the kitchen to grab a cold one from the fridge before heading up to my room to chill for a while.

When I turn around, Savannah has materialized in front of me.

Sheesh. That girl moves around like a specter. Although this time, she's not alone.

"Hey, Gray." A cunning smile curves her lips as she glances at her friend. "You remember Lissa, don't you?"

Ummm, can't say that I do. But I'm smart enough to keep that information to myself. Instead, I give the tall brunette a chin lift in greeting and twist off the cap of my beer before lifting the bottle to my lips.

"Hi, Gray." Lissa beams and gives me a flirty little wave with her fingers. "It's been a while."

Wait a minute...

Oh, yeah...right. I stand corrected, I *do* know this girl.

Well, shit.

Lissa is Savannah's best friend. They do everything together.

And I do mean *everything*, if you catch my drift.

Narrowing my eyes, I glance at Savannah. There's a smug smile stretched across her pretty face. This move is a calculated one. As much as I admire her tenacity, the answer is still the same.

No dice.

I'm not interested.

Savannah's gaze stays locked on mine in silent challenge. I think she's trying to pull a Jedi mind trick thing on me, but it's not going to work.

"It's so crowded down here, don't you think?" Her red-tipped fingernails trail lazily over the deep V of her shirt. My attention automatically drops to her cleavage, which is on prominent display. "Maybe we should take this party of three up to your room and have a little fun?"

I'm going to be completely honest. It's not in my nature to turn down no-strings-attached sex when it's offered. Especially when it involves two beautiful women who are known to have a few eye-crossing tricks up their sleeves. But as I hold Savannah's gaze, I realize that I have zero interest in getting naked with either of them.

That alone is an indicator as to how deep I'm in with Whitney. The realization should terrify the crap out of me and send me running straight into their waiting arms, but it doesn't. I've never been one for relationships. Whatever this is with Whitney, I'm interested in seeing where it leads.

Although, that will only happen if I can convince Whitney I'm worth taking a chance on. She might have gambled and lost on me before, but I'm not the same dude I was freshman year. If we're going to move forward in any kind of meaningful way, then she needs to trust me.

It never occurred to me that I hurt her until I caught a flash of pain in her dark depths while talking in my truck. A closed-off expression had entered her eyes. If I could rewind time and change the way I handled the situation, I would.

But that's not possible.

"Gray?" Savannah coos as she runs her hand over my chest.

I blink back to the present and realize that Savannah and Lissa have closed ranks around me. Each one clings to an arm. Their breasts are squashed against my biceps.

I clear my throat, trying to come up with an escape plan. "As tempting an offer as that is, ladies, I'm going to take a pass." I feign a yawn, unable to believe that it's come to this. "I'm pretty whipped after that game. And Coach is going to skate our asses off tomorrow morning. I need to be ready for it."

Savannah thrusts out her lower lip as she slowly rubs her titties back and forth against my arm. "Are you sure about that?"

"Yup, pretty sure. I need to catch a few Z's"

"If you're worried that your *girlfriend* will find out, don't be." Savannah sends her bestie a conspiratorial look as she runs her fingers up and down my chest. "We know how to keep a secret." She adds with a smirk, "Don't we, Lissa?"

The other girl bobs her head enthusiastically.

Even if that were true—which it's not—the answer is still no.

Before I can shoot her down one final time, Savannah takes matters into her own hands.

*Literally.*

Her fingers migrate from my chest to my abs before dropping to my junk. She grabs hold of me, giving my dick a firm squeeze. Her brows draw together when she doesn't find a raging boner fighting its way out of my pants.

I shrug. "Sorry ladies, I've got one girl on my mind." I let the *and it's not you* implication hang silently in the air. I may not have given voice to the words, but they both hear them loud and clear.

*Thank fuck.*

Savannah rips her hand away as if her fingers have been burned and swings around to her friend. "Let's go, Lissa." Her upper lip curls in disgust. "I'm sure we can find another guy who isn't so lame."

"I'm sure you can," I agree easily.

That remark makes her scowl intensify as she flounces from the kitchen with her sidekick in tow.

Well...that's one disaster narrowly averted.

I take a pull from my beer. I really need to get out of here before there are any more run-ins. Just as I'm about to leave the kitchen and head upstairs, Evert fills the doorway.

I groan.

It's obvious from the way he's glaring that there's something he needs to get off his chest. When he doesn't get right down to it, I impatiently arch a brow. I can just imagine what this is about. Or maybe I should say *who*. "Whatever it is that you have to say, spit it out."

That's all it takes for him to straighten to his full height and step toward me. "What the fuck kind of game are you playing with Whitney?"

Evert may be squat and built like a brick shithouse, but I'm tall and muscular. So we're evenly matched. I'd been pissed at the bar earlier when I'd found him talking to Whitney, but I'm over it. The last thing I want is to get into a fight with him. At the end of the day, he's my friend and teammate.

I'd like it to stay that way.

"You've got it all wrong, Monroe. I'm not playing any games." I'm tempted to tell him about the fake-dating situation but decide at the last moment to keep that information to myself. It's none of his damn business. Evert may have feelings for Whitney, but nothing is going to happen between them. He needs to accept it and move on.

His lips flatten into a thin line as he sneers, "There's no damn way you're interested in being with one chick. And even if you were, Whitney isn't your type. She actually has a working brain. She's not a piece of ass you can screw around with." He jerks his head toward the living room. "Stick with the puck bunnies. They're more your speed, McNichols. They'll fuck your brains without expecting anything in return except a good time."

My brows snap together, and my fingers tighten.

*Who the hell does this guy think he is?*

"Last time I checked, Whitney wasn't any of your concern." I take a step forward and add, "She's mine. So back the fuck off and stay there."

His jaw clenches as he stabs a finger in my direction. "That's where you're wrong, because I'm making it my concern. Whitney's a nice girl. She doesn't deserve to be jerked around by you."

*Where the fuck is all this coming from?*

"I don't plan on jerking her around," I growl. How many times tonight am I going to have my past shoved down my throat?

He snorts, and the sound scrapes against my nerves. "Please...I've lived with you for the past two years. I've seen just how much pussy you've boned, and I'm telling you to leave Whitney alone. Stick to girls who understand how to play the game. Whitney isn't one of them."

Before I can fire off another shot, he stalks from the kitchen, leaving me to stand there with my dick in hand.

It's not a good feeling.

Does everyone around here think I'm a complete asshole where women are concerned?

It's probably best not to answer that.

# WHITNEY

*J*'m camped out on the second floor of the library. I've been here for two solid hours and I'm totally in the zone. There's a business book splayed open alongside my computer and I'm tapping away at the keyboard. The words are flowing from my brain right out the tips of my fingers.

I love when that happens.

This upcoming week is going to be a real killer. There's a paper I'm trying to crank out, so I'll probably be here for the next couple of hours. And then I have a test on mergers and acquisitions. I go over the chapter until my eyes feel gritty. For the most part, I enjoy my business classes, but there are times when they can be bone-dry and slogging through the material feels like a herculean task.

After a while, I check my phone, noticing that another thirty minutes has slipped by in the blink of an eye. Just as I decide to take a five-minute break and stretch, my cell chimes with an incoming message. I roll my shoulders and glance at the screen.

My belly does a little flip when Gray's name pops up.

*Need 2 talk 2 u.*

After the other night at the bar, I'm back to avoidance mode where he's concerned. It's far safer to keep my distance until everything in me settles. I fiddle with the phone, tempted to ignore the message.

When I don't respond, another text pops up.

*Hola?*

I glare at the silver device in my hand, not putting it past Gray to bombard me with texts all afternoon. The guy is ridiculously persistent.

And no, it's not an attractive quality.

All right, maybe a little bit.

Begrudgingly, I tap out a quick reply.

*Sry. Busy. Can't talk.*

There.

That should do the trick.

I shove the phone to the corner of the table and prepare to dig back in. I've made a lot of progress this afternoon, but I still have a long way to go. So I need to get cracking.

Just as I start a new chapter on financial adjustments to inflation, another text flashes across the screen. This time, I decide not to respond. I've got too much work to plow through to get tangled up with Gray. Five minutes slowly creep by and I realize that I've reviewed the same paragraph three times.

Arghhhh!

I slide the phone toward me and peek at the message.

*It's important!*

*Importante!*

I set the slim cell aside with more force than necessary.

Seriously, how imperative could it be?

Exactly. It's not.

I don't have time for Gray McNichols.

Naturally, he doesn't get the hint.

*Answer ur phone*

*Hello?*

*R U there?*

*Heeeeellllllllooooo!!!!!*

*Knock, knock*

*Who's there?*
*Banana*
*Banana who?*
*Knock, knock*
*Who's there?*
*Banana*
*Banana who?*
*Knock, knock*
*Who's there?*
*Orange*
*Orange who?*
*Orange you glad I didn't say banana?*
*Ha-ha, I love that joke!*

I grit my teeth. I'm seriously going to kill Gray when I get my hands on him. But what I'm not going to do is respond to his irritating texts. Although, that doesn't mean I'm getting any work done either. Leave it to a dark-haired hockey player to ruin my mojo.

*Grrrr.*

I glance at the clock on my phone. Great. Now I've lost a good twenty minutes because of him. How can I be expected to work under these conditions?

I need to forget all about how annoying Gray can be and focus on the task at hand. I roll my shoulders and move my head from side to side to rid myself of any lingering tension. Then I lean back in my chair, close my eyes, and stretch my arms overhead, reaching for the ceiling. I need to pull it together and refocus my attention.

"Hey, buddy!"

My eyes pop open as I stifle a yelp of surprise. My heart beats into overdrive. I straighten on my chair, only to find Gray parked across from me.

*What the—*

My brows lower at the sight of him. As much as I'd like to cling to the hope that this is some kind of delusion, I know it's not. Already my senses are being assaulted by the woodsy scent of his aftershave.

155

Damn him for always smelling so delicious. "What are you doing here?"

Unaffected by my curt demeanor, Gray leans forward, resting his elbows on the table before loosely tangling his fingers together. "You may not realize this, but I've been trying to get a hold of you for the last thirty minutes."

I lock my jaw and nod, spreading my arms wide so that it encompasses the table along with my materials. "That's because I'm doing a little something called studying. Perhaps you've heard of it?"

He cocks his head thoughtfully. "Hmmm. I don't believe I have." With wide-eyed innocence, Gray rests his chin on his hands. "It sounds utterly fascinating. Tell me more."

Instead of answering, I change the subject. "How did you find me?"

His sparkling blue eyes dance with mischief as if he's loving the give-and-take of our conversation.

I almost shake my head in disgust.

*What am I thinking?*

Of course he's loving this. Annoying me is one of his favorite pastimes.

His smile broadens until his dimples pop. "Your roommate was most helpful in securing your location."

*Katelyn.*

You better believe she's going to catch hell about this when I get home. She shouldn't be giving out my whereabouts to random dudes. And the not-so-random ones like Grayson McNichols.

I relax against the chair and quirk a brow. "And this behavior doesn't strike you as stalkerish?"

"Not in the least." Gray shrugs and taps his fingers on the table. "Aren't you my girlfriend?"

That's a trick question and he damn well knows it. "Do you really want me to answer that?"

His grin broadens as his eyes ignite with humor. "Absolutely."

"Well," I huff, "if you want to get technical—"

"Which I do," he cuts in smoothly.

"Then yeah," I grumble, folding my arms across my chest, "I guess I'm your girlfriend."

With a smug look, he points a finger in my direction. "Precisely. I'm glad we were able to straighten that out."

I shake my head and pinch the bridge of my nose in frustration. Arguing with him isn't going to get me anywhere. So I decide to change tactics. "Is there a reason you hauled ass to the library to bother me?"

Taking his sweet damn time, Gray leans back on his chair and folds his arms behind him so that his dark head rests against his laced fingers. And just like that, I'm distracted by the way his well-defined biceps bunch and flex.

Say what you want about the guy, but he has amazingly sculpted muscles and I for one can totally appreciate that.

Even if I don't particularly want to.

"Now that you mentioned it, there *is* a reason I was trying to get a hold of you."

*Ugh. Get on with it already!*

When Gray doesn't immediately launch into an explanation, I give him a *come-on* gesture with my hand by circling my wrist a few times. Any moment I'm going to leap across the table and strangle the life out of him.

"Are you going to tell me what's going on," I ask in a voice filled with boredom, "or are we going to play a game of fifty questions for the rest of the afternoon?"

He unfolds his arms and digs around in the front pocket of his khakis before pulling out a small, rectangular piece of paper. Silently, he slides it across the table so that it lies in front of me.

I glance suspiciously at the paper before meeting his hooded gaze. "What's that?"

He shrugs, but a smile hovers around the corners of his lips. "Why don't you take a closer look and find out?"

Clearly he's up to something. I resist for roughly twenty seconds before picking up the thick piece of paper and glancing at it.

What I find is a ticket.

Two of them.

My eyes widen, and I jerk my head up to meet his gaze.

Is this a joke?

If it is, it's not funny.

"How did you get these?" I whisper hoarsely.

A huge grin breaks out across his face, making his dimples wink, although this time I barely notice. My heart feels like it's going to pound right out of my chest. "It's all about the connections, baby." He gives me a wink. "And I've got them."

I shake my head in wonder. "They must be damn good connections because Coldplay has been sold out for months. I couldn't get tickets the morning they went on sale."

"I know," he says smugly.

I'm at a total loss for words.

"So…are we going or what, Winters?"

I press my hand to my chest and gasp, "You want to take *me* to the concert?"

He rolls his eyes as if I'm too dense for words. "Who else would I take?"

I rip my gaze from him to glance at the tickets. It feels like I'm holding something infinitely precious in my hands. "I'm sure you have a lot of options." Like most of the female population at Hillsdale.

"I'm not interested in taking anyone else." He pauses for a beat and his eyes grow serious. "You're the only one I want to spend time with."

Unsure how to respond to the enormity of that, I drop my gaze to my phone. "But the concert starts in three hours!"

He slaps his palms against the table. "Then we better get a move on, right?"

Do I really have to think about this? I've been dying to see Coldplay ever since they announced the tour dates. It was a major bummer when I couldn't get tickets. But spending time alone with Gray doesn't necessarily seem like a good idea either. Especially after what happened the other night. As soon as the guy lays his hands on me—not to mention his lips—I melt into a puddle of goo.

*Every.*

*Single.*

*Time.*

It's totally demoralizing.

"So, what's it gonna be, Winters? Are we doing this or not?" Rather cagily he adds, "Did I mention they're tenth row seats?"

*What!*

I nibble at my lower lip with indecision.

*I shouldn't go...*

*I should stay at the library and study.*

But how am I supposed to resist the chance to see Coldplay? They're my all-time favorite band.

*Argh!*

Decision made, I slam my textbook shut and give a sharp nod. "Okay, let's go."

When he grins, I realize that I've just sealed my fate.

I am in so much trouble.

Oh, who cares! All that matters is that I'm going to see Coldplay!

*Yay!*

Dreams really do come true!

# GRAY

$\mathcal{N}$ ot that I'd ever tell Whitney this, but I pretty much had to sell my soul to the devil to get those concert tickets. It was totally worth it though, and I'd do it all over again in a heartbeat.

Whitney has her hands in the air and is singing along with Chris Martin as he croons one of their most popular songs. I've never been much of a fan.

But you know what?

Their music is decent and I'm enjoying myself. My arms are wrapped around Whitney's waist as she leans against me. I'd listen to Coldplay 24/7 if it meant holding her like this on a regular basis.

I glance at her, unable to imagine spending time with anyone else. I love the feel of her warm weight in my arms. Especially when she's all loose and relaxed. It makes me want to see her like this more often. And it makes me want to be the guy she lets her guard down with.

The *only* guy.

I almost shake my head at such a rogue thought. I might be twenty-three years old, but this is the first time I've taken a girl out on a legit date.

That's ridiculous, right?

Well, it's true.

I spent my high school years strengthening my leg and working on my stride. I lived at the ice rink and the gym my parents installed in our basement. Mom and Dad shelled out big bucks for me to work with the best trainers and private skating coaches in the area. I figured that I owed it to them to focus on hockey to the exclusion of everything else.

And that's exactly what I did. I wasn't out partying like my friends. It's doubtful I'd be where I am today if I hadn't dedicated myself a hundred percent to getting back to where I was before the accident.

After I graduated from high school, I spent two years playing juniors. By that time, I'd worked my ass off and was ready to cut loose and have some fun. Especially since I spent those two years living away from home. When you play for a minor league hockey team, there's going to be groupies. Lots of them. That's where I got my first real taste of celebrity. I was like a kid in a candy store, balling every chick I could get my hands on. It's surprising my dick didn't shrivel up and fall off from overuse. The second year was more of the same. By the time I started at Hillsdale, I was still making up for lost time and dipping my wick every chance I got. There was so much pussy, and I sampled it all.

As much as I've enjoyed the perks that go hand-in-hand with being a Division I hockey player at Hillsdale, I've never felt the urge to settle down.

Until now.

My feelings have shifted during the past few weeks. And that has everything to do with Whitney.

I should probably slow my roll and think about what I'm doing.

After graduation, I'll be headed to the NHL. At the moment, my agent is in talks with several teams, but where I end up is anyone's guess. The last thing I need is a relationship weighing me down. My agent keeps reminding me to keep things light.

*Fluid.*

That's never been a problem for me.

But I blinked, and everything changed.

Letting Whitney go isn't an option.

My arms tighten around the dark-haired girl. Her back is aligned perfectly against my front. I'd be lying through my teeth if I didn't admit that I'm sporting major wood. Every time she wriggles her backside against my groin, I have to fight the natural inclination of my body.

I'm keeping that shit locked down tight because this night isn't about me. It's about Whitney. It's about showing her that I'm more than she's always thought I am.

But will it be enough to change her opinion?

That's the million-dollar question.

# WHITNEY

est.
        *Concert.*

*Ever.*

I'm still riding high when we leave the venue and head to the parking lot. My hand is tucked safely in his larger one as we weave our way through the throng of concert goers. Once we find his truck, Gray opens the passenger side door and I slide inside. He jogs around the front and hops in next to me. The engine roars to life and then we're on the road, driving toward campus.

I'm so lost in thought, replaying every spectacular moment of the last couple of hours, that it takes me a while to realize we're not headed in the right direction. I glance around, but it's dark and we're out in the middle of nowhere. I have no idea where we are. And I haven't been paying attention. I'm still thinking about Chris Martin.

God, but he's dreamy.

I glance at Gray. "Aren't we going home?"

He flicks a look in my direction before his gaze darts back to the ribbon of road stretched out in front of him. "I want to take you somewhere."

I arch a brow and ask in a not-so-joking tone of voice, "Is this a place where you could easily dispose of a dead body?"

He chuckles and sends an amused smile my way. "Hardly, Winters."

I wait for him to fill me in, but he remains frustratingly tight-lipped. "So where are we headed?"

He jerks his head toward the windshield. "It's just up the road a bit. We'll be there soon enough."

I press my lips together. "I'm not going to lie, you're making me nervous, McNichols."

"Good." He pauses for a beat. "Just trying to keep you on your toes."

I might have grown up around here, but I have no idea where we are. My sense of direction has become discombobulated in the dark. My attention fastens on the window, looking for any signs of familiarity. After about ten minutes, we turn off the main stretch of road onto an unmarked gravel one.

My fingers dance nervously on my thigh as I glance at him from the corner of my eye. "Um, are you sure you're not looking to dump a body?"

Gray chuckles but doesn't respond, which only jacks up my nerves as my mind starts to spin.

We travel silently for another mile or so until I finally glimpse lights in the distance. At least we're somewhere near civilization.

"Just tell me where we are." I've had enough of this game. If I'm being completely honest, I'm a little freaked out.

"Look." He points at the windshield as his teeth flash in the darkness. "The airport is up ahead."

My brows knit as the lights loom closer. "Are we taking an unexpected trip?"

He parks the truck near a chain link fence and cuts the engine. "Come on, Winters, where's your sense of adventure?" Not waiting for a response, he exits the vehicle.

I gulp and consider hitting the locks, but Gray pocketed the keys so I'm not sure what good that'll do me. Maybe he's going to murder me after all. At least out in the open, I can run for my life. Before I can decide what to do, he's already walked around the front of the truck and is pulling open the door.

There must be a panicked expression flitting across my face because he laughs and extends his hand. "I promise that I have no intention of chopping you up into tiny pieces."

I snort. "Isn't that what a homicidal maniac would say to throw off suspicion?"

"Probably." His gaze stays locked on mine. "Guess you're just going to have to trust me."

A couple of weeks ago, trusting Gray McNichols would have been completely out of the question.

Now...

I'm not so sure.

Tentatively, I place my fingers in his hand. As soon as I do, he grasps them and helps me from the truck. I used to think that Gray had the manners of a Neanderthal, but that hasn't turned out to be the case. Every time I'm with him, he opens the door for me.

Once my feet are planted solidly on the dirt-packed earth, I tug my hand free, needing to put a bit of distance between us. At the concert, I'd been so wrapped up in the music that I hadn't thought too much about the way Gray was holding me in his arms. I hadn't been focused on how natural it felt.

But now, without Chris Martin to distract me, I'm acutely aware of it. I'm nowhere near ready to reconcile the feelings that are growing inside me to the ones I've always had for Gray.

As soon as the contact is broken, I shove my hands into the pockets of my jeans and glance at the airstrip on the other side of the fence. There are loose loops of barbed wire strung across the top.

My narrowed gaze slices to him as I nervously tap my foot. "If you think I'm climbing over that, you're out of your mind."

His eyes flicker from my face to the chain link barrier. "Hell, no. Do you think I have a death wish?"

Everything in me gradually relaxes as the sound of crickets chirping and the hoot of a lone owl fill the silence. Since Gray hasn't been a fount of information, I prod, "If we're not climbing over the fence, then what are we doing here?"

He jerks his head toward the back of the truck. "Come and see." When I don't move, he opens the backseat passenger side door and pulls out an armful of blankets before walking around to the rear. He lowers the tailgate, hops up, and drops the covers. Then he hunkers down and spreads them out.

Yanking my hands out of my pockets, I cross my arms over my chest and continue to watch. The foot tapping becomes more insistent with the passing of each second that slides by. "Exactly what do you think is going to happen here?"

He cocks his head to the side and squints. "Well, I was kind of thinking that you'd like to reimburse me for a night out on the town."

My jaw drops as I screech out an unintelligible sound at the top of my lungs.

"Jesus H. Christ, Winters, settle your ass down." With a laugh, he points to the sky. "This is the best place to see the stars." He shrugs, suddenly looking self-conscious. "I thought it might be nice. A little peace and quiet after all that noise."

*Gray McNichols wants to stargaze?*

I blink and shuffle my feet toward the tailgate. Unsure what to say, I grumble, "Coldplay is not *noise*. If you honestly think that, then this fake relationship is never going to work."

He pops up to his full height and closes the distance between us. Then, just like he did when I was exiting the vehicle a few minutes ago, he extends his hand. His fingers swallow mine up as he hoists me onto the bed of the truck as if I weigh nothing at all.

Once I've found my footing, he breaks the physical connection and takes a seat on the makeshift bed. Then he eases back and rests his head on a bunch of wadded up blankets.

Silence settles around us as I shift my weight, uncertain what to do.

"You waiting for a formal invitation, Winters? 'Cause I can extend one if you'd like."

Ugh!

An aggravated noise vibrates deep in my throat as I plonk down next to him. With a bit of side-eye cast in his direction, I straighten out and tentatively lay my head next to his. It takes a few moments to get comfortable and stop fidgeting. I avoid looking at Gray or thinking about how close he is or how intimate lying here beside him feels. Instead, I stare at the sky.

As soon as I do, all of my reservations fall away. The air rushes from my lungs as I take in the bright pinpricks of light that are painted across the velvety canvas overhead. "Wow," I breathe in amazement.

"Yeah." His voice is surprisingly devoid of smugness. Nothing but quiet awe fills it.

Even though we're alone and I could probably scream my head off and no one would hear, I drop my voice to a whisper. "This is so beautiful."

He turns his head until I feel the burn of his gaze. "It really is."

A burst of pleasure explodes in me, but I quickly tamp it down and focus on the sky. "Why aren't the stars this bright by us?"

"There are too many lights from the city. You have to go out into the country to see this."

A bolt of electricity zips through my body as our gazes collide. Nerves flutter to life like a swarm of butterflies in the pit of my belly. "Thanks for bringing me here. This is really spectacular."

"I'm glad you like it," he says in an equally hushed tone.

His hand finds mine and when he laces our fingers together, it feels natural. Silently, we stare at the tiny lights shining overhead. Needing to focus on something other than the feel of Gray's hand wrapped around mine, I search the sky for constellations.

There's the Big Dipper.

And the Little Dipper.

The North Star.

That's about all I remember.

I'm so caught up in stargazing that I don't notice the plane that takes off from the airfield until it's directly overhead. My limbs stiffen as a scream wells in my throat. It's so close that it feels like I could reach up and stroke the bottom of the plane. I release my breath as it roars over us, flying off into the distance.

Gray squeezes my fingers as his gaze meets mine. A grin lights up his face. "Pretty incredible, huh?"

"Oh my God, that was so cool!" I laugh as my heart thumps madly against my ribcage.

"There'll be more," he says. "We just have to wait."

Once the noise of the plane fades into the distance, another comfortable silence falls over us. This has turned out to be one of the best nights of my life. What I can't wrap my mind around is that it's all because of Gray McNichols.

How is that possible?

Less than a month ago, I wanted nothing to do with him. He was the one guy I avoided at all costs.

My gaze travels over his angular face with its strong cheekbones and stubborn chin. Usually he's all smiles, his dimples winking. But that's not the case right now. There's an oddly sober expression on his face. Which is for the best. Every time those little indents pop, an unwanted punch of attraction tugs at my lady parts.

Most guys couldn't be labeled as beautiful, but Gray falls easily into that category. I don't know if it's the short dark hair and piercing blue eyes that grab your attention right from the start. Or the sexy smile that springs so easily to his lips. Maybe it's the sheer size of him. The easy grace he carries himself with. All I know is that the first time I caught sight of him on campus, I couldn't rip my gaze away. I'm certainly not the only one who feels that way about him.

I've been crushing hard on Gray since freshman year. After our ill-fated hookup, I buried my feelings deep down and avoided him like the plague. When forced to be anywhere near Gray, I alternately ignored or sniped at him.

That's called self-preservation, and I'm good at it.

But now...

I don't know.

Everything feels different between us.

As if sensing the direction of my thoughts, Gray turns his head until our gazes catch. A shiver of anticipation skitters down my spine as his attention drops to my lips. When my tongue darts out to moisten them, a groan rumbles from deep in his chest. It's as if his control snaps and suddenly, he's rolling toward me. Before I can catch my breath, his mouth slides over mine.

There's nothing hurried about this kiss. It unfurls lazily, as if we have all the time in the world to explore one another. He lavishes attention on my upper lip before doing the same to my bottom, nibbling at the corners until I'm groaning with need. This caress is just as devastating, if not more so, than the ones that have come before it.

"You have no idea how much I want you," he mutters.

Yeah…I kind of do, because I want him with equal intensity.

The way his mouth brushes over mine scatters all of my thoughts to the wind. Forming a coherent response feels impossible, but he doesn't seem to care. Gray goes back to stroking me as our tongues tangle. He props himself up on his elbow until he can lean over my body, his weight pressing me into the blankets. My arms twine around his neck as one of his hands slips beneath the hem of my shirt to gently strum my bare belly.

After a few caresses, he pulls back. It's not much, just enough to search my eyes. "Is this okay? Do you want me to stop?"

Panic fills me and my arms tighten around him in response. I shake my head, needing to feel his warm lips coasting over mine.

Instead of delving back in, he nibbles his way across my cheek, nipping at my jawline. I bear my throat as he sucks at the delicate skin of my neck. His hand continues to stroke my belly before slowly inching its way up my ribcage until he can palm my breast through the silky cup of my bra. His lips work their way down my collarbone as his fingers delve inside so they can caress my nipple. The little bud stiffens at his gentle plucking.

Oh God…that feels amazing.

A moment later, his hand disappears. Just as I open my mouth to protest the absence, he shoves my shirt up until it's bunched against my throat. Then he lifts my bra so that my breasts are freed from their confines. The cool air rushes over my heated flesh and I shiver, my nipples tightening into diamond-hard points. A choked sound rumbles up from Gray as his eyes fasten on my chest.

"Fuck, you're so perfect," he murmurs thickly, sounding as drugged as I feel.

A snort of disbelief escapes from my lips.

"What?" His gaze slices to mine. "You don't believe me?"

"I'm far from perfect," I force myself to admit. "I don't exactly have a lot of boobage going on."

He shakes his head. "It doesn't matter. You're fucking perfect. There's not a night that goes by that I don't dream about your tits."

The fierceness shining from his bright blue eyes as he leans down and captures one of my stiff peaks between his lips is almost enough to make me believe him. I whimper as he sucks the bud deep in his mouth. It's as if there's an invisible string connecting my nipple to my core. Every tug of his lips reverberates throughout my pussy and my panties flood with need. My back arches off the blankets as I tunnel my fingers through his hair, pressing him closer. I have little doubt that come morning, I'll regret every moment of this. But right now, it feels much too good to curtail.

With a pop, he releases the tiny bud. Then he leans over and licks the other hardened tip with the velvety softness of his tongue.

*Good Lord in heaven above.*

That's the only coherent thought zipping through my frazzled brain. The way he's able to stoke my body to life is nothing short of amazing. But that's always been the problem with Gray. He might have moved on in the blink of an eye after our hookup, but he did a damn fine job of worshipping me while we were together.

*Too damn good a job.*

Just like he is now.

I bite my lip, knowing that I should end this before it goes any further. I've been down this road before, and it won't end well for me. But instead of pushing him away, I tug him closer. He moves down my body, licking a fiery trail from my ribcage to my belly. Our gazes lock, and I shift restlessly.

Gray pauses, as if asking for permission, and I jerk my head into a tight nod. He unsnaps the button of my jeans and slowly drags the zipper down. The metallic clicking noise sounds absurdly loud in the silence that surrounds us.

He slips his hand down the front of my jeans and beneath my panties. I arch as he cups my heat and squeezes me possessively. His fingers glide over the seam of my lower lips. Already my flesh is slick with arousal. Wanting to give him greater access, I widen my thighs. His fingers ghost over me. I arch, wishing he would stop toying with my body and slide inside my pussy. Instead, he continues to tease, whipping me into a fever pitch. He glides from the bottom of my slit to the top before feathering across that throbbing little bundle of nerves.

I whimper with the fierce need he's fueled in me. Gray growls before his fingers disappear from my body and then he's yanking my jeans and panties further down my thighs, but it's not enough. With a sob of frustration, I shove at the material until it's bunched around my ankles. Only then are my legs able to fall open.

Gray rears back until he's able to look his fill. His gaze licks over every inch of me.

"You're so fucking beautiful," he murmurs thickly before pressing a kiss against my clit. I groan as his tongue swipes over the tender flesh. Everything about this moment is perfect.

His tongue continues to lazily skate over my core. I squeeze my eyes tightly shut, almost dizzy with the pleasure he's rousing within me.

"Your pussy is drenched," he growls.

He's right, it is.

"Is this what I do to you?" His tongue swirls more insistently around my clit.

When I don't respond, he asks harshly, voice full of crushed gravel, *"Is it?"*

"Yes," I moan.

The rasp of his tongue strokes over me, and I whimper as pleasure continues to unfurl in my core.

"I could eat you up all night," he murmurs.

*Gaaaaaah.*

I don't think I could withstand that kind of sweet torture. Barely am I hanging onto a thread. It's only a matter of time before I splinter apart into a million jagged pieces.

Gray's dark head hovers over my center, his warm breath feathering against me. With his thumbs, he spreads my lips and laps at my soft flesh, spearing his tongue deep inside. The movement has me arching my back, trying to spread my legs wider. A fine tremble wracks my body as he continues to push me toward the precipice. When I can't stand another moment, he buries his face against my clit. His teeth scrape over it and I whimper. My fingers thread tightly through his thick hair, holding him in place as he nibbles at me.

*"Gray, please..."*

"Open your eyes," he commands.

I pry them apart and he easily captures my gaze with his own. When one thick finger slowly slides inside my heat, I nearly come off the bed of the truck.

I'm so close to splintering apart. I want nothing more than for this wave to crash over me, dragging me to the bottom of the ocean. A scream builds at the back of my throat. Its release feels imminent. This kind of mindlessness that is clawing at my insides is uncharted territory.

"Not yet," he whispers harshly. "Don't come yet."

My teeth sink into my lower lip to stifle the orgasm from bursting free. My body quivers as everything goes whipcord tight. I'm not sure how much longer I can contain it. I whine as my fingers dig into his scalp. Instead of easing up, he continues to lick me, sucking my clit into his mouth. His finger strokes my warmth rhythmically.

*I.*

*Can't.*

*Take.*

*Much.*

*More.*

I can't—

*"Now, Whitney."* He bites down on my clit in a way that makes me lose control over my body. *"Come now."*

With a hot rush of pleasure, I shout out the most intense orgasm I've ever experienced in my life. A massive plane fills my vision as the belly of it flies directly overhead. The loud rumble of the engine drowns out my screams. My body bows off the bed of the truck as I shudder. It feels as though every nerve ending has been electrified.

Long after these sensations dissipate, Gray continues to nibble at my swollen flesh. He circles my clit with lazy strokes as I stare sightlessly up at the stars painted across the dark night sky. They sparkle and shine more brightly than before.

I'm so thoroughly sated that it feels as if I could slip into a coma. It takes effort to shake off the lethargy as I glance at Gray. Everything about this moment feels hazy and dreamlike. The way his gaze stays pinned to mine while he licks at my soft flesh sends a thrill to the tips of my toes.

"Did that feel good?" he asks.

A slight chuckle escapes from me.

*Feel good?*

That's the understatement of a lifetime. Nothing has ever felt better. I don't know if I could adequately describe what just happened.

"It was amazing," I whisper roughly.

The corners of his lips lift into a grin as he presses one last kiss against my clit. "I like feeling your pussy throb against my mouth when you come."

My eyes flare.

"You're so creamy." With a growl, he buries his face against my core. "I don't think I'll ever get enough."

The feel of his lips, tongue, and teeth against my sensitive flesh is nothing short of pure bliss.

Reluctantly, he pulls away before tugging my panties and jeans into place. He leans down and places another soft kiss against my navel. Then he moves up my body, sucking one stiff peak into his mouth before lavishing the same attention on the other. With careful fingers, he pulls the cups of my bra down and straightens my shirt.

Heat fills my cheeks as I stare at him. The shiny evidence of my pleasure is all over his mouth and chin.

*Oh God, what have I done?*

I wince, realizing how easily I gave myself to him.

As if reading my thoughts, his eyes narrow and he shakes his head. "Don't you dare regret this." He smacks a kiss against my mouth before sucking on the plump lower lip. Once he releases it, his tongue delves inside my mouth. Even with the regret that has crept in, I find myself opening for him.

The taste of my own arousal floods my senses.

*That shouldn't be so sexy.*

"Do you taste that?" he whispers.

"Yes." It would be impossible not to.

He pulls back, and I whimper from the loss of him, which is crazy because I just experienced the best damn orgasm of my life. I should be completely sated. But still…I want more.

I want his kisses.

I want his mouth roving hungrily over my body.

I want him to make me so mindless that I forget about the remorse that's threatening to take root.

"That's what I do to you." Fierce possessiveness sparks in his eyes. "I make your pussy cry with need."

His words are so dirty and yet such a turn-on.

One hand strokes down my body until he can cup my tender flesh. He squeezes my core, making it throb to life again with just one touch.

"And then I licked up all your tears," his lips ghost over mine, "until there was nothing left."

With that, he plunges his tongue deep inside my mouth, dragging me under yet again. Any embarrassment or regret evaporates. We continue kissing until Gray rolls on to his back, pulling me along with him. I curl against his body as his arms wrap protectively around me.

As wrong as I know this is, I can't bring myself to care. Not when I'm lying against the steely strength of his chest and can hear the steady thumping of his heart. In this moment, everything feels strangely perfect.

Tomorrow will be soon enough for reality to crash down around my head. For now, I'm content to lie in Gray's arms and stare at the starry sky and think about just how amazing this night turned out to be.

# GRAY

"Hey, McNichols!" a random dude calls out as I arrive at Whitney's apartment building with a cup of coffee held in each hand. "Let me grab the door for you!"

"Thanks." I give him a chin lift for doing me a solid.

"No problem." He beams, looking thrilled to be of assistance. "I can't wait for the season to start! I saw the scrimmage last week. It was a great game. What did you score? One goal?"

"Two," I correct, unable to help myself.

Hey, if you're going to talk about my stats, at least get them correct.

"Oh, right!" He shakes his head, looking impressed. "That second goal at the end of the third period was pretty sweet."

"Yeah," I chuckle as we walk through the lobby, "it was. We barely pulled that win out of our asses. We're going to have to step it up a notch if we want to make it to the Frozen Four this year."

Failure isn't an option. We're going all the way, baby.

"With Bresnik as goalie, I can't imagine you not making it to the championship. He's freaking insane." The guy goes a little starry-eyed. "The two of you out there on the ice are a dream team."

Got that right.

"Bresnik's a machine," I agree easily.

We shoot the shit for a few more minutes before he gives me a wave and takes off. I hit the call button for the elevator with my elbow. Once the car arrives, I push the button for the third floor. Just as the doors are about to slide shut, a hand reaches in and halts it. Two chicks jump onboard. They're gossiping about a girl they know and the douchebag boyfriend she's dating when one glances over at me. Her eyes widen as she elbows her friend in the side. The second female frowns before glancing my way. Then they're both staring.

This behavior isn't out of the ordinary. The notoriety of playing hockey at Hillsdale makes me a minor celebrity. I'll admit that when I played juniors, the attention went to my head. Now I'm used to it and take it in stride.

The one who first recognized me clears her throat. "Hey, aren't you Gray McNichols?"

"Yup." I give them each a pleasant smile, hoping I'm not trapped in here with them for long. I hate to sound like a conceited prick, but I know exactly how this is going to play out. And I'm not interested.

The other chick perks up with excitement. "Oh my God, do you live in the building?"

I shake my head and jiggle the drink containers in my hands. "Nope, just bringing my girlfriend coffee." The word girlfriend slides easily from my lips. I'd be lying if I didn't admit how much I like the way it sounds. More than that, I like referring to Whitney as my girl-friend. I like the claim of ownership it gives me.

Does that make me a chauvinistic pig?

Possibly.

But I don't give a damn.

In fact, I like it so much that I should probably find a way to make the situation permanent. Although, that's easier said than done. The girl wants no part of me.

Maybe I should amend that statement.

She likes the way I make her feel, but that's about it.

"You really have a girlfriend?" The first female rakes her gaze over my body in a way that almost makes me feel violated. "Lucky girl," she murmurs wistfully.

"Yup." I almost snort. I'd freaking love for someone to tell her that. "Maybe you know her? Whitney Winters?"

The second chick nods eagerly, her eyes brightening with recognition. "She's in one of my business classes. Super nice girl. She's given me her notes a few times."

"Yeah," I say with a smile, "that sounds like her."

Before they can pepper me with more questions, the elevator doors slide open, and I hop out on the third floor.

"Bye, Gray!" they call out in unison.

"Take care."

I walk down the hallway and find Whitney's apartment easily enough. I jostle the cups around, tucking one against my chest and forearm so I can free up a hand to knock. A few moments later, the door swings open and Whitney stands before me in all her sexy glory. Her long, dark hair has been swept up into a messy bun at the top of her head and she's wearing black-rimmed glasses.

Fuck me, she looks gorgeous.

Good enough to eat.

That has my mind tumbling back to last night. I shove that thought quickly from my head before I pop a boner. Her beauty has a way of knocking me off balance. Couple that with her smartass mouth, and you can understand why I've never been able to evict her from my mind.

Whitney's eyes widen at the sight of me before skittering away. Her body tenses as she shifts her weight from one foot to the other. It doesn't take a rocket scientist to figure out that she's embarrassed about what happened between us at the airfield.

Which is exactly why I'm here. If I give her enough room, she'll avoid the hell out of me.

And I'm not about to let that happen.

Last night was freaking awesome, and I'll be damned if I let her push me away. Not when I'm beginning to gain traction. I've never wanted a girl the way I want Whitney.

This feeling…it's totally foreign. I'm not sure how to handle the situation, but my instincts are screaming at me to proceed with caution. So, for the time being, that's exactly what I'm going to do.

"Oh, hi." Nerves thread their way through her voice. Her gaze meanders to mine before she jerks it away again. "What are you doing here?"

"I thought you might need a coffee before class." I shrug, attempting to keep it casual. Like I just so happened to be in the neighborhood and thought I'd swing on by. But I have a feeling there's a needy look on my face that gives away all of my inner thoughts. Best to lock those down tight so I don't scare her off. Whitney doesn't trust me. After our disastrous hookup freshman year, I don't blame her.

She studies the cup in my hand like it's a rattlesnake that could strike without the least bit of provocation. Her eyes narrow with distrust. It's a look I'm intimately acquainted with.

"You brought me a coffee?" she repeats.

"Yup." I smile, well aware that it'll make my dimples pop. I have no idea why girls love those little indentations. But you can bet your damn ass that I'm going to pull out the heavy artillery if needed.

And right now, it's warranted. There's a distinct possibility that Whitney is going to slam the door in my face.

Her brow furrows. "Why would you do that?"

"Because I kept you out late, and you have an early morning class."

Her cheeks go up in flames at the mention of last night. My gaze drops to her mouth and I'm so damn tempted to kiss the wariness right out of her. I want her warm and pliant in my arms, just like she was in the back of my truck. And my kisses seem to have that effect on her.

Instead, I keep my distance, because she's liable to junk punch me.

A whimper escapes from her lips as my gaze darts to her widened eyes. "Gray—"

"Yeah?" Everything in me goes on high alert. I take a step forward, closing the space between us.

Whitney clears her throat and mumbles, "I think we should talk about last night."

Those eight little words kill the arousal rushing through my veins.

I know exactly what's coming, and I'm ready for it.

*What?*

You didn't seriously think that Whitney was going to swoon at my feet because I just so happened to give her the best damn orgasm of her life, did you?

*Please, people...*

"Sure." With a nod, I force my tense muscles to loosen. "What do you want to discuss?"

I'd be more than happy to talk about how she was screaming my name at the top of her lungs in the bed of my truck.

Almost reluctantly, Whitney steps aside, allowing me into the apartment. I glance around, interested to see what the place looks like. It's not huge, but it's nicely decorated. A couch, chair, coffee table, and television make up the living room. She pads on bare feet and takes a seat on the chair, tucking her feet beneath her. I'm left with no other choice but to park myself across from her on the couch.

What she's doing isn't lost on me. This girl is trying to put as much physical distance between us as she can. I'll allow it for the time being but not much longer. I set the coffees on the table between us and sit back, wanting to appear relaxed and unconcerned.

Whitney twists her fingers in her lap. She looks so uncomfortable that I almost take pity on her. That being said, she's crazy if she thinks I'll let her off the hook so easily.

"I, um, wanted to thank you again for the tickets last night." Her dark eyes brighten, flooding with excitement as her unease fades. "The concert was amazing. A once-in-a-lifetime experience."

As far as I'm concerned, what happened afterward was the once-in-a-lifetime experience, but I keep that little tidbit to myself. "I'm glad you enjoyed it."

She nods enthusiastically, her spine relaxing one vertebra at a time against the chair. "I really did." For a moment, she pauses while fiddling with the edge of her white shorts, which reveal a tantalizing amount of sun-kissed skin.

It's distracting as fuck. I'm having a hard time concentrating on what she's saying.

Whitney tilts her head. "Did you know that Coldplay was my all-time favorite band?"

She'd like for it to be nothing more than a coincidence, but that's not the case. "You mentioned it the morning after we partied together."

Her brows draw together. "I did?"

"Yeah," I chuckle, "you tried to tell me that Coldplay was a super band."

The memory floods back to her and her mouth falls open. Her voice drops as it fills with surprise. "You remembered that?"

"Yup."

She blinks with uncertainty. "I don't understand," she murmurs slowly. "Did you already have tickets?"

"No, but I was able to get my hands on them." Then I add, because I don't want Whitney to feel indebted, "It wasn't a big deal."

"Those tickets were sold out within fifteen minutes. They were impossible to get," she mutters. "Trust me, I know because I checked everywhere." She shifts on the chair. "Well, unless I was willing to pay a thousand dollars." Her eyes widen as she claps a hand over her mouth. "Please tell me you didn't pay that much for them," she whispers through her fingers.

I'm not sure what she wants me to say, so I keep my lips firmly pressed together.

"Gray?" she squeaks, her voice rising in disbelief.

When I don't respond, she explodes. *"Oh my God, why would you do that?"*

"Because you wanted to see them."

Whitney jumps to her feet and paces in front of the chair she just vacated. Her brows are tightly knitted together. She spins on her heel toward me, confusion written across every line of her face. "I don't understand what's happening here."

There's a desperation weaving its way through her voice that tells me how uncertain she is about the situation.

I hold my hand out to her. "Come here, Whitney."

She draws her lower lip into her mouth to nibble on it. After a moment of hesitation, she steps toward me and places her fingers in my hand. As soon as she does, I tug her until she falls onto my lap. She lets out a gasp as her hands go to my shoulders for balance. My arms slide around her hips to keep her locked in place. If I know Whitney, once she hears what I have to say, she'll be off like a shot.

"I bought the tickets because I knew how much you wanted to see them in concert. And it made me happy to do it for you."

Her eyes widen.

Before she can hurtle any questions in my direction, I force myself to continue. I need to get this all off my chest. No matter what happens, I want Whitney to know how I feel about her. "I've always regretted that we hooked up freshman year."

When hurt flashes across her face, a string of curse words fall from my lips. I'm fucking this up, and that's the last thing I want to do.

Frustrated with myself, I shake my head. "What I meant to say is that I knew who you were, and I was interested, but I didn't want a girlfriend. I wasn't ready for that kind of commitment. We shouldn't have had sex. I knew it was a mistake but couldn't resist the temptation. Afterward, I felt like shit because I'd fucked things up. I wanted you, couldn't stop thinking about you, but there was no way for me to make it right. Hurting you was the last thing I wanted to do." Quietly, I add, "I don't blame you for hating me, but I'm hoping you can move past it. I like you, Whitney. And I want to spend more time with you."

I shift as nerves prickle at the bottom of my gut. I've never felt more vulnerable or exposed in my life. Even when I was laid up in a hospital bed, I never felt this helpless.

A full minute ticks by and she doesn't utter a peep. When I can't take another moment of silence, I plead, "Whitney, say something."

*Say anything!*

I'm sweating bullets over here. Not that I deserve it, but come on, throw me a bone. Sure, I might be a few years too late, but I'm trying to make this right.

She shakes her head, still looking gobsmacked. Her mouth opens and everything in me tightens, waiting for a response. But then she snaps it shut again and my heart crashes to my toes.

*Well...I guess that's my answer, isn't it?*

The sad thing is, I've had girls profess their undying love for me and I've brushed it off.

I've brushed *them* off.

This is the first time I've opened up and put myself out there. I'd have to be a real dumbass not to see the irony of the situation. Here I am, baring my soul to a chick who clearly doesn't reciprocate the sentiment.

*Just kill me now.*

I need to get out of here. I can't take the way she's gaping at me.

This really blows. And I'll be damned if I ever do it again.

Fuck that shit.

Before I can lift Whitney off my lap and dump her ass on the couch so I can get the hell out of here and lick my wounds in private, her hands find their way to my cheeks. She turns my face, forcing my gaze to meet hers.

When I refuse, she whispers, "Gray, please look at me."

*Hell, no!*

I shake my head. This was a stupid idea. I shouldn't have bothered.

"Gray!" She chuckles.

*Oh my God! She's laughing at me?*

And now my humiliation is complete.

Instead of letting go, she shocks the hell out of me by pressing her lips against mine. After a moment, she pulls back enough so that our gazes can lock.

"Thank you for the apology," she whispers. "It means a lot to me."

"I'm sorry for how I treated you," I grumble. "Especially afterward."

"Did you really mean what you said about always thinking about me?"

I huff out an exasperated breath.

*Seriously? Why does she think I've been annoying her for the last three years? Sheesh.* "Whitney, I've never been able to get you out of my head."

Her lips lift. "Good, I'm glad."

"Oh?" I cock a brow, waiting for a reciprocal declaration, which doesn't seem forthcoming. "So," I clear my throat, "is there anything you'd like to say to me?"

Her expression turns contemplative before she flashes a grin and shakes her head. "Nope."

My brows lower and I frown. "There's *nothing* you want to say?"

"Ummm…" She blinks innocently. "Thank you for telling me how you feel? I appreciate it."

I lock my jaw and bite back a growl of frustration. "That's it? There's nothing else?"

She snaps her fingers and smiles. "Actually, there is something."

*Well, fucking finally!*

"You're right, I needed a little caffeine before heading to class this morning. Thanks for the coffee." She gives me a sassy wink. "You're a special guy, Gray. A good friend."

*A special guy?*

*A good friend?*

Did she seriously say that?

I stare in horror as my mouth falls open.

*That does it! I'm out of here!*

Just as I'm about to toss her from my lap, Whitney bursts out laughing. "I'm kidding!" When she places her hands on each side of my face, I refuse to make eye contact. "Come on, Gray," she says cajolingly, laughter simmering in her voice. "You can't blame me for wanting to screw with you a bit. You totally deserve it."

Oh, this girl is going to get it.

I glare.

Whitney chuckles and presses her lips to mine. Between kisses she admits, "I feel the same way. That's why I spent so much time trying to keep my distance. What happened freshman year hurt."

All of my anger and embarrassment melts away. My arms snake around her body and haul her close. I hate that I caused her even a minute's worth of pain. She never deserved it. "I'm sorry, baby. I wish I could go back and do things differently, but I can't."

"You're right. The past can't be changed." A sexy glint sparks in her dark eyes. "But I'm sure there are ways you can make it up to me in the future."

I like the sound of that. Especially if it involves getting her naked.

"Oh, yeah?" In one smooth move, I flip us around and press her into the cushions until I'm stretched out on top of her. "What'd you have in mind?" I nibble at the delicate skin of her throat until she groans and writhes beneath me. "A little something like last night?"

The thought of going down on her is enough to give me a raging boner. I love the way she tastes. And I want more of it.

Just as she's about to answer, the door to the apartment swings open. Two voices fill the air. One is Katelyn's and the other is a dude. The guy's voice sounds suspiciously familiar, but I can't place it. My mind is too clouded to think straight.

Whitney stiffens beneath my body. Instead of pulling me closer, she shoves at my chest. "Get off," she hisses.

And just like that, sexy time is over.

Figures.

There's a bit of banter before everything around us goes silent.

And when I say silent, what I really mean is that the sounds of people getting it on fill the room. Sexy time might be over for us, but not for these two. I smirk as my gaze meets Whitney's wide eyes. Then I waggle my brows and jerk my chin in their direction.

*Getting turned on?* I mouth.

She grimaces and swats at my chest.

My shoulders shake with laughter as I pull back and allow Whitney to scoot up to a sitting position. We both peek over the edge of the couch and stare at the couple who is making out like this guy is about to get shipped off to war. One of his hands is shoved up Katelyn's shirt and going to town on her boob.

All right...this is getting weird.

Clearly, we need to let them know that they have an—

Whitney gasps and the couple jumps apart. Katelyn stares at us with a dazed expression on her face.

Then I get a good look at Casanova.

*Well, well, well. Who do we have here?*

*Evert fucking Monroe.*

Unable to resist, I smirk and move closer to Whitney.

Katelyn turns about fifty shades of red as Evert glares at me. I don't know if he's still pissed that I'm pursuing Whitney or if he's mad that we've interrupted the daytime action he was about to close the deal on.

Probably both.

Since no one has uttered a sound, I clear my throat and say nonchalantly, "Hey, Katelyn." A grin lifts my lips as I take in my teammate. "Monroe." I slowly run my tongue over my teeth. "Seems like we've interrupted something here." I get to my feet and pull Whitney up with me. "Whit and I were just about to leave." I glance at her. "Right, babe?"

"Um, yeah."

When she remains frozen in place, I squeeze her fingers. "Why don't you grab your bag, and we'll head out." I give Katelyn and Evert a wink. "Let's give these two crazy kids a bit of privacy."

Galvanized into action, Whitney sprints to her room, grabs her bag, and beelines for the door. Not about to be rushed, I take my sweet damn time grabbing our coffees and trailing after her.

"Now," I say, my gaze bouncing between the pair of them, "don't go doing anything I wouldn't do."

Which—let's face it—isn't much.

An embarrassed groan rumbles up from Katelyn's throat as I press my lips together so that I don't burst out laughing before slamming the door shut behind me.

Guess I don't have to worry about Evert fucking Monroe going after Whitney. Looks like he's moved on.

As soon as I step into the hallway, Whitney meets my gaze and we both lose it.

And that, my friends, is how you start the morning off with a bang.

# WHITNEY

*I* glance around the restaurant as the hostess seats us at a small table for two near the window. In a way, it feels like we've circled back to the scene of the crime. A little more than a month ago, I was pulling up in front of Calliope's to meet my dad after spending the night in Gray's bed.

How did I go from hating him to dating him?

None of this makes any sense.

And yet...

I wouldn't have it any other way. What I've found with Gray feels special.

"Your server will be with you in just a moment," the hostess says with a smile.

"Thank you," I murmur as Gray does the same.

As soon as she disappears, he reaches across the table and snags my fingers. That's one thing I love about Gray. He's so free with his affection. It's like he always wants to be touching me. When we walk around campus, his arm is slung around my shoulders or he's holding my hand.

Our gazes collide and a zip of energy hums through my veins. It's always been like that between us, but now there's an added layer to it. A deeper, more meaningful connection.

This isn't just me crushing on him. This is me falling for him.

Hard.

*Oh my God, did I just think that?*

Am I really falling for Grayson McNichols?

Am I totally crazy? Especially after everything that's happened between us?

Gray squeezes my fingers, drawing me out of my head. "What are you thinking about?"

Ha!

As if I'm going to share that with him. I need more time to mull this over. I clear my throat, giving him a partial truth. "Just how weird it is that we're a couple."

"Hmmm. *Weird?*" He quirks a brow. "Is it possible that you meant to say amazing instead?"

I chuckle and glance at our entwined fingers in order to escape his penetrating stare. He's right. This *is* pretty amazing. But still...it's weird as well. "Did you ever think we'd get together?" I waggle a finger between us. "Because I never saw this coming."

Not in a million years.

"I..." His voice trails off as the waitress stops by our table to take our drinks order. Once she leaves, Gray picks up the thread of our previous conversation. "I don't know. Hockey has always been the most important thing in my life. It's taken up every spare moment of my time. And I never wanted anything to get in the way of that." Looking restless, he glances around the crowded restaurant.

Is he having regrets?

Is that why he asked me to dinner?

To gently break the news to me?

My heart clenches as I lay my other hand on top of his. "I get it," I say softly. "You don't have to apologize for having goals. You've worked so hard to get to the NHL. Nothing should stand in the way of that."

Including me.

Gray releases a breath before shaking his head. "What I'm trying to say is that after the accident, my dreams are what kept me motivated. I didn't want the distraction of a relationship. It never seemed worth it." He shrugs. "But I don't feel that way anymore. I want this." He moves his hand around until he's able to squeeze my fingers. "I want *you*."

"Really?" My insides turn to mush as a hopeful note fills my voice.

He lifts my hand to his mouth and brushes a kiss against my knuckles. "Yeah. It's always been you."

I tug my hand free and rise to my feet before coming around the table.

"Whitney?" His brows draw together. "What are you—"

Once I'm beside him, I lay my palms against his cheeks and lower my lips to his. He growls as his arms snake around my waist, hauling me onto his lap.

As soon as his mouth collides with mine, everything around us fades to the background. It's like we're alone in a world of our own making. All I'm cognizant of is Gray. Slightly out of breath, he pulls away. There's a heated look simmering in his blue depths. One that makes my core tighten in response.

"You know, it's not like we've ordered dinner yet." His gaze falls to my lips. "Maybe we should grab the check and get the hell out of here. I just want to get you alone."

That sounds like the best idea I've ever heard. I'm about to nip at Gray's sexy lower lip when I hear—

"Whit? Is that you?"

*Holy crap, that sounds like—*

When I whip around in shock, my forehead bangs into Gray's nose.

"Ow!" he mumbles, hands flying to his face as I scramble off his lap.

*Oh.*

*My.*

*God.*

Please tell me this isn't happening.

189

Heat floods my cheeks as I stare at my father. "Um, hi Dad." I glance at Gray's mom, who stands next to him. Her lips are pressed together as if she's fighting back a smile.

Oh, the horror.

"Hello, Veronica," I mumble, wishing the floor would open and swallow me whole.

No such luck.

She gives me a wink and then turns her attention to her son. "Grayson." She beams a full-on smile at him. "You seem to be doing rather well."

"Hi, Mom," he grunts and flicks his eyes to my father. "David."

I glance at Gray and bite my lip. His fingers are still pressed against his nose. "Are you all right?"

"Yeah," he says, sounding nasally. "I'm fine. No worries."

Tentatively, he removes his fingers and I realize there's blood smeared beneath his nostrils. "You're bleeding!" I must have knocked him harder than I realized. Forgetting all about our parents, I grab a linen napkin from the table and dab at his nose. "Tip your head back," I instruct quietly, stroking his hair with my other hand.

My gaze shifts from his nose to his eyes. "I'm so sorry," I whisper. Could I feel more like a doofus?

Nope.

One corner of his mouth hitches. "It's fine, babe. Trust me, I've taken far worse beatings on the ice."

Closing my eyes, I shake my head. This was supposed to be a nice dinner and it's turning out to be a disaster.

With bloodshed.

Dad clears his throat impatiently. "I think Grayson will live. Maybe you should return to your seat, Whit."

Oh, right. I almost forgot about them. I'm tempted to brush my lips across Gray's mouth but resist the urge. It's as if he knows what's going through my head because he winks at me as I slip onto my chair and fold my hands demurely on my lap.

One small consolation is that we're seated at a table for two—otherwise I suspect they might join us.

Dad stuffs his hands into the pockets of his slacks and rocks back on the heels of his wingtips. "We certainly weren't expecting to run into you guys here." His gaze bounces between us as he swipes his tongue across the front of his teeth. "Have you ordered dinner yet?"

Gray and I speak at the same time.

"No, not yet."

"We were just about to grab the check."

Dad's eyes narrow as I glance at Gray. Heat floods my cheeks. Any moment, I'm going to burst into flame.

"Oh?" He glares at the younger man. "You weren't going to have dinner?"

I keep my mouth firmly closed as Gray clears his throat. "Umm, we both—"

"Let me guess…" With a look of annoyance, Dad taps his finger against his chin. "You both have a lot of homework to do?"

Gray snaps his mouth shut and mutters, "Yeah. Something like that."

The smile my father gives Gray is thin and tight. "I think you can push that off for an hour to have dinner with your parents." Dad's penetrating look shifts my way. "Don't you think so, buttercup?"

Oh boy. He's trotting out the pet name he used to call me when I was a kid.

"Yeah," I murmur, my gaze flicking apologetically to Gray, who looks none-too-pleased with the change in plans, "that works."

Dad snorts and mutters, "You're damn right it does."

Veronica rubs my father's back in an attempt to calm him down. A smile simmers on her lips.

"I'll let the hostess know that we'll need a table for four." With that, he stalks to the front of the restaurant.

When he's a safe distance away, Veronica releases a chuckle. "Well, this should certainly be enjoyable."

I catch Gray's sullen gaze.

Enjoyable seems like the last thing this dinner will be.

# GRAY

*W*hitney's hand is firmly ensconced in mine as I haul her from the restaurant and into the parking lot. It's like we're two fugitives running for our lives, trying to get the hell out of Dodge before we're caught and dragged back inside Calliope's. Knowing the reason for it, she chuckles, trying to keep pace with me.

Two freaking hours...

That's how long David kept us. Every time I glanced at my phone and began to make noises about leaving, he ordered something else off the menu. First dessert. Then coffee. Then another coffee, which he took his sweet damn time drinking.

Currently, I'm rocking a major case of blue balls. If I don't alleviate the situation soon, they just might explode.

And that would not be good for business.

As soon as we reach the truck, I push Whitney against the door and I'm on her before she can draw in a full breath. I can't wait another freaking second to have my mouth on hers. Despite David's best efforts, my need for Whitney has been building all night long and I've got to have a small taste until I can get her alone.

A gasp leaves her mouth as my lips crash into hers. My tongue sweeps across the seam of her lips and she immediately opens. With our mouths fused together, I align my body against hers, wanting to be as close as possible. My erection juts insistently against the softness of her belly and I groan, wishing we weren't in such a public space.

Between kisses I mutter, "Fuck, baby, I want you so damn bad." I can't remember wanting a girl the way I want this one. She's all I can think about.

"Mmmm," she says in agreement. "Maybe we should take this to my place before our parents walk out and detain us any longer." She grins as I nibble at her mouth. "Do you really want my dad inviting us back to your mom's house for a fun-filled night of board games?"

*Argh.*

David had actually thrown the idea out there before Mom shut it down with a laugh and a firm no.

The conclusion I've drawn is that Whitney's father doesn't want me anywhere near his daughter.

*Well, David, that's too damn bad.*

"Your abso-fucking-lutely right." I glance toward the entrance and reluctantly step away from her. "We need to get out of here before they take care of the bill."

It's a fifteen-minute drive to her apartment. With a growl of frustration, I smash my lips against hers, stealing one more kiss for the road.

Whitney's mouth is addictive.

I yank open the door and hustle her gorgeous ass inside. Then I race around the front of the truck and hop in the driver's seat. With my foot pressed against the accelerator, I peel out of the parking lot and head toward campus. There's no way in hell we're going back to my house.

With my luck, Savannah will be lying in wait to ambush me. That damn girl needs to move on. I'm trying to be a nice guy regarding the situation, but she isn't getting the hint that I'm no longer interested.

"You need to slow down," Whitney says with a laugh, placing a hand on my thigh. "It's going to be difficult to have sex if we're both dead."

I snort but don't bother to glance in her direction. My eyes are laser focused on the road stretched out in front of us. Right now, I'm a man on a mission.

Believe it or not, we haven't slept together.

We've been making out like crazy, but I've been holding off, not wanting to rush her until she's ready. Whitney needs to understand that I'm willing to wait for as long as it takes. I'll wine and dine the fuck out of her, because what we have is more than just screwing.

But tonight...it feels right. The sexual tension between us has been building. I think we're both on the verge of spontaneous combustion.

I make about a dozen traffic violations on the way, but we arrive safely at her apartment in less than ten minutes, which has to be a record. I throw the truck into park before shooting out of the cab like a shot. Then I'm yanking open Whitney's door and hauling her into my arms before striding up the walkway toward the lobby.

"Gray," she shrieks, "put me down! I'm fully capable of walking on my own two feet."

I smack a kiss against her lips. "Hell, no. You're staying right here in my arms."

"You're crazy," she sighs, nibbling at my mouth.

*Gahhhh.*

Tonight, I plan on making her mine. Maybe we hooked up freshman year, but what's about to happen between us now is different. It means so much more.

We pass by a few people in the lobby. They openly gawk as I grin and tell them to have a good night as if there's nothing out of the ordinary going on. Whitney buries her face against my chest in embarrassment. By the time we reach her apartment, I'm barely able to contain myself. I'm on the verge of busting out of my pants, but I want to make sure this is good for her.

Tonight is all about Whitney.

When I had sex in the past, it was all about me. Girls would spread their legs, get down on their knees, wanting nothing more than to make me happy. Not that they didn't leave completely satisfied... please, I'm not that big of a jackass. But still, the whole experience revolved around my pleasure.

And I loved it.

Reveled in it.

After the grueling pain of the accident, the physical therapy that followed, and hours I put in at the rink and gym to get back to where I was, it felt like my due.

What I have with Whitney couldn't be any further from that. I find myself wanting to please her instead of myself. I might have fucked my way through the female population at Hillsdale, but this is the first time a girl has actually mattered.

This is the first time I'm going to make love to a woman.

And that, my friends, is a scary thought, but an amazing one as well.

I kick the door closed with my foot and scan the apartment. It's dark inside, which hopefully means we're alone. With Whitney cradled in my arms, I beeline for her room and set her down in the middle of her queen-sized mattress. For a long moment, I stare at her as she meets my gaze with trusting eyes. My heart swells with an emotion I'm unable to identify. There's no way I'm going to say it's love. It's a little too early for that kind of declaration, but it's getting damn close.

I drag a hand over my face, knowing I can't fuck this up. This girl means too much to me. Hell, she means everything.

"You sure about this?" Before she can answer, I add, "Because we don't have to do anything. We can wait." I clear my throat. "*I* can wait."

Do I want to wait?

Hell, no.

But I will.

I'll wait for as long as she needs me to.

Whitney's lips lift at the corners as she scrambles to her knees. When she holds her arms out, I step toward her. She flattens the palms of her hands against my chest. "I want this, Gray. I want *you*."

"There's no reason we have to rush this." I draw in a deep breath before slowly releasing it, willing everything inside me to settle.

Her features soften. "I know. And I appreciate that, but I'm ready."

Her fingers go to the hem of her shirt and in one swift motion, she yanks it over her head and tosses it to the floor.

My gaze dips from her eyes to her silk-covered breasts. Instead of the pink polka dot bra she wore the last time, this one is a teal cheetah print. I don't know how it's possible, but my dick becomes even harder. Whitney smiles as if she's aware of how crazy she drives me and is enjoying every damn minute of it.

"Fuck baby, that's sexy," I groan. "Please tell me you're wearing matching panties."

"I don't know." She gives me a coy look from beneath the thick fringe of her lashes and shrugs. "Guess you'll just have to find out for yourself."

Those words are all it takes to unleash my inner beast. With a growl, I take another step forward and gently press her to the bed. My fingers zero in on the button of her jeans before dragging the zipper down and peeling the denim to her thighs.

And...

*Ding, ding, ding, we have a winner!*

Matching.

"You look so freaking hot." With hasty movements, I strip off her pants and toss them to the floor. My mouth waters as I eat her up with my eyes. She looks like a fucking angel with her dark hair spread out and her nearly naked body showcased in the matching teal bra and panty set.

I can only shake my head for being such a dumbass freshman year.

How fucking lucky am I that another dude didn't snap her up?

I clench my hands at my sides, wanting nothing more than to tear off her underwear and have at her, but we've reached the portion of the evening where I need to keep my baser instincts under strict lock and key. I have to take my time and do this right.

When I don't immediately fall on top of her, Whitney props herself up on her elbows and slowly spreads her legs wide.

My eyes arrow to her panty-covered pussy. "Aww, come on," I groan, dragging a hand through my hair. "You're not playing fair. Can't you see that I'm trying to keep a lid on things?"

A sly smile spreads across her face. "You don't need to do that. I've waited long enough and I'm not waiting any longer."

"*You've* waited long enough?" A gurgle of laughter erupts from my lips.

She's gotta be joking, right?

I've been beating the meat for a solid two weeks so I wouldn't maul her the first time we had sex. And yet, all the energy I've previously released isn't doing a damn bit of good when faced with her perfection.

All I can say is if this girl wants me, she's got me.

I crawl on the bed and maneuver between her thighs. She whimpers, her head falling back when I press a kiss against her core. "As much as I love these, they've got to go." I hook my fingers under the elastic band at her hips. She lifts her ass off the mattress as I pull the flimsy material down her legs, tossing it over my shoulder.

With Whitney exposed, I resettle myself. I've been dying for another taste of her. She whimpers as I lay a kiss against the top of her slit. Without me asking, she spreads her legs wider. Wanting to take my time, I lick and nip at her inner thighs, pressing sweet kisses against her outer lips. When I ghost over her center, she arches, trying to inch closer. I grin as frustration erupts from deep in her throat.

"What's wrong?" I ask innocently. "You don't like this?"

"I love it, but I need more," she moans, twisting beneath me and clawing at the covers. "You're driving me crazy, Gray."

Still propped on her elbows, Whitney lifts her head so she can watch the way I touch her. Our gazes cling as I give her pussy a long lap with my tongue. A drugged expression settles over her features.

"Again," she murmurs huskily.

Wanting nothing more than to please her, I continue to glide over her core. Her body shudders as I stab my tongue in her softness and nibble delicately at her clit. A guttural groan leaves her lips as I suck the tiny bundle of nerves into my mouth.

She's so fucking responsive to my every touch.

When her body begins to tighten, I back off, giving her little kisses until she relaxes again and her fingers release the bedspread she's been clutching. I do this over and over, whipping her into a frenzy before allowing it to dissipate, wanting to draw out every last shred of pleasure for as long as possible. Only when Whitney is on the verge of sobbing, pleading with me to let her come, do I suck her clit into my mouth and give it a hard tug.

She bows off the bed as an orgasm slams through her. My name is like a fervent prayer on her lips. It's the best damn sound in the world.

When her pussy finally stops pulsing and I've licked every last drop of cream, I crawl up her body and give her a kiss. A smug smile curls my lips at the satisfied expression on her face.

"Feel good, baby?"

She grunts out an incoherent response and I chuckle.

*You're damn right I did that, thank you very much.*

The need to be inside her pounds through me. I roll to the side and sit up, stripping off the shirt before going to work on the jeans. By the time I'm down to my boxer briefs, Whitney has fought her way out of her orgasmic haze. She sits up and pushes me against the bed, sliding one long leg over my torso so she's able to straddle me.

My eyes cross at the feel of her core pressed against my boxers. I flex my hips and stroke my dick against her. It won't take much for me to go off like a shot. "This isn't going to work unless I take these off."

Her head falls back as I rub my length against her heat. "I'm aware. I just wanted to be the one to do it."

Far be it for me to deprive her—and myself—of the pleasure.

Whitney leans forward. Just when I think she's going to kiss me, she pauses. Her warm breath drifts across my lips. With our gazes locked, her tongue darts out to swipe at me before she draws my lower lip into her mouth.

I groan when she releases my flesh.

"I hope you're ready for the same tortuous treatment you gave me." An evil smile settles across her face. "Turnabout is fair play, right?"

My hands go to her hips, holding her firmly in place as I arch my pelvis, sliding my cock against her pussy.

Christ...these boxers need to go. I want to feel her naked flesh pressed against me.

"How about I get inside you and then you can torture me all you want?" I cajole. "Sound like a plan?"

"Nice try...but I don't think so."

My fingers dig into her hips as I grind myself against her. She moans before reaching around and unsnapping her bra. The silky material slides down her arms, revealing high, tight titties. As soon as she tosses the garment to the floor, my hands go to her breasts, squeezing the soft weight in my palms.

"Come on, baby," I whine like a little bitch. "I need to be inside you." All I can think about is her slick heat wrapped around my cock. The thought makes me want to come all over myself.

Whitney's teeth scrape against my jaw before she licks her way down my throat and across my chest. Her tongue swipes across one flat nipple before sucking it into her mouth. My hands slide through the silky strands of her hair, loosely holding her in place. Then she kisses her way over to the other and laves it with the same attention.

I groan as she takes her time, nibbling her way from my ribcage to my abdominals. She's right about this being torture. I don't know how much more I can withstand. She arrives at the waistband of my briefs before slowly peeling them down my hips. With every strip of flesh that is revealed, she kisses the bared skin until she reaches her destination. One hand strokes over my erection before cupping my balls.

*Fuck.*

*Me.*

After what feels like an eternity, Whitney tugs at my boxers until my cock springs free. She makes a little humming noise deep in her throat.

Appreciative, perhaps?

Let's hope so.

Her eyes lock on my hard flesh as she lowers her mouth and swipes her tongue across the bulbous head before sucking it into her mouth. Then my dick is disappearing between her lips.

Goddamn, that's sexy as fuck.

I squeeze my eyes tightly closed as pleasure explodes through my body.

She does this over and over until I'm gritting my teeth and silently reciting the alphabet—backward—in an effort to draw this out for as long as possible.

Releasing me, her tongue laves my balls with lazy strokes before it's back to licking the tip of my cock like it's a lollipop. When she flattens her velvety softness against the underside of my dick, I know it's game over.

"Whitney," I groan, "I'm going to come. I want to be inside you when that happens."

Around my girth, she whispers, "You are inside me."

That might be true, but I want inside that sweet pussy of hers. I've been dreaming about it for nearly three years. When she doesn't budge, I sit up and slide my hands beneath her arms, lifting her off me.

My erection pops free from her mouth and she pouts. "I wasn't done."

"The hell you are," I growl and flip her onto her back so I can settle between her thighs.

*Fuck...*

*Condoms.*

With a groan of frustration, I stab a finger in her direction. "Don't move one damn muscle!" Then I roll off the bed and grab my jeans, rifling through the pockets until I find the square foil wrapper I'd stuffed in there earlier.

She raises a brow. "Came prepared, did you?"

"I came prepared for *you*, baby." I rip open the packet and slide the rubber over my erection. "*Just you.*" I don't want her to ever doubt that.

Whitney's mouth lifts, and she spreads her thighs wide, giving me a little glimpse of heaven. For just a moment, I admire the view. The lips of her pussy are swollen from her orgasm and I can't wait to slide between them.

How am I ever going to get enough of her?

Whitney crooks a finger in my direction and I grin, crawling onto the bed before lining up the head of my cock with her opening. She spreads her legs wider as I slowly push inside her tight heat until I'm buried to the hilt.

*This*...this right here is the best damn feeling in the world. Being inside her is even better than I remembered. Her pussy fits my dick like a glove. I haven't moved a muscle and already I can tell this won't last long.

Being a one pump chump isn't something I want to add to my resume. Then she'll have every damn right to call me out on my weak stroke game.

Whitney wraps her arms and legs around me so I'm flush against her body. Sweat breaks out across my forehead as I slowly flex my hips. Normally, when I'm fucking a chick, I close my eyes and concentrate on the pleasure rolling through my body. But this time, I lock my gaze on hers. I want to see every emotion as it flickers across her beautiful face.

Whitney arches as I move against her, our bodies in perfect harmony. It doesn't take more than a dozen strokes for her to constrict around me, strangling my dick with her tight sheath. Neither of us look away as she groans out her orgasm and I dive headfirst off the cliff after her.

With one last flex of my hips, I collapse on top of her. Her warm body cradles my softening length. Fuck me, I don't want to pull out.

Already I know that what just happened between us has ruined me.

Nothing will ever feel as good as this.

# WHITNEY

$\mathcal{J}$'m hauling ass across campus when I hear my name called. Recognizing the voice, I turn and see Evert jogging to catch up with me.

Once he reaches my side, he gives me a tight smile. "Hey. I was hoping I'd run into you today. Are you busy? Do you have time to grab a coffee and talk?"

"Hey, yourself," I greet. "Actually, I was just on my way to speak with Dr. Levinstein before class starts. If you want, we can walk together to Thorson."

"Sure." With a nod, he falls in line with me. "That works."

Evert is such an awesome guy. I had a feeling that he and Katelyn would click, and I wasn't wrong. What makes the situation even better is that Evert and Gray are friends. There hasn't been time for all of us to hang out together, but I'm looking forward to it. Maybe we can grab dinner or see a movie sometime this weekend.

I give him a bit of side-eye as we push our way through the crowd of students moving across campus like cattle. The easygoing smile he usually wears is noticeably absent.

When he remains silent, I clear my throat. "It's really cool that you and Katelyn are together."

"Oh, yeah," he mumbles. A frown settles on his face as he breaks eye contact. "That just kind of happened."

That wasn't *exactly* the response I was expecting. I thought maybe he was going to thank me for hooking them up.

If he doesn't want to talk about Katelyn, then maybe this has to do with the class we have together. "So, what's up?"

"I don't know how to say this," he mutters, unease flickering across his face. "So, I'm just going to get to the point."

"Ummm, okay."

"You shouldn't be hanging out with Gray McNichols," he blurts.

*"Excuse me?"* My mouth falls open and I shake my head, wondering if I misheard him.

Evert presses his lips into a thin line. "That guy is all wrong for you."

I stop in the flow of traffic and stare at him in surprise. "Why would you say that?" Gray is one of Evert's teammates and they share a house together. I thought they were friends.

Guess not.

Before I realize what's happening, Evert wraps his fingers around my upper arm and is dragging me off the path and onto the patch of grass next to it. "When I first heard you two were seeing each other, I thought it was a joke. Everyone knows that McNichols doesn't date. He uses girls before throwing them away like dirty Kleenex."

I wince at the ugly analogy before tugging my arm free from his grip. Evert isn't telling me anything I don't already know. Gray *has* blown through a lot of girls at Hillsdale.

And I was one of them.

But…

Everything is different now, isn't it?

Unwilling to dwell on those troubling thoughts, I push them from my mind.

Why is Evert bringing this up?

What business is it of his?

I shift my weight as my hand tightens around the strap of my messenger bag. "I appreciate your concern, but my relationship with

Gray is strictly between the two of us. It's not something I'm going to discuss with you."

He huffs out a breath as his shoulders fall. "Look, maybe I'm not saying this the right way, but I don't want to see you get hurt. Especially by someone who has such a shitty reputation where women are concerned. I care about you, Whitney." His voice drops. "*A lot.*"

The air shifts between us as awkwardness descends.

Unsure how to respond, I give him a strained smile and lay my hand on his arm. Evert and I have been friends for a while. As much as I appreciate his concern, he needs to back off. I'm more than capable of taking care of myself. "Thank you. You're a good friend, but you don't have to worry about me."

"That's the thing..." He glances away before admitting, "I'd always hoped we would be more than just friends."

Bewildered by the admission, the smile slides off my face as I yank my hand away so that we're no longer touching. *"What?"*

Evert takes a step closer. Paralyzed by shock, I stay rooted in place.

"I've liked you since freshman year." Evert's cheeks flood with color as he jerks his shoulders. "I guess, maybe, I'd always hoped you would figure it out and return the feelings."

I bite my lip as my eyes meander to the pedestrian path and the business hall that looms in the distance. I want to end this conversation before he says anything else that will make the situation worse than it already is.

"I'm sorry," I murmur, shifting my weight. "I didn't realize." My mind quickly flips through the years. How did I miss this?

"Maybe if I'd spoken up sooner, you'd be with me instead of McNichols."

It never crossed my mind to consider Evert as anything more than a friend. Plus, Katelyn has liked him for a while. I would never break girl code and go after a boy that one of my friends was interested in.

"I don't think that would have made a difference." The truth is that I never stopped liking Gray. As much as I didn't want him taking up residence inside my head, that's exactly what happened. "I don't understand why you're bringing this up." I gulp and force out the rest. "What about Katelyn? I thought you guys really hit it off."

He shrugs as his gaze skitters away. "She's fine." There's a pause before he mumbles, "But she's not you."

It's almost painful to swallow past the thick lump that has settled in the middle of my throat. I don't want to see Katelyn get hurt. And I don't want to be the reason Evert causes her pain.

I wrack my brain, desperate to fix this situation. "Maybe if you took the time to get to know her better, you'd see just how great she is." The last thing I want to do is spill any of my friend's secrets, but I want Evert to know how much she likes him. Hopefully, it'll make a difference. "Katelyn is really into you." When his expression doesn't change, I add, "She has been for a while."

"I know," he says flatly, "but she's not the one I want."

Any hope I had of Katelyn finally getting her man comes crashing down around my head.

When she finds out, she's going to be devastated.

"I'm sorry," I repeat stiffly, "I don't feel that way about you." I shuffle my feet, hating him for putting me in such a shitty position. I'd always thought Evert was such a nice guy, but now...

Not so much.

"If you don't have feelings for Katelyn, you need to be upfront with her. It's not fair to lead her on."

His shoulders slump under the weight of my words. "Yeah, I know. It's just that I'd hoped maybe you would see us together and get..."

*Jealous.*

*Oh my God!*

Filled with disgust, I take a hasty step in retreat. "I need to get to class."

Before I can turn and run, he grabs my arm to hold me in place. "Just think about what I've said." His green-colored eyes plead with mine. "Give me a chance to show you how good we could be together."

I shake my head as hysteria bubbles up in my throat.

*Is he seriously crazy?*

"Katelyn is my best friend." Fury ignites inside me. "I would *never* hurt her like that."

"But I don't have feelings for her," he repeats, brows snapping together in annoyance. "I never have. It's always been you, Whitney."

"I'm sorry. Nothing is ever going to happen between us." With a tug, I jerk my arm from his grip and stagger backward.

The further I get from him, the easier it is to breathe. Evert's eyes hold mine as I stumble onto the walking path. I bump into a guy and mumble an apology before turning and sprinting away as fast as my legs will carry me. The heaviness of what he admitted drags me down.

I have no idea what I'm going to do about this situation.

# GRAY

"**M**om?" I holler, slamming the front door closed behind me. "Are you home?" I had a couple of hours between class and practice and thought I'd stop by. Maybe, if she's not busy, we could have dinner together.

You know, just shoot the shit.

Catch up.

Spend a little mom-son bonding time with one another.

Fine…that's a lie.

I'm here to suss out more information regarding her relationship with David. Breaking them up hasn't been as easy as I'd thought it would be. It's been about six weeks since they let the cat out of the bag, and I still don't like it.

"In the kitchen," she calls out in response.

With a determined stride, I head to the back of the house. Mom is at the stove, stirring a pot. I grind to a halt and close my eyes, inhaling the fragrant aroma. If there's one thing I miss about living here, it's Mom's homecooked meals. She's a fantastic cook. The shit I nuke in the microwave at school is in no way the same.

I slide onto a stool at the long stretch of island. "Whatever you're making smells fantastic."

She turns and smiles. "Smothered porkchops with mashed potatoes and corn."

My belly rumbles as my mouth waters. "That's one of my favorites."

"I guess it's a happy coincidence that you dropped by." She grabs the mitts before taking the large red pot and popping it into the oven. Then she moves around the island. "Any reason in particular that you decided to stop home?" She wraps her arms around me for a quick hug before settling next to me.

You bet your ass I have an agenda. But I'm not about to launch into it within minutes of walking through the front door.

Instead, I shrug, going for nonchalant. "Just thought I'd see how you were doing." I give her my most winning smile. "Plus, I was hoping you were making something good."

"If you'd given me a bit of notice, I would have whipped up a dessert."

I groan.

*Damnit.*

She's right. I should have called instead of planning a sneak attack. "Next time," I promise.

"It's nice having you so close." Mom hoists her smile as emotion fills her eyes. "I'll miss you next year when you're gone."

"You could always sell the house and move where I end up."

She nods as a thoughtful expression crosses her face. "I suppose that's a possibility to consider down the road, but I'm going to continue working for a few more years." She hesitates before adding, "Plus, there's David to consider."

Just hearing his name makes me grit my teeth. It's not that I don't like David. He seems like a perfectly fine dude.

For a different woman.

Not my mom.

I'd planned on waiting until after dinner to broach the subject, but she's given me the perfect opening, so I'm taking it. Clearing my throat, I delve right in. "I know we haven't really talked about it, but I thought you and Dad were trying to work things out."

Surprised by the change in topic, her eyes widen before she glances away.

An uncomfortable silence falls over us and I begin to wonder if she's going to respond to the question. But then she straightens her shoulders and nods her head.

"You're right. We haven't really talked about it and I'm sorry for that. Your father and I should have sat down with you to discuss the situation." She pauses as her gaze searches mine. "I know you were hoping that Dad and I would get back together..." Her voice trails off.

When she doesn't continue, I raise a brow. "But—"

She lays her hand over mine. "But it's not going to happen."

A lump of nausea settles in the pit of my belly as I shake my head. "Why not?"

"There are a lot of reasons." A regretful smile twists her lips. "I think the biggest factor is that your father and I got married when we were really young. Instead of growing together, we grew apart and started living separate lives. Neither of us wanted it to happen. We spent a lot of time working on our differences in counseling, but, in the end, they were too insurmountable to overcome."

The breath rushes from my lungs.

I have no idea what to say.

Her eyes fill with sympathy. "I'm sorry, Gray." She squeezes my fingers as if that will soften the blow of her words. "We really did try to make it work."

I might be twenty-three years old, but I'd been holding out hope that my parents would work their shit out. It was so much nicer when it was just the three of us. Dad has had a few girlfriends since he and Mom split up, and it's weird. There's nothing more awkward than showing up at his apartment and finding a random chick chilling on the couch.

And now there's David, who doesn't seem to be going anywhere. At least the girls Dad dates don't stick around very long. A couple of months at the most. I don't bother getting to know them or their names.

There's no point. They're not permanent.

"Well," I bite out, feeling uncharacteristically pissed off, "maybe you should have tried harder."

Her face falls and hurt blooms in her wide eyes, which makes me feel like a real prick.

I love my mom. Whenever I've needed her, she's always been there for me. She's the one who schlepped me to physical therapy appointments and doctor's visits for years. Once I'd gotten strong enough to skate, she's the one who drove me to the hockey rink six days a week. Not to mention all the other mom-things she did for me while growing up.

The last thing I want to do is lash out and inflict pain.

Embarrassed by my outburst, I scrub a hand over my face. "Sorry, Mom. I didn't mean it like that." I shift uncomfortably on the stool and glance away, unable to hold her searching gaze. "It's just that..." Unsure what to say, my voice dies.

"You wish your family were together." Wetness shines brightly in her eyes, which makes me feel like a bigger asshole. "I get it." She sniffles. "And more than anything, I wish I could give you that."

*Aww, hell.*

"Don't cry, Mom," I plead, "I'm sorry." Obviously, I shouldn't have opened my big fat mouth.

"I know what you're going through. Grandma and Grandpa divorced when I was ten." She gives a helpless shrug. "There's nothing worse than being shuffled between two households and never quite feeling like you belonged in either. That's the last thing I want for you." She draws in a deep breath before expelling it. "It wasn't a decision either of us made lightly. You have to know that I tried everything I could to salvage our marriage." She drags her gaze from mine. "It just couldn't be saved. No matter how much we both wanted it to work."

"I'm sorry, Mom." I glance at my fingers, which are clenched so tightly that the knuckles have turned bone white. "I shouldn't have brought it up."

"No, it's all right. If you have questions, then I'm glad we could talk about them."

"You sure about that?" I ask jokingly, attempting to lighten the mood.

"Absolutely. I know it's not easy to discuss these kinds of topics, but it's important that we communicate honestly with one another. You're the most important person in my life, Gray. I want you to be comfortable with how I'm choosing to move on." She glances away as her voice becomes hesitant. "If you think this relationship with David is moving too quickly, then I'll slow things down."

This is exactly what I'd been hoping for. It's the reason Whitney and I pretended to be involved in the first place. And here Mom is, offering to slow-track their relationship even though I know she doesn't want to.

"You really seem to like him," I mutter reluctantly, hoping that I'm off base. But I know I'm not. I can see it in the way she lights up every time she mentions his name or when they're together. Now that I think about it, she never did that with Dad. It seems like she and David have a lot of interests in common. They like doing the same kinds of things. She and Dad didn't. He liked to sit around and watch sports or go out with his friends.

A silent war breaks out in my head.

The words are there. It wouldn't take much to force them out. As far as I can tell, I've got two options. I either bite my tongue and say nothing, or I pull the plug on their relationship.

Fuck me.

There's no doubt about it—adulting sucks.

# WHITNEY

*W*ith a sigh, I shut the apartment door and lean against it. Thank God this day is almost over. As much as I'm dreading this conversation with Katelyn, I don't feel like I have much choice in the matter. I can't allow Evert to spend more time with my friend if his feelings aren't genuine.

And they're not. He made that abundantly clear this afternoon.

I shake my head, still shocked by everything that had tumbled out of his mouth.

Who the hell uses one girl to get to another?

That's so messed up.

My hands tighten into fists as I think about Evert. I'd seriously like to wring his neck. The real kicker is that I'd always thought he was such a nice guy. Well, nothing could be further from the truth.

"Hello?" I call out, shoving away from the door and walking into the living room.

Is it terrible to hope that she isn't home? Then I can push off this conversation until later. Like tomorrow. Maybe by then, Evert will have come clean and told Katelyn the truth himself, saving me from having to get involved in this mess.

"I'm in here," she chirps.

Her cheerful voice sends my heart plummeting.

*Damn.*

It's obvious that Evert hasn't owned up to being an asshole.

I peek inside Katelyn's bedroom, surprised to find her putting the finishing touches on her outfit. Her makeup is on point and her blond hair has been straightened so it hangs like a shiny curtain around her face. She's wearing a cute denim skirt paired with a navy-blue V-neck top that hugs her curves.

"Wow. You look really nice."

"Thanks." A smile lights up her face as her gaze meets mine. "I'm just about to head out for the night."

"Oh?" I'm almost afraid to ask where she's going.

Katelyn claps her hands together as she bounces on the balls of her feet. "Evert asked me to go to a party with him."

*Double damn.*

My teeth sink into my lip as I worry it. Before I can gather my thoughts and figure out how I'm going to broach the subject with Katelyn, she says, "I think tonight's the night."

*"What?"* I squeak. Please tell me that she's not going to—

"Yes!" she blurts. "I'm going to sleep with him."

I stifle a groan and shuffle from one foot to the other as my brain cartwheels. "Don't you think it's a little soon for that? You just got together a few weeks ago."

Katelyn shoots a frown in my direction. "Wow! Hypocritical, much? I mean, you had a one-night stand with Gray and weren't even in a relationship."

Well, yeah...

I scrub a hand over my face and try again. "I know, but this situation is different. Maybe..." My tongue darts out to moisten my lips. "Maybe you need to slow things down and make sure it isn't a mistake."

Annoyance flickers across Katelyn's face as she turns toward me. Clearly, she doesn't like the advice I'm trying to dole out. The last thing I want to do is ruin this for her. But how can I let her sleep with a guy who admitted that he's using her?

No matter what I do, Katelyn is going to get hurt.

Hands planted on her hips, she glares. "Slow things down? Why are you trying to talk me out of this? You know how much I've always liked Evert. And after more than a year, he's *finally* taken notice. Taking this relationship to the next level isn't a mistake." She huffs out a breath. "Why can't you just be happy for me?"

Nausea churns in the pit of my belly. I don't know what to do.

Is it possible that Evert will change his mind and develop feelings for Katelyn? She's a great girl. He would be lucky to have her as a girl-friend. Maybe now that I've told him there's no chance for us, he'll move on.

*"Well?"* Katelyn snaps, cutting into my thoughts.

But...what if that doesn't happen?

What if he just continues using her?

And I could have stopped it from happening when I had the chance?

Ugh. I wish there was more time to think this over.

"Whitney!"

But there isn't. I don't have any other choice. I owe it to Katelyn to be honest. Even if it hurts.

"I ran into Evert before class today," I say carefully.

Her expression turns wary as she shakes her head in confusion. "And?"

It would be so easy to backtrack at this point, but I can't bring myself to do it. I clear my throat and push out the rest. "He admitted to having feelings for me."

An uncomfortable silence crashes over us.

"Katelyn," I whisper, taking a hesitant step into her room. "Did you hear what I said?"

My voice jolts her from her stupor, and she narrows her eyes. "Let me see if I understand this...Evert told you that he has feelings for *you?*" Her words are deliberate and halting. *"Today?* He told you that *today?"*

I press my lips together and jerk my head into a tight nod. I don't want to give her any more information than necessary. The less damage I inflict, the better it'll be for both of us. "Yes."

She spins away, only to stare out the bedroom window. I can't see the expression on her face or tell what she's thinking, but I know she's upset.

Unsure what to do, I pad across the room and lay my hand on her shoulder, giving it a gentle squeeze. "Are you okay?"

She whirls toward me, abruptly knocking my hand away. Anger leaps to life in her eyes as she forces out a humorless laugh. "No, I'm not all right."

Everything inside me wilts. "I'm sorry, I thought you should know what he said. I don't want him using you to get to me."

As soon as the words are out of my mouth, I realize they're a mistake. Two red flags stain her cheeks as a furious glint ignites in her eyes. "Because no one could possibly want to go out with me unless they were trying to get to you?"

"No!" I gasp. "That's not what I said!" I would never do anything to hurt Katelyn. I've always had her back. How could she think otherwise?

Her glare intensifies. "Actually, you did. You said that Evert was using me to get to you."

"Katelyn," I squeeze my eyes tight, trying to think of a way out of this mess, before forcing them open again, "you're twisting my words."

"Why are you trying to ruin this for me?" she snaps. "Are you jealous?"

*Seriously?*

"Of course not!"

Ignoring my protest, she continues. "It's not enough that you have Gray McNichols—now you want Evert Monroe?"

"No!" This couldn't possibly be going any worse! All I'm trying to do is be a good friend. "I had no idea Evert felt that way about me."

"Whatever, Whitney." She rolls her eyes. "I don't believe one word you're saying. Evert likes me. He's not using me to get to you." Her upper lip curls. "I never realized how full of yourself you were."

*"What?"* How did this conversation end up going sideways like

this? I'm not the bad guy in this situation. But that's exactly what she's painting me out to be. "Come on, you know that's not true. I told you what he said because I don't want to see you get hurt. That's all. I have no interest in Evert."

"Good. Keep it that way." She glances at the mirror one last time, but there's no longer any joy in her gaze. Avoiding eye contact, she grabs her purse and stalks past me.

My mouth falls open as I stumble after her to the living room, where she slides her feet into a pair of wedge sandals.

*Wait a minute...*

"You're *still* going to meet up with him?"

"Yeah, I am." She throws a sullen glare over her shoulder. If looks could kill, I'd be dead on the spot. Where is all this anger coming from? "I'm not going to let you ruin this for me because you're jealous."

*Oh my God...why isn't she listening to me?*

"Katelyn, I promise this has nothing to do with jealousy!" I shake my head and try one last time to reason with her. "Please, don't leave. Let's finish talking this out."

She glances impatiently at her phone as it dings with an incoming text message. Her body vibrates with anger as she lifts her gaze to mine. "We have nothing more to discuss."

"But—"

Before I can say anything more, Katelyn slams out of the apartment. As she does, the door rattles on its hinges, making me wince.

No matter how badly I thought the conversation might go, that was so much worse.

# GRAY

$\mathcal{I}$ catch a glimpse of Whitney's dark head as she ducks into Bean Blast, one of the coffee shops on campus. A smile springs to my lips. I don't even bother trying to fight the contentment that floods through me at the sight of her. Instead of heading to class, I detour, wanting to steal a kiss before we go our separate ways for the rest of the day.

As soon as I enter the shop, I find her in line, staring at the phone in her hand. It takes five steps for me to close the distance that separates us. Her long hair is pulled up into a messy bun.

Goddamn, but that's sexy.

Then again, everything about this girl is sexy.

She's got it all going on.

Looks, brains, and a sassy mouth that I find entirely too kissable.

Not to mention that she's fuckable as hell.

I sneak up behind her and press a kiss against the bared column of her neck. As soon as I make contact, she swings around. A small smile tugs at the corners of her lips when she realizes that it's me.

"You almost lost a of couple teeth there, buddy. You should know better than to sneak up on a girl like that."

I grin, aware that my dimples will flash and she'll melt like a puddle of goo on the coffee shop floor. Just like I suspected, I see the instant she softens. Realizing what happened, her eyes narrow.

"Maybe you should try using those for good instead of evil every once in a while," she grumbles.

"Now why would I want to do that," I lean forward and press my lips to hers for a quick kiss, "when it's so gratifying to be evil?"

Chuckling, she nips my chin with sharp teeth. "Just as long as I'm the only one you're using them on."

"Deal." I give her a wink and change the subject. "I stopped at home and saw my mom the other day."

Interest flickers in her eyes. "Oh?"

"Yeah...we actually had a good talk." I pause and admit, "She's really into your dad."

"If it makes you feel any better, he's just as into her." She tugs her bottom lip with her teeth, and I'm tempted to reach over and nibble at it. "I haven't seen him this happy in a long time."

"Mine, either." I glance away, still not entirely comfortable with Mom moving on. It's weird to see her with a man who isn't my dad. I'm not sure how much I like it. And I'm willing to bet that Whitney feels just as conflicted. It's doubtful she wants another woman replacing her mom. But...

I scratch the back of my neck as I throw out the idea. "Maybe we should just leave them alone. There's nothing that says their relationship will work out long-term."

Relief washes over her features. "I was thinking the same thing. If they end up staying together, then we'll deal with it. And if they don't, we have nothing to be concerned about." Her gaze tentatively searches mine. "Right?"

I nod, happy that we're both on the same page. Letting this go feels like a huge load off my mind. I don't want to do anything that will hurt my mom. If she's found a good guy who makes her happy, then maybe I just need to roll with it.

Unable to resist, I pull Whitney into my arms. "You know, if we hadn't tried to break up our parents, we wouldn't have gotten together." When she laughs, I nip at her neck, inhaling her sweet scent. "You never would have bothered to give me the time of day."

"That's probably true," she admits, pressing closer.

"So, maybe in a weird way, we owe them for dating in the first place."

A grin lights up her face as Whitney smacks a kiss against my lips. "I think we should keep that information to ourselves, don't you?"

Laughter bubbles up inside me. I think her dad would bust a nut if he found out. "Yeah, probably. But, come on...you have to admit that it'll be a funny story to tell later down the road."

"Sure," she agrees, lips brimming with humor, "*way* down the road."

The bell over the door rings as another customer enters the shop. I glance over and see Katelyn. As soon as she spots us standing in line, her eyes go wide, and her lips flatten. I raise my hand in greeting, but she spins around and stalks out of Bean Blast without acknowledging my presence. My brows slam together as I watch her disappear into the crowd outside.

*What the hell was that about?*

Unsure what's going on, I glance at Whitney. There's a devastated expression on her face as she stares at the empty doorway.

When she remains silent, I slip my fingers beneath her chin so I can angle her face toward mine. "What's up with Katelyn?"

There's a long pause. Whitney shakes her head as if unsure how to explain the situation before finally admitting, "She's angry with me."

"Well, yeah," I snort, "that much is obvious." A blind man could figure that out from the tension that had gathered in the small shop. The frostiness in Katelyn's eyes had been palpable.

"I was hoping this would blow over," she murmurs, "but it hasn't."

"Did you two get into a fight?" For some odd reason, Whitney is being stingy with the details.

"It wasn't exactly a fight," she hedges, glancing away, which instantly makes me suspicious.

I get the feeling she's purposefully leaving out pertinent information. Impatient to get to the bottom of what's caused the rift between

Whitney and her friend, I cock a brow and wait for her to elaborate. If she thinks I'll just drop the subject and move on, she's wrong. I can be like a dog with a bone when the circumstances call for it.

Whitney is saved from having to explain as we step up to the counter. I order a coffee for myself and an iced mocha latte for her. After I pay for the drinks and leave a tip, we move to the side to wait.

"I don't want to tell you," she reluctantly mutters.

My brows shoot up.

*Why the hell wouldn't she want to tell me what's going on?*

*How bad can it be?*

"All right," I grumble, folding my arms over my chest, "now you have to fill me in."

She groans.

This is seriously killing me. I just want her to spit it out so I can solve whatever problem is going on and we can all move on with our day. There's no way the situation can be as bad as she's making it out to be. In a few days, whatever bullshit is going on between the two girls will blow over.

"Promise you won't get mad?" she asks.

I narrow my eyes. "How can I promise something like that when I don't know what you're going to tell me?"

"Ugh!" She swats at my chest with a burst of frustration. This relationship might be new, but I can tell she's getting all jacked up and that's the last thing I want. "Can't you just promise?"

"Fine, you have my promise." I shake my head. "Sheesh."

Her gaze skitters away as anxiety threads its way through her voice. "I ran into Evert a few days ago."

Even though questions bubble up inside me, I'm smart enough to keep my trap shut. At least until she gets the whole story out.

"He, um, doesn't think I should be involved with you."

My hands tighten as my temper skyrockets. I'm barely able to keep from exploding.

*What a freaking little bitch.*

It's one thing to voice his concern to me. It's quite another to go behind my back and talk smack to Whitney. That makes me want to beat the shit out of him.

Teammate or not.

Can't say I've ever felt that way before.

Un-fucking-believable.

"What else did my good buddy Evert have to say?" I congratulate myself on staying calm and keeping my voice level. Trust me, it's not easy. Already my mind is trying to puzzle the pieces together. The last time I saw Evert and Katelyn, they'd been mauling each other at the apartment. Honestly, I'd thought we'd all moved on.

Me and Whitney.

Evert and Katelyn.

Apparently, that's not the case.

I should have known better. I'd realized a while ago that Evert had a thing for Whitney. Who knows just how long he's had his eye on her?

She clears her throat and mutters, "He admitted that he's only with Katelyn to make me jealous."

And there you have it. No wonder she wanted to secure a promise that I wouldn't go ape shit.

Well, guess what?

I'm pissed as hell.

"The fuck you say?" I ground out, holding onto my temper by a thread.

Several heads swivel in our direction. "Sorry," I mutter, raising my hand apologetically.

Once our coffee comes up, we grab the cups and head out the door. By the time we hit the path and are walking toward our ten o'clock classes, I've figured out how everything went down with her roommate.

"Obviously you told Katelyn about the conversation," I say flatly.

"Yeah." Misery fills her face as she jerks her head into a nod. "I didn't want to, but what choice did I have? I couldn't let my best friend continue to see a guy who's using her."

"You did the right thing." I slip an arm around her waist and tug her close. "All you were trying to do was be a good friend. At some point, Katelyn will realize that."

"You think so?" Cautious optimism enters her voice.

"Yeah, I do. But it might take time," I admit reluctantly. I hope for Whitney's sake that Katelyn comes to her senses and realizes she was only trying to protect her.

She leans against my chest and sighs. "I hate this," she murmurs as we walk across campus.

I drop a kiss on the top of her head. "I know. And I'm sorry." If I had my way, I'd beat Monroe to a bloody pulp for putting Whitney in this untenable situation.

What a douche.

But I can't do that. Not without upsetting Whitney.

"I appreciate you saying that, but none of this is your fault."

"I know, but I hate to see you hurting like this. If I could fix it, I would."

A chuckle escapes from her lips.

Confused by her response, I glance at her. "What? Did I say something funny?"

"No, I just..." Her voice trails off as she clears her throat. "I never expected you to be this...thoughtful. It's actually nice."

She peeks at me from where she's tucked against my chest. Uncertainty swims in her eyes and my heart swells with emotion.

In all honesty, I never expected it myself.

But there's always been something about Whitney that pulled at me. No matter how much I tried to suppress it, I found myself gravitating toward her. Whatever this is between us, it's a game changer. And I don't want it to end.

So...no matter what I have to do, I'm going to be there for my girl. And if that means helping her solve a bunch of bullshit with her friend, then that's what's gonna happen.

# WHITNEY

*A* full week slides by and still Katelyn won't speak to me. If I'm at the apartment, she's conspicuously absent. She's not around when I go to bed at night, and she's gone when I get up in the morning. If she comes home at all. My guess is that she's shacking up with Evert. I've tried texting and calling, but she refuses to respond.

In hindsight, I never should have mentioned my conversation with him. That was a mistake. I should have kept my mouth shut and just let the chips fall. I'd thought I was being a good friend.

Clearly, that's not the case. All I've done is drive Katelyn into the arms of the guy I was trying to protect her from.

Lesson learned the hard way.

I'm two pages into the paper I'm writing for my Investment Portfolio Management class when the door to the apartment opens. My heart stutters as I jump from my chair and race to my bedroom door just in time to see Evert and Katelyn head into her room.

"Hey," I blurt, hovering awkwardly in the doorway, "do you have a minute to talk?" I don't bother glancing at Evert. As far as I'm concerned, he doesn't exist. Ever since he divulged his feelings for me, we've been ignoring each other.

The look Katelyn levels in my direction as she drags Evert into her room is enough to freeze my blood. "No, sorry. We're busy." As if to punctuate her words, she slams the door with more force than necessary.

I blink back the tears, not wanting to let them fall.

I don't know what to do about our living situation. Katelyn refuses to talk to me. The thought of us not speaking for the rest of the year fills me with dread. There's no way I can live like this.

Within sixty seconds, the bedsprings in her room are squeaking. My eyes widen in horror. I should go to my room and slam the door. Instead, I stand rooted in place.

*Oh.*

*My.*

*God.*

*Are they seriously doing it while I stand in the hallway?*

As if to answer that silent question, Katelyn moans and the squeaking picks up speed. I'm not the one who should be embarrassed, and yet heat floods my cheeks. I'm tempted to grab my bag and get the hell out of here. I don't want to see either of them when they're finished with what they're doing.

*Ewww!*

But I'm not going to do that. I refuse to be chased out of my own home.

Snapping to awareness, I spin on my heels and stalk into my bedroom before slamming the door shut. When that doesn't muffle the sound of them knocking boots, I stuff noise cancelling earbuds in and go back to working on my paper.

But I can't concentrate.

With a huff of frustration, I lean against the chair and stare at the ceiling. All I want to do is clear the air between us and move on. This is the first real fight we've ever had, and it sucks.

After an hour, my belly grumbles and I decide to take my chances and fix myself dinner. I tentatively pull out the earbuds and cock my head, listening for any sounds of life.

Or sex.

But there aren't any. The apartment is shrouded in silence.

Maybe they finished up what they were doing and took off. I crack open the door and peer at Katelyn's bedroom across the hall. Her door is still closed. My shoulders fall. I'm guessing they're still in there doing God knows what.

*Ugh.*

Impatient to eat, I tiptoe to the kitchen and pull out everything I need to make a sandwich. It won't take more than five minutes and then I can hightail it back to my room until Evert leaves. Thinking about him makes my jaw lock. We used to sit by each other in class and talk all the time. Now, he won't meet my eyes. Which is fine by me. I have nothing to say to the big jerk.

It blows my mind that I misjudged him. Then again, look how wrong I was about Gray. The one I thought was a decent guy has turned out to be an asshole. And the one I pegged to be a womanizing asshole has turned out to be the complete opposite.

I layer a few slices of smoked turkey, swiss cheese, light mayo, and a pickle, before topping it with a second piece of whole wheat bread. Voilà, I've got a delicious sandwich. My belly grumbles and I realize how famished I am. Just as I'm about to bring the concoction to my mouth for a gigantic bite, my roommate's door swings open and Evert saunters out. Katelyn trails after him. Her hair is disheveled and she's wearing yoga pants and a T-shirt.

Their unexpected presence has my appetite pulling a disappearing act. No longer hungry, I lower the turkey and swiss to my plate.

Evert spears me with a spiteful look as he grabs Katelyn and pulls her into his arms. Then he attacks her face with his mouth. Not caring that they have an audience, she throws her arms around his neck and hangs onto him for dear life.

My face scrunches with disgust. I stare at them as they go at it like a pair of cats in heat. I want to rip my eyes away from the disturbing scene but can't. Nausea churns in the pit of my stomach.

What the hell is wrong with these two?

In a way, I understand what Evert is doing. It's like he's trying to get back at me. Or hurt me. Maybe he's still trying to make me jealous.

But Katelyn?

I don't get her behavior at all. It's like she's had a lobotomy. She's not acting like the girl who was once my best friend. The sad thing is, I'm not sure we'll be able to come back from this.

Filled with revulsion, I grab my plate off the counter and head to my bedroom. Just as I pass them, Evert untangles himself from a clinging Katelyn.

He smacks another kiss against her swollen lips. "I'll catch you later."

"Okay," she sighs, staring at him like a lovesick schoolgirl.

Evert doesn't spare me another glance as he heads to the apartment door, closing it behind him. Katelyn stares after him, lost in her own world. Does she even care that we're barely on speaking terms?

Is this how little our friendship means to her?

It's disheartening.

Maybe now that Evert has taken off, Katelyn and I can sit down and have a heart-to-heart. It seems crazy that we could lose our friendship over a jerk like Evert Monroe. But that's exactly what's going to happen if we don't get the situation straightened out.

If Katelyn wants to date Evert, she can have at it, but I don't want anything to do with him. If she were thinking clearly, she'd dump his ass. Although, after the display I just witnessed, that's not going to happen. Katelyn finally has the guy she wants and she's not going to give him up.

Even if it causes a rift in our friendship.

No longer hungry, I return to the kitchen and set the plate on the counter. Katelyn ignores me. It's like I'm not even there. A feeling of hopelessness fills me. I'm not sure if there's any point in talking with her, but I have to try. At least one more time. I don't want to give up on our friendship yet just.

"Do you have time to talk?"

The dreamy expression disappears from Katelyn's face as she glares. I almost flinch at the fierce look she aims in my direction.

Time has not softened her stance toward me one bit.

"I guess," she mutters unenthusiastically.

Needing something to occupy my hands, I grab a bottle of water from the fridge and glance at her. "Do you want anything?"

Katelyn folds her arms across her chest and shakes her head. "No, thanks." Then she moves into the living room and plops down on the chair. "Can we just get this over with?" she snaps, studying her finger-nails. "I've got a lot of reading to get through tonight."

Her callous attitude sends another jolt of pain through me. I'm beginning to doubt if there's anything I can say or do that will change the trajectory of our friendship. We've been through so much together. Maybe that means more to me than it does to her. "Yeah, sure. I'll try to make this as quick as possible."

Indifference is etched across every line of her face. "Great."

How did one stupid boy wedge his way between us? It seems ridiculous. Apparently, solidarity and friendship mean nothing to Katelyn.

I settle on the couch across from her and attempt to gather my scattered thoughts. When she continues to glower like I'm her worst enemy, I shake my head in frustration. An apology had been poised on the tip of my tongue, but her cold-hearted demeanor makes me swallow it down and choose a different route. "Does it bother you at all that we're barely on speaking terms?"

She flicks her gaze at me and shrugs.

"Katelyn, we've been friends for three years." I pause, allowing those words to sink in. "Does that mean anything to you?"

A tiny crack in her armor becomes visible as she bites her lip and glances away.

"Yeah," she mutters, "it does."

My rigidly held shoulders droop as tension slowly leaks from them. "Then talk to me," I plead. "Tell me what's going on. Let's work through this." Honestly, it shouldn't be this difficult.

Her narrowed gaze slices back to mine and anger wells in her voice. "You want to know what's going on?"

I nod. Anything is better than her icing me out.

Even her fury.

"I care about you, Katelyn. You're one of my best friends. I would never do anything to deliberately hurt you." I search her eyes for a spark of our old friendship, but there's nothing. "I hope you realize that."

She snorts. "Just so you know, I asked Evert about what you told me. He said that you were lying. You're jealous that we got together, so you turned everything around on him." Her upper lip curls in disgust and she glares at me like I'm a bug smeared across her windshield. The more she talks, the more her voice escalates. "All Evert was trying to do was warn you about Gray being a manwhore." She rolls her eyes. "Like you didn't already know that. You're the one who kept telling me what a player he was. And now you don't want to hear the truth." She shakes her head. "You're really pathetic, you know that?"

I blink, unable to believe that she's hurtling such hateful words at me. *Who is this girl?* Because I don't know anymore.

"How can you say that?" I thought we were friends. We might be fighting, but still...

You don't speak so cruelly to a person you care about.

Not bothering to answer my question, she sniffs with distain. "I didn't want to say anything, but I totally agree with Evert. Gray is going to use and abuse you." Her voice hardens, becoming razor-sharp. "Just like he did freshman year. He's not a long-term kind of guy. Unless of course, he's cheating on you left and right." She shrugs as if she couldn't give a shit about what happens to me. "Then maybe."

My heart cracks wide open and everything spills out. "Katelyn," I whisper with a dumbfounded expression on my face, "what the hell is wrong with you?"

There's not a drop of remorse in her eyes as she unflinchingly holds my gaze. "Oh, come on! You can't be that stupid! Everyone on campus knows that Gray McNichols is a player." Then she tosses my own words back in my face. "You've always said that Evert is one of the nicest guys you've ever met. He's not the one out screwing every girl who will spread her legs for him." She pauses before taking one final jab at me. "That's *your* boyfriend. Not mine."

I feel like I've been sucker punched.

When I remain silent, she rises to her feet. "Are we done here?"

"Yeah," I wheeze through the pain, "we're done."

All I had been trying to do was protect Katelyn. I didn't want to see Evert hurt her or take advantage of the feelings she had for him. And yet, all they've managed to do is turn everything around on me. Somehow, I've become the bad guy.

I have no idea what will happen between those two, but as far as I'm concerned, they can figure it out for themselves.

I'm done.

With both of them.

# GRAY

"Fuck, dude, that test sucked." Collins scowls as we leave the science building behind. "I might have tanked it."

"It was definitely messed up." There were a few answers that I had to pull out of my ass. Which doesn't bode well for me. Collins, on the other hand, is completely full of shit. He always goes off the deep end after an exam. When he whines about bombing a test, it usually means he pulled off a B. Maybe an A. It's annoying as hell.

Since we're both Forensic Science majors, we usually end up having at least one class together every semester. It's always helpful to have someone to borrow notes from. The test Collins is bitching about is for Inorganic Chem II. Trust me, it's just as difficult as the name implies. Collins isn't looking to play professional hockey after college; he wants to get into forensic entomology.

Yeah…I have no idea what the hell that is either.

"Maybe you shouldn't have been out drinking last night," I remind him. Then again, Collins could show up blackout drunk to an exam and still blow the curve for all of us. He's one smart motherfucker.

"Yeah, well, it had seemed like a good idea at the time," he mutters. "And I thought I had everything down. I've been pulling all-nighters for a week straight and needed some time to chill." He taps the side of his head. "You know, let everything marinate for a while."

"How'd that work out for you?"

"Hopefully better than I think it did," he grumbles, brows beetling together.

"Hong Chow's tests are always brutal." You know it's bad when you walk into an exam and don't remember learning key pieces of the material.

"Let's hope there's a curve," he adds. "That's probably the only thing that will save my ass."

*Yeah, right.*

Collins is so full of shit his eyes are turning brown. He'll end up graduating summa cum laude.

Just as we catch the path that leads across campus, Collins elbows me in the side and jerks his chin toward the grassy knoll. "Uh-oh, looks like there's trouble in paradise." He snorts. "That didn't take long."

I follow his gaze until it lands on Katelyn and Evert. Everything in me tightens.

*Evert fucking Monroe.*

I promised Whitney that I wouldn't kick his ass, but the temptation is strong. Especially after she relayed the latest convo that went down between her and Katelyn.

I don't know what Whitney is going to do. If her relationship with Katelyn doesn't improve, she won't have any choice but to move out. I was totally joking around, trying to yank David's chain, when I mentioned us moving in together second semester, but now...

That's exactly what might happen.

My eyes narrow as I watch the drama unfold. Evert shakes his head and walks away. Eyes filled with tears, Katelyn reaches out and grabs hold of his arm. With an impatient expression on his face, he shakes her loose and leaves her standing on the crowded path.

"And another couple bites the dust," Collins says with a shrug. "This is exactly why I don't do relationships. Chicks are nothing but problems."

I elbow him in the ribs. "That's not true." It wasn't so long ago that I was voicing the same sentiment, so I can't exactly get on him for it.

"Yeah, right," he scoffs. "I don't need that kind of drama. I've got enough going on."

"Like a failed Inorganic Chem test?" I say, trying to needle him.

He points a finger and grins. "Precisely."

From the corner of my eye, I watch Whitney's friend slump onto one of the benches that line the walkway and bury her face in her hands. I'm so tempted to ignore her. Whatever went down with Evert is none of my damn business. More importantly, that girl has been a total bitch to Whitney. If I had my own place, she would already be moved in. That thought gives me pause and I have to shake my head to clear it. This relationship is moving at warp speed.

Collins jostles me in the side, breaking into my thoughts. "You want to grab some grub before we head home? I'm pretty sure we need to make a run to the grocery store. The only thing in the fridge is beer and Gatorade. And I'm trying to stay away from liquid lunches. It messes with my mojo out on the ice."

I chuckle, but my gaze is still pinned to Katelyn.

*I should walk on by.*

*This isn't any of my business.*

*Fuck...*

As much as I don't want to get tangled up in the Evert/Katelyn drama, I can't leave her sitting there, bawling her eyes out. The only reason I'm stopping is because all this BS is affecting my girl. Otherwise, I wouldn't bother. As far as I'm concerned, Katelyn deserves exactly what she gets.

Evert is a complete dick.

And she hasn't turned out to be the friend Whitney thought she was, either.

"Can't," I sigh. "There's something I need to take care of first. I'll meet you back at the house."

Collins shrugs. "Fine, I'm stopping by the Union and picking up a sub. You want one?"

I shake my head. "Nah, but thanks."

"No problem, man. I'll catch you later," he says with a wave of his hand.

As Collins disappears through the crowd, I turn toward Katelyn. My step falters when I get a good look at her face.

Great…she's still crying.

I groan, dreading this even more.

I really hate all this emotional bullshit.

Collins is right. This is one of the reasons I avoided getting involved in a relationship. Who needs this crap?

Except…

Whitney is worth it.

One thing is for certain, that girl is going to owe me big time. And I'm looking forward to payback. Especially if it's in the form of a BJ.

Like a man marching toward certain death, I reluctantly close the distance between us before gingerly settling on the bench. As soon as I do, Katelyn's head whips up and she swipes at the tears streaming down her cheeks.

"Gray?" Her brows slide together. "What are you doing here?"

She looks stunned to see me, and I have to admit, I'm equally surprised to find myself here.

"I saw you and Evert…" my voice trails off as I shrug awkwardly. "I wanted to make sure you were all right."

Her cheeks flood with color as she bites her lip and looks away. "Yeah, I'm okay."

Awesome! Glad to hear it. If it's all good in the hood, then I'm out of here. I've done my good deed for the day. I'm not going to lie, it feels pretty damn amazing to be a caring member of humanity. Maybe I'll catch up with Collins and enjoy that sub.

Just as I rise to my feet, Katelyn says with fresh tears filling her eyes, "Evert broke up with me."

*Aw, hell.*

I fall back onto the bench. Guess I won't be enjoying that sub after all.

"What happened?" I force myself to ask.

She blinks rapidly, trying to wrangle her emotions under control so she doesn't fall apart. Which, trust me, I appreciate. Like most men, when it comes to overly emotional females, I have zero idea how to comfort them.

With shaking fingers, she swipes at a stray tear. "He said that he likes me but isn't interested in having a girlfriend right now." She sniffles loudly. "He wants to keep things casual."

Just like I said...complete dick.

Katelyn loses the battle she's been waging and buries her face in her hands again. Her shoulders shake as she sobs uncontrollably.

I wince, pretty damn sure there's ugly crying going on.

"I feel like such an idiot," she moans between shuddering breaths. "I really liked him."

Ugh.

What the hell am I supposed to do?

I reach out and awkwardly pat her shoulder. "There, there," I say in a soothing voice.

Clearly, I've bitten off more than I can chew. I know nothing about consoling hysterical girls over dickhead boyfriends. Or, in Evert's case, dickheads who were using a girl's roommate to get to the chick he really wanted. I wonder if Whitney would have any qualms about me beating the piss out of him now. I should probably ask. My fists are aching to rearrange his face.

"Maybe I should call Whitney," I mutter. She'll know how to handle this situation far better than me.

Katelyn's head whips up and I congratulate myself on being right about the ugly crying. It's pretty bad.

"No!" She shakes her head vehemently as more wetness leaks from the corners of her eyes. "Please don't call Whitney!" She groans, "I've been so terrible to her."

Brows lowering, I admit grimly, "Yeah, I know."

That comment only makes her cry harder.

"But she's your friend," I add begrudgingly, "and she'll probably forgive you."

Hope enters her red-rimmed eyes as she visibly perks up. "Do you really think so?"

I nod. Whitney has a heart of gold. Especially where her friends are concerned. "Yeah." That being said, I don't want to let her off the hook so easily. "You know that Whitney was only trying to protect you, right? She never meant to hurt you."

Another flush stains Katelyn's cheeks as she stares at her hands. "Yeah," she mumbles, "I realize that now." She falls silent for a beat. "But at the time, I didn't want to hear what she was saying. I wanted it to work out with Evert." She peeks at me from beneath wet lashes. "I had liked him for so long and didn't want anything to ruin it. But I should have listened to Whitney." Her voice wobbles with thick emotion. "She was right about everything. Evert was just using me."

"You need to talk with Whit. She'll understand."

Katelyn nods. "Yeah, okay." A hint of a smile lifts the corners of her lips. "Thanks, Gray. I feel bad for telling Whit that you were a manwhore who would break her heart."

I frown. "She didn't mention that part."

It's funny that being called a player never bothered me before. Now, that's the last thing I want Whitney to think I am.

Her mouth snaps shut, and her eyes widen. "Oh...um, sorry." Before I can say anything else, she jumps to her feet and hitches her backpack over one shoulder. "Thanks again, Gray. I'm going to take your advice and talk to Whitney." She chews her lower lip for a moment before leaning over and pressing a quick kiss against my cheek. Then she takes off, disappearing down the path.

All in all, I think that went better than expected. I lean back and lace my fingers together, resting my head against them.

I suppose if the NHL doesn't work out, I could always becomes a therapist.

Clearly, I've got some serious skills.

# WHITNEY

"*D*id you see the post on Facebook?" Dad asks excitedly.

I can't help but smile at the way his voice bursts with happiness. Any moment and the guy is going to break out into song.

"Yup, I did," I admit, curling up on the couch in the living room of the apartment.

While on vacation in the Virgin Islands, Dad popped the question to Veronica. They posted a cutesy selfie of him holding a sign next to her with the words *she said yes*.

Some of his exuberance fades. "Are you mad that I didn't call right away and tell you?"

"Of course not, Dad. I knew what you were planning to do. And I'm glad it worked out. Are you guys having fun?"

I might have had reservations in the beginning about this relationship, but I don't anymore. It's just going to take some time to get used to this new family dynamic, but I will. Eventually. Veronica is great. Other than my mom, I couldn't have picked a better match for him.

"We're having a fantastic time. The weather's beautiful and the food is amazing," he continues excitedly. "Maybe next summer, the four of us can come back for a visit. You'd love this all-inclusive resort. There's so much to do. They have all these planned activities."

*Next summer...*

*The four of us.*

That's eight months from now. Will Gray and I even be together at that point? For all I know, our relationship could end next week, or a month from now, or when we graduate from school. What's to say we won't break up when Gray gets drafted to the NHL? He's already admitted that he could end up anywhere in the United States.

And I have no idea where I'll be this time next year. I've always dreamed of living on the East Coast. New York. Boston. Or maybe Philadelphia. A big, bustling city with lots of energy and opportunities.

Am I really going to change my plans when we haven't made any promises to each other?

Am I going to blindly follow Gray?

*Would he even want me to?*

"Whitney? Are you there?"

Dad's voice snaps me back to the present.

"Yeah, sorry." I shake my head to clear it of those unwanted thoughts. "A trip to the Virgin Islands sounds like fun."

"It would be nice for you and Ronnie to spend a little quality time together. I think you two will end up discovering that you have a lot in common." There's a beat of silence. "She doesn't have a daughter, and I know she wants to get to know you better."

He doesn't come out and say *and you don't have a mother,* but the words hang in the air nevertheless. I'm sure Veronica and I will get to be friends, but no one will ever take Mom's place. It's just not possible. Needing fresh air, I pad across the living room and open the slider to the balcony.

Once outside, I inhale a lungful of oxygen before slowly releasing it back into the world. Then I drop onto one of the chairs at the tiny café table.

Dad clears his throat. "Actually, the real reason we're thinking about returning next summer is to tie the knot," he admits nervously. "You know, like one of those destination weddings."

My head spins. "Wow, Dad. That's, um…fast."

"When you're my age, you realize there's no point in wasting time. Plus," he says with a chuckle, "now that she's agreed to be my wife, I don't want to give her too much time to change her mind."

I can't tell if he's kidding or not. "You don't really think that would happen, do you?"

"No," he scoffs, "of course not."

"Oh, okay." I swallow down the thick lump that has settled in my throat. "I'm happy for you, Dad. You and Veronica seem good together."

"We are. When we get back to the States, we'll all get together for dinner. Veronica has taken a ton of pictures she wants to show you."

The slider from the living room opens and Katelyn pops her head out. When our gazes catch, she gives me a hesitant smile before raising a hand in tentative greeting.

Not only am I shocked that she's here, but I'm surprised by the gesture. After our last disastrous interaction, Katelyn has gone out of her way to avoid me. And I've given her a wide berth in return. The words she hurtled at me still sting. I'm nowhere near ready to deal with her poisonous tongue again.

It's disheartening to admit that Katelyn and I weren't as good friends as I'd always assumed.

With my attention focused on Katelyn, I say, "That sounds good, Dad."

"All right, buttercup, I'd better get going. We're just about to head down to dinner. I love you," he says just like he always does, and I return the sentiment.

Nausea swirls at the bottom of my belly as I pull the phone away from my ear and set it on the table. "Hey."

"Hi." Katelyn shifts her weight from one foot to the other and cautiously edges her way onto the balcony. She stuffs her hands into the pocket of her hoodie. "Do you have a moment to talk?"

"Sure." Now that I'm taking a good look at her, I can tell she's been crying. Her eyes are red-rimmed and her normally creamy complexion is splotchy. Even though I shouldn't care, I ask, "Is everything okay?"

As soon as the question leaves my lips, her eyes fill with tears.

She shakes her head before pulling out the other chair and dropping down onto it. "Evert said that he wants us to be casual."

What that translates to is that he wants to screw her whenever he feels like it without any kind of commitment.

*What.*

*An.*

*Asshole.*

Unable to hold my gaze, Katelyn glances away and clears her throat. "You were right about him, Whit," she admits quietly. "He was just using me to get to you."

If I thought her admission would bring me any kind of joy or vindication, it doesn't. In fact, it's the opposite. The last thing I wanted was to see my friend get hurt. And right now, she's in pain.

Instead of letting her twist in the wind, I reach out and lay my hand over hers before giving it a gentle squeeze. "I'm sorry. I know how much you liked Evert and wanted to believe in him."

Wetness streaks down her cheeks as she jerks her shoulders. "That's not an excuse for how I treated you." She swipes at the tears that shimmer in her eyes. "I know it doesn't make anything better, but I'm really sorry."

As much as Katelyn wounded me, I'm not sure there's anything she can say or do that will make it better. Evert lied and used her, and she chose to believe him over me, her best friend. As much as I love Katelyn and want us to be in a good place, it's going to take time to rebuild our friendship.

"Thank you for apologizing, but let's just forget about it."

Looking relieved, Katelyn nods and promptly changes the subject. "How's your dad doing?"

Even if things aren't necessarily the same between us, it feels good to clear the air and move on.

"They're in the Virgin Islands right now and he just asked Veronica to marry him. She said yes." My lips tug up at the corners as the conversation I had with Dad replays through my head. "So, I'd say he's doing pretty good."

I pick up my phone and show her the picture on his Facebook page.

Her eyes widen as she stares at the photo of the happy couple. "Wow. That was fast!"

I laugh, unable to resist thinking the same thing. "Yeah, it was. They're talking about getting married this summer."

Life is changing quickly. It's still difficult to imagine Dad married to anyone other than my mom. At least I'll have the rest of this school year to get comfortable with the new arrangement. Hopefully by the time it happens, it won't feel so odd. I should probably be thankful that they didn't get hitched while on the island.

"I can't believe you and Gray will be stepsiblings." A chuckle escapes as she shakes her head. "That is so hot!"

With a groan, I bury my face in my hands. Heat floods my cheeks as I force my gaze to meet hers. "I think the word you meant to say is *weird*. Not *hot*." Some people might think us being related and dating is sexy, but I don't.

It's bizarre.

And kind of creepy.

"I don't know, Whit." She waggles her brows. "I think it's hot as hell."

"No, it's not. My dad is marrying his mom and now Gray and I are dating. That's definitely weird."

My roommate grins, looking very much like the old Katelyn as a little bit of our friendship falls back into place. I'm glad we resolved the issue. This past week has been horrible.

The bright smile fades as she shifts on her chair and yanks her gaze from mine. "I'm sorry for what I said about Gray. He really *is* a good guy."

My eyes widen.

Am I seriously hearing this from her when she was so intent on bashing him a few days ago?

Katelyn shrugs and launches into the story from earlier this afternoon. "He saw that I was upset and came over to see if I was all right. Most guys wouldn't bother." She clears her throat. "After I blubbered all over him, he encouraged me to talk with you and work everything out."

She doesn't have to tell me that Gray is a great guy. I've seen for myself how much he's changed since freshman year, but this surprises even me.

It makes everything churning inside me more difficult to deal with. When it comes down to it, I have no idea what will happen with Gray. It's not like he has a long history of serious relationships under his belt. Maybe after a few months, the novelty of being tied down will wear off.

Under normal circumstances, I wouldn't worry about the future. I'd take this relationship one day at a time and see what comes of it. But our parents are getting married and that changes everything. Gray and I will forever be tied together, and we'll be stuck seeing each other at family gatherings.

I can't believe I'm even thinking along these lines. But...maybe it would be best for everyone involved if Gray and I parted ways while we're still on good terms. At this point, there's no harm and no foul.

Who's to say it would be that way in the future?

As much as I hate the thought of letting Gray go, it seems like the most sensible thing to do, given the circumstances.

# GRAY

*W*ith a frown, I stare at my phone.

Declined.

The call was declined, and Whitney isn't responding to my texts.

What the hell is up with that?

I'll let you in on a little secret. This whole boyfriend thing is harder than it looks.

A ball of unease settles in my gut. Here's what I do know—I'm not about to sit around with a thumb up my ass, trying to figure it out. If there's a problem, I want to hear it straight from Whitney.

So, I do the only thing I can and head over to her place. Just as I reach the lobby door of her building, her roommate exits. Luckily for me, there are no tears in sight.

Halle-fucking-lujah.

"Hey, Katelyn," I call out, catching her attention as I walk toward her, "is Whitney around?"

"Hi." She stops in her tracks as her expression wavers.

Which is definitely odd. After the solid I did for her the other day, we should be lifelong besties.

Apparently, that's not the case.

"Ummm…" She glances nervously toward the apartment building.

"Katelyn," I snap, pulling her attention back to me, "what's going on?" Clearly my instincts are spot-on. There's definitely a problem. And I'm going to damn well figure out what it is. "Why is Whitney avoiding me?"

Her eyes widen, and her mouth forms a perfect little circle. Not giving her the chance to come up with any bullshit excuses, I say, "What have I done to piss her off?"

I've been wracking my brain and can't come up with anything. All this boyfriend business is new to me, but I'm trying my best. That doesn't mean I'm not going to fuck up every now and then. Whitney needs to cut me some slack.

Katelyn's gaze skitters away as she mumbles, "You didn't do anything wrong, Gray."

And yet my girlfriend won't speak to me. So that doesn't really help.

"Okay...then tell me why Whitney is avoiding me."

Katelyn gnaws on her bottom lip for a moment before straightening her shoulders. Then she stalks to the building and keys in the entry code before holding open the door. She waves me in with a flourish and a tentative smile. "You need to talk with Whit."

"Excellent idea," I agree. *Finally*...something that makes sense. "Thanks."

It only takes a moment for me to jog up the stairs and arrive at her apartment. I give the door a few raps and wait impatiently for an answer. From the other side, I hear Whitney pad to the door before it's yanked open.

"Did you forget—" the question dies a quick death on her lips as her eyes widen. "Gray," she squeaks, "what are you doing here?"

Her less-than-thrilled greeting only confirms my suspicions and I fold my arms across my chest. "I came to see you, obviously."

"Oh." She drops her gaze, staring at her pink painted toenails. "You should have texted first."

Disbelief bubbles up in my throat.

*Is this girl serious?*

243

"I *have* texted and called, but you aren't responding." I pause for a beat and ask the question foremost in my mind. "Why is that?"

My gaze licks over her. Even though I'm unsure where we stand with one another, I have to fight the urge to drag her into my arms and hold her close. This relationship might be new, but the feelings I have for her are real.

A guilty flush blooms in her cheeks. "Ummm..."

Instead of giving me an explanation for the past twenty-four hours of stereo silence, she remains tight-lipped. After a moment of her barring the door, her shoulders slump and she steps aside. "You should probably come in, so we can talk."

Maybe I don't know my ass from a hole in the ground when it comes to relationships, but I realize that her saying we need to talk isn't a good sign. My heart thumps painfully as I follow Whitney into the living room. She takes a seat on the chair and I have no other choice but to settle on the couch across from her.

Unable to hold back any longer, the questions burst free. "What's going on, Whitney? You're not answering my texts or calls. Why are you freezing me out?"

The pit sitting at the bottom of my gut doubles in size with that startling realization.

*She's freezing me out.*

Instead of meeting my stare head-on, Whitney looks everywhere but at me.

Impatiently, I lean forward, resting my elbows on my knees. It feels as if my entire body is straining to get closer to her.

It takes effort to keep the panic from my voice. "Just be straight with me about what's going on."

A puff of air escapes from her mouth as she shakes her head and blurts, "I don't think we should see each other anymore."

My heart stutters. I don't think I've ever felt more blindsided. Not even in high school, when I made the mistake of skating with my head down and a big motherfucker from the other team trucked into me, laying me out flat on the ice.

"You…want to break up?" I ask slowly. My hand rises to my chest as I clarify, "With me?"

Her gaze slides reluctantly to mine. Her face is full of misery as she gives a sharp nod. "Yeah."

In the stifling silence of the living room, that one word sounds like a gunshot.

None of this makes a damn bit of sense. A couple of days ago, we were fine. What happened to change that?

My brows slam together as I shake my head. "Explain to me why you want to break up, because I don't understand."

She fidgets on the chair. "My dad proposed to your mom and she said yes." Whitney pauses, searching my eyes. When I remain silent, she snaps, "They're getting married, Gray! Probably this summer."

Ummm, okay. This isn't exactly a surprise. We both knew this was coming down the pike. So I don't understand why it's such a big freaking deal now that it's actually occurred.

"Yeah, that's usually what happens when a couple gets engaged," I say slowly, spreading my palms out in front of me. "They plan a wedding and get hitched."

Whitney squeezes her eyes tightly shut and whispers, "I know… but it's happening. They're really going to do it."

This entire conversation is confusing as shit. "Yup, they are." I shrug. "So what?" That can't be the reason Whitney has been avoiding me. Why would it matter? Hell, they were dating before we were.

"Our parents are going to be legally bound for the rest of their lives." She shakes her head. "Don't you get that?"

I drag a hand over my face in frustration as laughter falls from my lips. Is there anything funny about this situation? Hell, no. All we're doing is talking in circles and getting nowhere fast. "Apparently, I don't. I think you need to do a better job of explaining it to me."

Making an exasperated noise in her throat, Whitney throws her hands up. "Where do you see our relationship going?"

"I don't know," I mutter with a shrug. "It's too early to tell." But I have an idea of what I want to happen. Maybe I'm not ready to verbalize it just yet, but I'd like to see us stay together for the long haul.

A triumphant expression settles on her face as she stabs a finger at me. "Exactly!"

My brows snap together.

*Exactly what?*

This has to be one of the most maddening conversations I've ever experienced. I plow both hands through my hair in an attempt to hang on to the last of my patience. Losing it isn't going to help the situation. It'll only make matters worse. "Whitney," I growl, "you're not making a damn bit of sense!"

She huffs out a breath like I'm the one who's being dense. "Hypothetically, let's just say that we date for the rest of senior year, okay?"

I nod, liking the sound of that.

"And," she continues, "you get drafted. At this point, it could be anywhere. Boston, Minnesota, or Las Vegas."

She's right about that. I have no idea where I'm going or who I'll be playing for. So I remain silent, waiting to see where Whitney is going with this before I try to combat it.

"You know what happens then?"

No. But I have a feeling she's going to tell me.

"We break up," she says quietly as sadness fills her eyes. "Our parents will be together, and we'll be stuck having to see each other for the rest of our lives. What if one of us has hurt feelings? No matter what anyone says, breakups are never amicable."

I narrow my eyes as the realization of what she's doing slams me upside the head. "So...you think we should cut this off now before it goes any further?"

Whitney glances away, but not before I glimpse the wetness shining in her eyes. "Don't you think that's the smartest thing to do? I don't want to end up hating you, Gray. I'd rather end things now while there's no hurt feelings. Thanks to our parents, we're always going to be in each other's lives. I don't want it to be awkward when we have to see each other."

I can only stare at her in astonishment. "Please tell me you're not being serious."

She blinks with uncertainty. "Of course I am."

I shake my head and roar, *"That has to be one of the dumbest things I've ever heard in my life!"*

Whitney's eyes widen, and her mouth drops open. *"What?"*

"You heard me! Breaking up with me for no reason other than our parents getting married is just plain stupid!" I pause, trying to wrestle my emotions back under control. "And more than that, your logic is flawed."

She works her jaw a few times before slamming it shut. Her eyes narrow. "How so?"

"Because," I growl, hands clenching into fists, "there isn't going to be anything amicable about us breaking up, sweetheart. Not now or ever."

Her tongue darts out to moisten her lips as she stares owlishly at me. I congratulate myself on finally being able to render Whitney Winters speechless. Guess there really is a first time for everything.

"But—"

I shake my head and rise to my feet, walking around the coffee table. Her wide eyes track my every movement. When I hunker down in front of her and clasp both of her hands in my own, she draws in a sharp breath.

"Do you honestly think I could walk away from you?" What I feel for Whitney is unlike anything I've ever experienced before.

She glances away and shrugs.

"Then let me make it perfectly clear." I pause as her eyes slide back to mine. "You're the one I want to be with. *The only one.*" I can't imagine there ever being another girl beside Whitney. In a short amount of time, she's become my everything.

*Amicable, my ass.*

If we end up parting ways, it won't be on good terms.

As if arriving at the same conclusion, Whitney's shoulders slump. Silently, she leans forward until she can rest her forehead against my shoulder.

I wrap my arms around her, tugging her body against mine as I pick her up and flip us around so that she's curled up on my lap. Her face is burrowed against my neck as her warm breath drifts across my flesh, and it's the best damn feeling in the world.

One I'll never grow tired of.

"It took me long enough to win you over," I tell her. "You've got a screw loose if you think I'm going to walk away without a fight."

"But our parents..." she mumbles halfheartedly against my neck.

"Neither of them give a shit if we're together." I snort. "Hell, my mother already loves you."

She chuckles as her body melts against mine. "I hope you realize that my father doesn't feel the same way about you."

A smile tugs at the edges of my lips. Yeah, I'm aware of David's feelings. "Then I'll just have to win him over by showing him how much his daughter means to me."

Whitney lifts her face from my shoulder to meet my gaze. "Is that really what you want, Gray?" A hopeful light ignites in her eyes. "For us to be together?"

Whitney is one of the smartest people I know, but right now she's being as thick as a two-by-four.

"It's the only thing I want." I lean in and press a kiss against her lips. "You...you're what matters most to me. As long as we're good, everything else will work itself out."

Her lips feather over mine. "Okay."

I pull back, needing her to understand one more thing. "The next time you try shutting me out without telling me what's going on, you're going to end up with your ass spanked." I search her eyes as her face floods with color and her mouth falls open. "Got it?" When she remains silent, I nip her bottom lip between my teeth and tug it gently. Then I release it, giving her a wicked grin that's full of promise. "And trust me, sweetheart, I'll enjoy every second of it."

"You wouldn't dare," she breathes, looking surprisingly excited by the prospect.

I arch a brow. "Try me."

"Maybe I will." This time, she's the one reaching up, taking my lip between her teeth and giving it a sexy pull.

My cock stiffens, and I groan. The past twenty-four hours have been a real killer. All I want to do is bury myself deep inside her sweet pussy. And maybe spank her ass a few times for putting me through the wringer for no damn reason.

If the expression on Whitney's face is any indication, she understands that we're in this for the long haul.

This girl right here…she's mine.

*She will always be mine.*

And nothing is ever going to change that.

# EPILOGUE

## GRAY

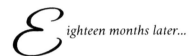 *ighteen months later...*

MY BREATH GETS CLOGGED in my lungs as I catch my first glimpse of Whitney as she pauses on the beach.

Fuck…she looks so beautiful, like a goddamn angel. I couldn't rip my gaze away if I tried.

Her long dark hair has been swept up to the top of her head. A few loose tendrils curl around her face. I've never known Whitney to wear much makeup, but it's been professionally applied for the occasion. As much as I wanted to keep her ass in bed, she spent all morning getting pampered at the spa.

Her gaze locks on mine as she proceeds down the makeshift aisle, each step bringing her closer to where I stand. Everyone else fades to the background until she's all I'm cognizant of. It's always like that with her. This girl is my fucking world. I have no idea how I lived so long without her by my side.

When her lips lift, I return the smile, giving her a wink as she closes the distance that separates us. As beautiful as she looks in the strapless swishy dress she's wearing, I can't wait to get her out of it.

Hell, maybe we can sneak off during the reception so I can get my hands on her.

It's almost like I can see our future playing out before my eyes. Instead of scaring the shit out of me, it only makes me more impatient to make her mine.

Wait just a minute...

Did you think that we were the ones tying the knot here?

*Fuck no!*

I'm nowhere near ready for that. And neither is Whitney.

David and *Ronnie*—yeah, I don't think I'll ever get used to that one —are getting hitched in the Virgin Islands. Friends and family have been invited for a destination wedding.

You should see the shocked expressions when they realize I'm dating my stepsister. It makes me laugh every damn time. Whitney doesn't seem to find it nearly as funny as I do.

Once Whitney makes it down the aisle, the music changes and Mom begins her procession with Grandpa Joe. Grandma Alice is parked in the first row. She's been taking slugs of bourbon from a silver flask she keeps hidden in her purse. I'm not sure who she thinks she's fooling. We all know it's there. Hell, if you've made it to eighty-four years old and want to have a few shots during the day, have at it.

As far as I'm concerned, you've earned it.

Aunt Marybeth, Mom's sister, doesn't feel the same way and keeps shooting Grandma exasperated looks when she takes a little nip. Alex, my cousin, is sitting next to his mom. I've noticed that he keeps staring at my girl.

Yeah, that's a no-go.

Obviously, I'm going to have to set him straight on that one.

*Get your own damn girl, buddy. This one is taken.*

Mom looks beautiful in a simple, blush-colored gown. More than that, she looks over-the-moon-happy. Her face is beaming, and she hasn't taken her eyes off David.

The officiant gives his spiel, and, before you know it, the happy couple is pronounced husband and wife. They kiss, and everyone cheers.

After that, the party moves to the open-air restaurant on the beach. There's dinner and dancing to cheesy eighties music. I keep Whitney by my side the entire time. She looks so fucking hot. I don't want my cousin getting any more ideas. I give him a sharp look as I wrap my arms around Whitney.

*Yeah, asshole, I see you. Keep those eyeballs to yourself before you lose them.*

I glance around the reception. Everyone's laughing, drinking, and having fun. Which means that this is the perfect opportunity for us to slip away unnoticed. I've had to share Whitney with our families since we arrived on the island—I need a little alone time with her.

I grab Whitney's hand and tow her toward the door. She stumbles after me on bare feet.

"Where are we going?" she asks, her voice sounding light and happy. I know she's had a few glasses of champagne this evening.

"You'll see."

By now, night has fallen, and the stars are out in full force. It reminds me of the night I surprised her with tickets to the concert and then afterward, staring up at the sky from the bed of my pickup.

That date was a game changer for me.

It's when I started falling in love with Whitney. Now, I'm so deeply entrenched that I don't ever want to be set free. I can't imagine a life without her in it.

We hit the sand and leave the boardwalk behind us. A silvery moon hangs heavily in the sky, sending cascades of light over the ocean. The rhythmic sound of the waves rolling onto the beach fills my ears.

This is the most perfect night, and she's the only person I can imagine sharing it with. When we're a few feet from the water, I drop down and pull Whitney onto my lap. My arms slip around her waist as I hold her close. A few strands of her hair whip in the wind, sliding across my cheek. Whitney snuggles against me as if she's just as content as I am.

I've worked for almost a decade to make it to the pros. Until I met her, I couldn't imagine anything ever meaning more to me than achieving that goal.

Last spring, I was drafted to the Detroit Red Wings.

Yeah…they're rivals with the Chicago Blackhawks, but you know what? I don't give a damn. I'm playing in the NHL. Every fucking day I get to live my dream. As awesome as it was to hear my name called during the draft, having Whitney by my side is what made it special.

After graduation, she came to Detroit and helped me pick out an apartment. I asked if she would be willing to relocate and move in with me. She agreed and found a consulting job working for a finance company in the suburbs. We've been shacked up ever since.

My life is pretty fucking sweet right now. There's not a damned thing I would change about it. And that has everything to do with the woman in my arms.

Whitney makes me a better man.

I nuzzle her neck as the warm wind sweeps over us. "You happy, baby?"

She turns her face toward mine and smiles. I see the contentment shining in her eyes. It's an amazing feeling to know that I have everything to do with it.

"Yeah, I am. Today was perfect, don't you think?"

I nod. "It was. And you were gorgeous."

"You didn't look so shabby yourself."

"I'll take that as a compliment."

She presses her lips against mine and whispers, "I love you."

"I love you, too." So freaking much that it hurts my heart. Maybe I'm rushing things, but I don't give a shit. I slip a hand inside my khakis and pull out the ring I picked out a month ago.

She gasps as I slip it on her finger. "Gray…what is this?"

"I want you to be my wife."

For a long moment, she stares at the emerald and diamond ring I've placed on her finger. Her eyes shimmer with unshed tears. I have no idea what her silence means, but a large, uncomfortable stone settles in my gut.

All right...maybe I jumped the gun by asking her to marry me so soon.

Maybe I should have waited until Christmas and gotten a few more months under my belt. Shit. How am I supposed to backtrack from this without looking like a complete fucko? We haven't talked a whole lot about getting married. I just assumed she'd be down with it. But from the look on her face and the fact that she hasn't said a word, I think I made a colossal ass out of myself. "Ummm, we don't have to—"

Whitney twists in my arms before placing her fingers against my mouth. "Shush."

My eyes widen.

She shakes her head and presses her lips together. More wetness gathers in her eyes until it overflows, sliding down her cheeks. "Yes. I'll marry you."

The air rushes from my lungs in relief. For a moment there, I wasn't sure how this was going to play out. "You will?"

She chuckles, and her gaze flicks from my eyes to the ring adorning her finger. "How could you think otherwise?" Her hands drift to each side of my face. "I love you so much. And more than anything, I want to be your wife. I want to spend the rest of my life with you."

There's a fierceness to her words that brings a thick lump of emotion to my throat that is impossible to swallow.

*Goddamn it...*

I clear my throat. "I love you too, baby. Forever and always."

She grins and presses her lips against mine. "Forever and always."

"So...what do you say we go back to the room and enjoy our hot tub and private pool?"

She nods before holding out her hand and admiring the way the moonlight catches the polished stones. "Yeah, I think a little naked time is warranted."

Just the thought of getting her out of that dress makes my cock stiffen. I jump to my feet with Whitney cradled against my chest. She squeals and twines her arms around my neck as I carry her down the beach.

And who knows?

Maybe next summer we'll be back for a wedding of our own.

For now, I'm going to enjoy making sweet love to my fiancée. The only thing she's going to be wearing for the rest of the night is the massive rock on her finger.

So, if you don't hear from us for a couple of days, don't get your panties in a twist. And don't, for the love of God, come banging on our door. 'Cause we won't be answering.

Now, go on…get the hell out of here and let us celebrate in private.


The End

# JUST FRIENDS

## REED

*W*ith a sigh, I collapse onto the couch in the living room of the house I share with a couple of guys from the hockey team and pop open a can of cold beer, guzzling down half of it in one thirsty swig.

Goddamn, but that hits the spot.

Know what else would hit the spot?

Yeah, you do.

It's the second week of September, and Coach Richards has us skating two-a-days, lifting weights, and running five miles for extra cardio.

As if we need it.

Oh…and he added yoga to this year's regimen.

Fucking yoga.

Can you believe that shit?

Let me be perfectly clear—I'm not into contorting my body into a pretzel and breathing deeply from my diaphragm. Sure, I get it. He wants us to work on our flexibility. And I'll do it, but that doesn't mean I have to like it.

Coach R is a total masochist.

Or is it sadist?

I can never keep those two straight.

No matter. Whatever kind of *ist* he is, the man thoroughly enjoys working our asses over. The only amusement I get is from listening to all the incoming freshmen piss and moan about what a tough schedule we have.

*Welcome to Division I hockey, boys. Buckle up, it's going to be a bumpy ride.*

Pile on fifteen credit hours and I don't have time for much else.

"Reed, baby, I've been waiting all night for you to return."

A curvy female drops onto my lap like an angel falling from heaven before she twines her slender arms around my neck and pulls me close.

I stand corrected. There's always time for *that*.

Hell, half the time, *that's* what gets me through the grind. Sex is an amazing stress reliever, and don't let anyone tell you differently. I'm way more chill after I've blown my load. And if I'm fortunate enough to do it twice in one night, then it's like I've slipped into a damn coma.

Pure bliss, baby.

Luckily for us, the Red Devils hockey team has its fair share of puck bunnies on campus who are always willing to provide some much-needed stress relief on a regular basis. God bless every last one of those ladies. They have no idea how much their *team spirit* is appreciated.

That being said, there are always exceptions to the rule.

And the girl currently cozied up on my lap is exactly that.

Megan thrusts out her lower lip in a sexy pout. "How is it possible that we've never hooked up before?"

The answer is simple. I go to great lengths to avoid her like a particularly nasty case of crabs.

She flutters her mascara-laden lashes and tilts her head. Her voice becomes lispy and toddler-like as she twirls a dark curl around her finger. "Don't you think I'm pretty?"

*Pretty?*

No, Megan is flat-out gorgeous.

Her long, black hair is as shiny as a crow's wing as it floats around her shoulders in soft waves. She has dark eyes that are tipped at the corners, giving her an exotic look. And her skin is sun-kissed all year round. And if that weren't enough to have any guy giving her a full-on salute, she's also got gravity-defying tits and a nice round ass.

Have I imagined fucking her from behind and smacking that bubble butt a few times before blowing my wad?

You bet Megan's perfectly round ass I have. The girl is a walking wet dream.

And from what the guys on the team tell me (because they're a bunch of loudmouth assholes who like to brag), she can suck a dick like nobody's business. That being said, I won't be finding that out firsthand anytime soon.

I've made it a point to steer clear of Megan because every time I look at her, I see Emerson.

And imagining that I'm nailing my best friend is a definite no-no.

When I don't immediately respond, Megan grinds her bubble butt against my junk—which is something I really don't need, because just the thought of Emerson alone is enough to have me popping wood.

It's a messed-up situation.

One that Em is blissfully unaware of. Which is exactly the way it needs to stay. She can't find out that I've got the hots for her. Emerson Shaw is one of the first friends I made when Mom and I moved to Lakefield the summer before freshman year of high school. And we've been tight ever since.

While I enjoy having a casual, friends-with-benefits relationship with a number of girls on campus, I've never considered sleeping with Em.

Okay, maybe I've *considered* having sex with her. It would be hard not to imagine stripping her naked and getting jiggy with a girl who looks like that, but I've never done anything about it.

I've screwed too many women not to know that getting naked changes a relationship. And I like Em way too much to risk sleeping with her. She's the one person who has always had my back. And let's face it, I can be a hell of a lot more honest with her than my teammates.

Can you imagine me baring my soul to those assholes?

*Exactly.* I'd never hear the end of it.

My friendship with Emerson also gives me all this insight into the female psyche that I wouldn't otherwise be privy to. It's like taking a peek behind the magic curtain. I'm not willing to throw that away when there are plenty of random chicks I can get my rocks off with.

Moral of the story? Friends are a lot harder to come by than hookups.

"Reed?" Megan nips my lower lip between her sharp teeth before giving it a gentle tug and releasing it.

I blink back to the girl wriggling around on my lap. "Yeah?"

Her hands flutter to my shoulders before settling on them. "You're so tense."

Damn right I am. All I can think about is Emerson, and that's all kinds of wrong.

"Let's go upstairs." Her tongue darts out to moisten her lips as she whispers, "I know *exactly* what will fix that."

If any other girl were making the offer, I'd already be dragging her up the staircase to my bedroom. But that's not going to happen with Megan.

I just can't do it. Maybe I'm not *technically* doing anything wrong, but it still feels like I'm breaking some kind of friendship rule. Emerson may not realize I'm thinking about her like that, but I do.

And that's all that matters.

Guess I'll have to find a different girl to get busy with. Preferably a flat-chested blonde with big blue eyes who doesn't resemble Em. Or maybe a redhead, just to mix things up a bit.

Megan's eyes light up when I set my beer down and wrap my hands around her waist, until I carefully remove her from my lap. "Sorry, sweetheart. I've got homework to finish up for tomorrow." I tack on the lie to soften the blow. "Maybe another time?"

Her face falls. "Sure, no problem."

Before she can pin me down on a time and place, I beat a hasty retreat from the living room and head upstairs. Once I've taken refuge in my room, I fire off a text to one of my go-to girls.

Fifteen minutes later, my booty-call for the evening strolls through the door.

Know what I like most about Candace?

The girl gets right down to business. There's no need for small talk, and that I can appreciate. I'm in the mood to fuck, not debate world politics or climate change.

The door hasn't even closed and Candace is already shedding her clothes. Since she hasn't bothered with a bra, her titties bounce free as soon as her shirt is discarded. Her nips stiffen right up when the cool air hits them.

It's a beautiful sight to behold.

Except...

Nothing stirs south of the border. Not like it did when I was thinking about a certain someone downstairs who shall remain nameless. But I'm not concerned. I just need to harness my mental capabilities and focus on the task at hand. Which is getting my dick to work properly.

I yank off my T-shirt and toss it to the floor as Candace flicks open the button of her teeny-tiny shorts before unzipping them. With her gaze locked on mine, she shimmies out of them.

And wouldn't you know it...

No panties in sight.

Just a gloriously bare pussy.

Works for me.

Well, that's what *normally* works for me.

At the moment, limp dick-itis has set in.

Once Candace has stripped down to her birthday suit, she struts her sexy stuff toward the bed where I've made myself comfortable. Her eyelids lower as a knowing smirk curves her red-slicked lips. I rake my gaze over her toned body.

The girl is absolutely perfect.

"I've missed you." She crawls across the mattress until her hands are resting against my bare chest. "I'm glad you texted."

She says that now, but it probably won't be the case when she gets her hands on my junk.

What the hell is wrong with me?

I thought this kind of thing only happened to older dudes. I'm way too young for Viagra. I've seen first-hand how that shit can mess you up.

As a joke last year, one of the jackasses on my team got his hands on a couple of those little blue pills and slipped them to one of the freshman players. The poor guy was sporting wood for days. Unfortunately, a trip to the emergency room became necessary. When Coach R was apprised of the situation, he reamed our asses good and threatened to bench the entire team for the season. We skated suicides until our legs practically fell off.

No, thank you.

Candy trails her purple-tipped fingernails down my chest before pushing me against the mattress and straddling my torso. Then she leans over and licks a wet trail down my body until reaching the waistband of my athletic shorts. This encounter is going to nosedive real quick if I can't get it up in record speed. Not knowing what else to do, I squeeze my eyes tight as an unwanted image of Emerson pops into my head.

Dark hair, lush curves, bright smile.

Candace chuckles as she pulls my hard length from my boxer briefs like it's a much-anticipated Christmas gift. "There's my big boy!"

I groan.

I am *so* screwed.

Want to read more? Check out Just Friends!

# KING OF CAMPUS

*Ladies, and a few guys as well, ;) keep those Roan King sightings pouring in. Especially the ones of him at football practice. Hot, sweaty, with an extra shot of gorgeous is exactly how I take my Roan King. Don't mind me while I type away with one hand... KingOfCampus.com*

"*H*oney," I holler at the top of my lungs before kicking the door shut, "*I'mmmm home!*"

Those words are met with a loud shriek as Lexie flies around the corner before hurtling her small curvy body at me. I'm given roughly two seconds to drop my bags in anticipation of impact. She's lucky I have fairly decent—

The breath gets knocked out of me as we both go crashing to the floor.

Apparently, reflexes are no match when that much force and weight are careening toward you at the speed of light. Physics, I'm guessing, is exactly how I end up sprawled on my back with my best friend and roommate spread out on top of me in our brand-spanking-new apartment. There's a completely manic light filling her big brown eyes. Matching the look, I can't help but beam up at her because it is so freaking good to see her gorgeous face.

It's been precisely fifteen months since we've been in the same room together. Actually, it's been fifteen months since we've been on the same continent. I spent my sophomore year of college studying abroad in Paris.

Needless to say, it was as amazing and spectacular as you'd imagine it would be. Even thinking about it leaves me with a tiny pang of nostalgia for the life I'd left behind.

"Damn, now that's hot! Can I snap a shot for my wallpaper?"

We turn to stare at the tall, good looking male grinning...or maybe the correct term would be—*leering* down at us. His eyes slide oh-so-slowly over our entwined bodies as if he's trying to singe this moment into his memory for all eternity. But it's not in a pervy way...what the heck am I saying? Of course, it's in a pervy way. Which is precisely when I realize that my dear friend, Lexie, seems to be missing the lower half of her outfit.

Yep...she's only wearing panties.

She smothers a giggle before clearing her throat. Rather impressively, her voice whips out in a perfect imitation of a mother scolding her three-year-old toddler. "You damn well better not snap a picture or you won't be seeing this ass for a very long time." To emphasize this point, she gives it a little shake and her boyfriend groans in response.

*"Please?"* There's a whole lot of whine filling his deep masculine voice. Which is kind of hilarious because he's well over six feet tall and is seriously broad in the chest and shoulders. This one is definitely all man. Lexie, of course, filled me in via Facetime on the football playing boyfriend she acquired about seven months ago. Needless to say, she wasn't exaggerating.

He's pretty damn hot.

If you're into big and muscly.

Which I'm not going to lie... I am.

"The mental snapshot you're burning into your brain will have to suffice."

Folding his muscular arms in front of an equally solid looking chest, he grumbles under his breath, "You always have to be such a hard ass."

Lexie gives me a little wink. "You wouldn't have it any other way, babe."

"True," he sighs in agreement, "very true."

Since Lexie isn't showing any indication of removing herself from my person anytime soon, I'm forced to point out the obvious. "You might want to get off me before your boyfriend has an embarrassing moment in his shorts."

I'm joking, of course.

Sort of.

"You don't have to get off on my account," he quickly chimes in as he continues to ogle us.

Lexie rolls her eyes at me.

"Have I mentioned just how hot you look in that thong?" His voice sounds all heated up and I'm seriously considering shoving Lexie off me before something unfortunate, not to mention awkward, happens and I'm no longer able to look this dude in the eyes again.

"Jeez, Lex, did you have to molest me while only wearing a thong?" No wonder her boyfriend is all but sporting a woody over there.

"Be happy you didn't arrive ten minutes later, I wouldn't be wearing anything at all."

I shake my head to loosen that mental image from my brain. "That wasn't something I needed to know."

Continuing to grin, Lexie smacks my lips with a big wet sloppy kiss. "Goddamn but I missed you, Ivy." Then she does her damnedest to squeeze the very life out of me before rolling gracefully to her side.

"I'm glad to be back, too." As the words automatically spill from my mouth, I realize that I don't necessarily mean them. There's a large part of me that wishes I were still living my life in Paris. With an ocean between me and my dad, I didn't have to dwell on him and the new family he created for himself so quickly after Mom died.

Dad's life carried on while mine fell apart. Even though it's been five years since she died, the ache still feels painfully tender.

Returning to Barnett means that I no longer have an excuse not to visit them.

Shaking those thoughts away, I realize I'm still sprawled on the carpeted floor. I blink my eyes a few times as a handsome face peers down at me before crinkling into a large friendly smile. I don't bother hoisting myself up just yet. Instead, I say in my most formal tone, "Mr. Sullivan, I presume."

His grin intensifies, making him appear even more striking than I'd originally thought. Lexie had gushed about how gorgeous her new guy was. And it's not like I didn't believe her, but it's obvious she wasn't exaggerating.

Like at all.

Because Dylan Sullivan is seriously hot.

Golden blond hair, deep brown eyes, sculpted jaw, and athletic body.

According to Lexie, he treats her like a total princess. Which is exactly how it should be. Lexie deserves someone who appreciates how smart, loyal, and gorgeous she is. She's a damn good friend and I'm lucky to have her in my life.

"The one and only," he beams in response, throwing a flirty wink in for good measure.

Oh, this guy is totally dangerous.

Could they be more perfectly suited to one another?

I absolutely love it.

"Umm, isn't your father Dylan Sullivan the first?"

He shrugs his broad shoulders. Self admittedly, I'm kind of a shoulder and arm girl myself. And Dylan Sullivan certainly has nicely chiseled ones.

"Shhh, you're ruining the moment, babe."

That being said, Dylan offers me a hand, which I grab hold of, before being hauled off the floor and set back onto my sandaled feet. I dust my backside off before my gaze slides to Lexie. The unexpected glassy sheen of tears shining in her big brown eyes has my own widening in confusion.

"Lex, why are you—"

I don't get a chance to wrap my lips around the last word before she's hurtling herself in my direction. Her arms slip around my body before tugging me close.

"I missed you, Ivy-girl," she whispers fiercely against my ear, "so damn much! Fifteen months is a long time to stay away. Don't ever leave me like that again."

I'm not normally an emotional person, but her heartfelt words have me choking up and I squeeze her to me.

She pulls back to search my eyes before admitting quietly, "I was afraid you might decide to stay over there."

That just goes to show you how well Lexie knows me. What I don't mention is that I tried my damnedest to make that happen. To finish out college, find a permanent place to live, a dance gig, all so I could postpone coming home indefinitely. Being back here, even though this is a new apartment, still reminds me that my mom is dead, and my dad has moved on and I no longer have a home to return to.

Not one that feels like home used to feel.

"I'm just so glad you're finally back."

"Me, too," I whisper as hot licks of emotion prick the back of my eyes. I hug her tightly one last time before releasing her.

Lexie and I have been best friends since fourth grade when her family moved in down the block from mine. We made it through middle and high school with our friendship intact and decided to apply at some of the same colleges so we could room together. Luckily, Barnett was on both of our short lists. It has a highly regarded fashion design program for Lexie and a kickass dance program for me.

There's absolutely no one in this world I can count on like Lexie Abbott. I'm actually a little ashamed of myself for failing to remember that. In trying to escape all the painful memories, I forgot about the good stuff, too.

Lexie backs up until she's standing directly in front of Dylan. As soon as she's close enough, he wraps those huge arms around her before pulling her flush against the front of his body. Looking ridiculously contented, he settles his chin on top of her head like he's done it a hundred times before.

Like it's the most natural thing in the world.

I can't help but feel thrilled that Lexie has found someone who appreciates the amazing woman she's grown into.

Unwilling to get anymore sappy than I already have, I shake my head. "Do you two come with barf bags? I've only been here for ten minutes and you're already making me sick to my stomach."

They both flash big cheesy grins at me. I want to roll my eyes before sticking my finger down my throat like I'm going to puke. "I suppose you're going to be practically living here with us?" Yep, I can already see how this will go. Dylan will be our unofficial apartment mascot.

With big innocent eyes, she says, "Didn't I mention that Dylan lives in the apartment next to us with two guys from the football team?"

"Nope," I shake my head, "you definitely did not mention that. I guess that makes things convenient."

"Totally convenient," Dylan adds with a sly grin aimed in my direction.

This time, I actually roll my eyes. "So which room is mine?"

In her exuberance, Lexie all but jumps out of Dylan's arms before leading me down a short hallway. As I trail after her, I'm reminded that she's only wearing a thong.

I mean, sure, she has a great ass but still...

"Er, maybe you should put your shorts back on before you give me the grand tour." Out of the corner of my eye, I see Dylan open his mouth. My narrowed gaze slices to his. "Don't even say it," I warn.

Biting her lip, Lexie stifles another laugh before dashing into her bedroom. In twenty seconds flat she rejoins us sporting tiny white shorts. Then she leads the way into a sunny little room before doing her best auto show model imitation as she gestures with wide sweeping movements to all the wonderful amenities my room has to offer.

She points toward the two large windows lining the wall. "Look at all the gorgeous sunlight that pours in!" Then she throws open the bi-fold closet doors. "And a humongous closet for all the clothes you brought back from Paris." Her arms drop to her sides as she swivels toward me. Her auto show model imitation is forgotten in lieu of possible new stylish European clothing. "You *did* bring me back some clothes, right?"

For a moment, my eyes travel around the room, taking everything in. It's not huge by any means but after living in Paris, it sure feels like it is. I'm used to about a third of the space. So this feels pretty damn luxurious. I can't imagine what I'm going to do with all this space to myself. Then my eyes fall to the double sized mattress shoved up against the far wall and my heart actually swells with unfettered joy.

Oh my god, it's so big! I've been sleeping on a twin bed for the last fifteen months. I literally can't wait to spread out on that huge mattress. Maybe roll around a bit. Make some snow angels...minus the snow. Already I'm looking forward to hitting the sheets tonight.

I spent a little more than eight hours on a plane with a two-hour layover in Amsterdam. And France is six hours ahead of us. So, I'd like nothing more than to fall into bed for a nice long nap.

When I don't respond, a thread of worry weaves its way through her voice. "Ivy?" Her concerned tone snaps me right out of my thoughts.

"Of course I did," I say. "There's a short, thigh length pleated skirt, two hand woven scarves, one cashmere sweater, a gorgeous black knit top and these creamy trouser pants that your ass will thank me for."

If watching Lexie sprawled out on top of me, wearing nothing more than a lacy little thong and a tank top is Dylan's idea of a wet dream, hearing about all the beautiful clothes I brought back from Paris is hers. We're talking flushed cheeks and dilated eyes.

And yes, it's entirely possible Lexie could have an embarrassing moment in her shorts. Although I hope not.

"Oh, I can't wait to see them," she squeals in delight, practically jumping up and down with unbridled enthusiasm.

Fashion design is Lexie's life. She was a budding fashionista way back in middle school before I ever cared about what top went with what bottoms. Thank goodness for Lexie or I probably would have been much more of a walking fashion disaster than I was.

I scraped together enough money and perused a few vintage boutiques to find unique pieces I knew she wouldn't be able to get here in the States. I hope she loves them half as much as I think she will.

"What about some hot French lingerie?" her boyfriend asks.

Since Dylan is standing directly behind Lexie, she doesn't bother turning around to admonish him. Instead, she rams her elbow into his gut. He grunts in response. If she hadn't done it, I probably would have.

"Just stand there and look pretty," she mutters under her breath.

My lips twitch because he is definitely pretty.

Lexie gives me a little wink as if she can read my mind. "Don't let his good looks fool you, he's smart, too."

Of course he is.

Because gorgeous and smart are exactly the kind of guys Lexie attracts. While I, on the other hand, had the sad misfortune to fall for a hot athletic jerk who assured me he was going to remain faithful to his study-abroad-girlfriend when in actuality, he started hooking up with other girls as soon as above-mentioned-girlfriend was out of the country.

I've had the last fourteen and a half months to get over Finn McKenzie. And I have. I am totally over him. Unfortunately, he's been calling and texting almost relentlessly for the last week, which means he's been occupying my thoughts way more than I'd like.

Perhaps I should say he's been *trying* to call and text. I haven't bothered to pick up his calls or respond to his rather lengthy and apologetic text messages. I mean, can you seriously believe that? The guy has some nerve reaching out to me after what he did. Is he so delusional as to think we're going to pick up where we left off now that I'm back at Barnett?

Apparently, he is.

We'd been together for about six months before I left for Europe. And yes, I knew having a long-distance relationship would be difficult, but I was willing to give it a shot. I'd grown to like Finn. I hadn't been gone more than two weeks when Lexie Facetimed me about what Finn had been busy doing...which had been, in case you're wondering, other girls.

And that, my friends, had been the end of that.

Lexie's advice was to forget about my cheating asshole of an ex by hooking up with a bunch of hot French guys.

I hooked up with two semi-hot French dudes and buried myself in dance which was the reason I'd been accepted to study at the Conservatoire de Paris in the first place. After a few months, my heartache lessened. I stopped thinking about Finn, my dad, his new wife, their kids, and I concentrated on soaking up everything I possibly could.

It took some time to adjust but after two months, I found myself with an amazing new life in a city renowned for its art and culture. There was no way I was going to allow anything to ruin this once in a lifetime opportunity. Right around the year mark, I stopped thinking about Lexie and returning to Barnett University and started wondering if maybe I could live here for the rest of my life.

Or, at the very least, the next few years.

When I mentioned this possibility to my dad, he made it perfectly clear that he would not be footing the bill for a life in Paris and said, in no uncertain terms, he wanted me back at Barnett come August. Undeterred by his directive, or perhaps because of it, I'd searched for enough scholarship and grant money to pay for me to continue studying in Paris. Needless to say, I hadn't been able to pull it off which is exactly why I was back at Barnett for my junior year.

"So, do you like it?"

My eyes swing back to Lexie who is standing there with all this hopeful expectation lighting up her face. A tiny smile tugs at the corners of my lips because it really is good to see her after all this time apart. "It's absolutely perfect."

Looking very much like the best friend I left behind fifteen months ago, a huge grin spills across her beautiful face before she hurtles herself at me for a third time.

Want to read more of Ivy and Roan's story? You can buy King of Campus here -) https://books2read.com/u/bPX7WY

# ABOUT THE AUTHOR

Jennifer Sucevic is a USA Today bestselling author who has published twenty New Adult novels. Her work has been translated into German, Dutch, and Italian. Jen has a bachelor's degree in History and a master's degree in Educational Psychology. Both are from the University of Wisconsin-Milwaukee. She started out her career as a high school counselor, which she loved. She lives in the Midwest with her husband, four kids, and a menagerie of animals. If you would like to receive regular updates regarding new releases, please subscribe to her newsletter here- Jennifer Sucevic Newsletter (subscribepage.com) Or contact Jen through email, at her website, or on Facebook.
sucevicjennifer@gmail.com
Want to join her reader group? Do it here -)
J Sucevic's Book Boyfriends | Facebook
Social media links-
https://www.tiktok.com/@jennifersucevicauthor
www.jennifersucevic.com
https://www.instagram.com/jennifersucevicauthor
https://www.facebook.com/jennifer.sucevic
Amazon.com: Jennifer Sucevic: Books, Biography, Blog, Audiobooks, Kindle
Jennifer Sucevic Books - BookBub